Readers love *Refraction* by JODI PAYNE AND BA TORTUGA

"This is an amazing story and is as intriguing as the title suggests."
—Diverse Reader

"…a gripping read that is full of passion, hot loving, and some amazing characters and settings…."
—Rainbow Book Reviews

"…this first-time collaboration by BA Tortuga and Jodi Payne was very interesting. Together they created two characters in Tucker and Calvin who were very opposite, so they have to find a way to compromise, understand and trust each other."
—The Novel Approach

By JODI PAYNE

Creative Process

With BA Tortuga

Heart of a Redneck

COLLABORATIONS
Refraction
Syncopation

Published by DREAMSPINNER PRESS
www.dreamspinnerpress.com

By BA Tortuga

Best New Artist
Bombs and Guacamole
Boys in the Band
Fighting Addiction
Latigo
Living in Fast Forward
Long Black Cadillac
Mud, Movies, Bullets, and Bulls
Old Town New
Private Dances
Rainbow Rodeo
Rough in Wranglers
Say Something
Seashores of Old Mexico
Stetsons and Stakeouts
Things that Go Bump in the Night

DREAMSPUN DESIRES
#6 – Trial by Fire
#30 – Two Cowboys and a Baby
#65 – Two of a Kind
LEANING N
#16 – Commitment Ranch
#42 – Finding Mr. Wright
TURQUOISE, NEW MEXICO
#53 – Cowboy in the Crosshairs

LOVE IS BLIND
Ever the Same
Real World

RECOVERY
Refired
Slip

THE RELEASE SERIES
The Terms of Release
The Articles of Release
Catch and Release

ROAD TRIP
Road Trip Vol. 1
Road Trip Vol. 2

SANCTUARY
Just Like Cats and Dogs
What the Cat Dragged In

STORMY WEATHER
Rain and Whiskey
Tropical Depression
Hurricane

THE WILDCATTERS
Oil and Water

With Jodi Payne

Heart of a Redneck

COLLABORATIONS
Refraction
Syncopation

Published by DREAMSPINNER PRESS
www.dreamspinnerpress.com

JODI
PAYNE
AND
BA
TORTUGA

SYNCOPATION

Published by
DREAMSPINNER PRESS

5032 Capital Circle SW, Suite 2, PMB# 279, Tallahassee, FL 32305-7886 USA
www.dreamspinnerpress.com

This is a work of fiction. Names, characters, places, and incidents either are the product of author imagination or are used fictitiously, and any resemblance to actual persons, living or dead, business establishments, events, or locales is entirely coincidental.

Syncopation
© 2019 Jodi Payne and BA Tortuga.

Cover Art
© 2019 Aaron Anderson.
aaronbydesign55@gmail.com
Cover content is for illustrative purposes only and any person depicted on the cover is a model.

All rights reserved. This book is licensed to the original purchaser only. Duplication or distribution via any means is illegal and a violation of international copyright law, subject to criminal prosecution and upon conviction, fines, and/or imprisonment. Any eBook format cannot be legally loaned or given to others. No part of this book may be reproduced or transmitted in any form or by any means, electronic or mechanical, including photocopying, recording, or by any information storage and retrieval system, without the written permission of the Publisher, except where permitted by law. To request permission and all other inquiries, contact Dreamspinner Press, 5032 Capital Circle SW, Suite 2, PMB# 279, Tallahassee, FL 32305-7886, USA, or www.dreamspinnerpress.com.

Trade Paperback ISBN: 978-1-64080-798-3
Digital ISBN: 978-1-64080-797-6
Library of Congress Control Number: 2018951847
Trade Paperback published February 2019
v. 1.0

Printed in the United States of America
∞
This paper meets the requirements of
ANSI/NISO Z39.48-1992 (Permanence of Paper).

To our wives.

Chapter One

"Oo-eee!" Oh praise Jesus, that felt like motherfucking heaven. Colt let the guitar rest, dangle from his fingers, the burning of the skin under his calluses promising to make tomorrow earned hell. It was worth it. Every fucking second of it. The music had poured through them all like they was all Robert Johnson hisself.

"Damn. Damn, that was fine, Boudreaux. You can play with us anytime, right boys?" Little Mel was sweating like a whore in church, her braids and mandolin dark with their good work. Hank Bennett and Mr. Bill were in the same boat. They'd laid down their tracks, wrote some, and then started jamming again. That last piece?

Lord, Lord.

Babies would be made under that song.

"I 'preciate it. For reals." Colt didn't know no one here, but he knew music, and he knew jamming, and he knew when it was right.

"You want to go get some food? You have to be starving, boy." Mr. Bill grinned at him, gold tooth shining, and Colt nodded.

"Yessir. I got a hollow leg, me. I could eat." He couldn't believe he was here, not really. Not here starving, either, but here making music because someone wanted to pay his happy ass to do it.

Him.

"Come to New York, Colt. You'll play some studio gigs, write some songs. It'll be fun."

What? He was gonna say no? What else did he do? He picked and played.

So here he was, 'til Nathan said to do something else. This place was like a dream, and he found himself going from little room to studio to little room, over and over. He'd traveled some—Dallas, New Orleans, Houston, San Antonio—but this place was... different. Cool and exciting, but he'd never felt so small.

He pulled his gimme cap on and put his guitar away with a smile. He'd reckon it. He'd managed fine so far, hadn't he? Yessir. And he was loving all the different folks, all the different styles. All the music.

No wonder men sold their souls for this.

"Great work, guys!" The guy who worked the booth bebopped in, grinning like a gator. "The sound rocked."

Little Mel grabbed the guy up in an embrace, and, damn, he sorta disappeared into her.

Whoa.

"Dang, Mellons. You gotta give a brother a chance to bail out before he suffocates in there."

Little Mel laughed, the sound rich. "You're on the wrong team, Timmy, honey. You're the only one that complains."

Timmy grinned at her and winked. "Hey, I totally got that whole last track even though you were just jamming. It was pretty sweet." The guy started cleaning up, pulling mics and dressing cables.

"Boudreaux can find one hell of a hook."

Colt bowed at her words, making a show of it. "La, it's a good job."

"Timothy Webb. Timmy." Timmy stuck his hand out for a fist bump. "You can't fake it and keep up with this crew. That was pretty boss, dude."

"Colt. Pleased and thank you." He didn't have an ounce of fake in him. Just music and a little bit of wild child.

"Now, if you're eating with them, you might find it harder to keep up. Especially with Mr. Bill. He can totally put it away." Timmy packed the mics into a crate and put the cables on top. "You guys using this kit tomorrow, or should I break it down?"

"Can you jam tomorrow, Cajun?"

"Surely do. Just point and shoot my happy ass, Mr. Bill." He didn't have any other reason to be here, and no one had said he was going anywhere else.

"Right on. I'll leave it, then. Just need the pickups." Timmy crawled all over the drum kit, pulling the electrics to lock them up. "Colt, just leave your cables be. You want to lock up your instrument with everybody else's babies, that's okay by me. So you don't have to carry it around? I keep the key, and I'm first in, last out of here."

"Yeah?" He looked to Little Mel, because this one wasn't his acoustic, but she was special. She was his, and she spoke to his heart. The acoustic spoke to his soul.

"It's cool, man. Seriously. It's safer here than sitting by your feet at a diner."

"Right. Thanks, boo. I appreciate it for true." He shot Timmy a grin. "You want food too?"

"You know it. I'll join you guys in a few. Just gotta wrap up here. Hank, you want to show the newbie where you keep your toys on the way out?"

"Oh, I suppose I can handle that. C'mon, Colt, I'll show you the locker." Hank hauled his ass off the chair like he was made of stone. Had to be seventy if he was a day.

"I'll catch up, dude. Shake Shack?"

Little Mel nodded. "I'm in, honey. We'll see you there."

He followed Hank, a melody tickling around behind his eyes, something happy and old, something his granny had sang to him, once upon a time.

"There's some sweet stuff in here. Trust me, your guitar will be in good company." Hank opened a door, which looked like any other door, but the door behind that one had a handle crank like a bank vault. The old man gave it a shove, and it swung open the rest of the way by itself, opening into a large, brightly lit room. There was a double row of guitar hangers on the far wall, and shelves with just about everything else imaginable on each side. Percussion instruments, strings, drum kits, a couple of leather jackets, a pair of cowboy boots. "This whole place could burn down and this thing would still be standing. I keep a bunch of my gear in here. I don't know who half this shit belongs to, but Timmy does."

"Merci, Vieux. This is sweet. Never seen nothing like this." They weren't near so fancy, back home.

"Welcome to the Big Apple, friend. Check out the pictures on the way out, get a little perspective. This isn't exactly a small operation."

"Big, small—whatever. I just want to pick." The Big Apple. Why an apple? Huh.

Hank waited for him to hang up his guitar and then followed him out. "You will, if you keep up like you did today. Something you may or may not already know? Make friends with Timmy. He makes it easy, so it's not like you have to try very hard. But he sits at that console every day whether you're here or not. And if you're not but someone that needs someone like you is? Timmy's your best friend."

They met up with the rest of the band in the lobby.

He filed that away. Friends he could do. Shit, he liked folks. He loved music. He loved folks that loved to play. All good, so far as he went.

The Shake Shack was crazy as all get-out. Loud and busy, burgers and dogs, and since this was Times Square, everyone was there. Suits, little kids, hipsters, uniforms, you name it. Sorta felt like New Orleans, but with less blues.

They'd only just sat down when Timmy arrived. He gave everyone a wave and got in line to order, head down and texting.

"So your manager sent you up here to us?" Hank asked, pulling at his cheese fries.

"Yessir. I come up from Houston, last, laying down gospel tracks. Good work, that." It soothed the soul, even if they'd all spent the late nights so fucked-up on grain alcohol that he swore he was gonna go blind.

Hank nodded and looked at Little Mel. "He's working for me. You?" Colt reckoned this was Mel's band, best he could tell. And he was pretty clear that today's session was an audition of sorts. That's how things usually worked out.

"You know it. We can finish this album out, if you're willing."

"Yes, ma'am. As you want. I'm easy, me."

"He's easy, him." Mr. Bill laughed, poked Colt with his elbow. "Just playin' with you, son. You can pick with me any day."

"Hank, you remember that dancer we did a mix for a couple of months ago?" Timmy worked his way into the table between Mel and Hank.

"The bad-boy ballet kid?"

"Yeah, dude. Him. Kyle? He just texted me. I cut him a couple more CDs from the master. He's coming to pick them up."

"He was a trip and a half. I guess it did okay?"

"I think he's going to let us know." Timmy picked up a hot dog covered in vegetables. Something about that didn't make no sense. "I guess they're keeping you, dude? If not, you'd have totally split by now. This crew is pretty straight shooting."

"I guess so. I like being kept okay." He was easy that way.

Hank laughed, elbowed Little Mel. "He's just like Timmy, all laid-back and whatever, dude."

"Hey! Timmy!" A guy in a big sweater and a mop of dark hair waved from the doorway.

"Kyle. Dude." Timmy waved his friend over.

"Duuuude." Kyle grinned, teasing. "Good to see you." They exchanged some complicated handshake and ended with a bro hug. "What the hell are you eating?"

"It's that veggie dog thing."

"Really, Timmy? Go with a cheeseburger next time. Hey, Hank." They shook hands.

"Kyle. This is Little Mel, Mr. Bill, and over there is our new picker, Colt Boudreaux."

Kyle shook hands and grabbed for Colt's last. "Pleasure."

Strong and warm and Colt's body tightened, the sudden rush of want surprising the shit out of him. *Huh. Pretty.* "Pleased."

Sit, boo, and watch you. Folks is folks and no one might want to know you swing the rainbow way.

Then again, he kind of thought Kyle held his hand, and eyes, just a little too long.

"I got your CDs, man." Timmy dug around in his messenger bag.

"Oh, great. Thanks." Kyle gave his hand an extra squeeze before letting go and taking the CDs from Timmy.

He set to his french fries, letting the greasy saltiness soothe his belly.

"So, Timmy, I've got another project to talk to you about. Do you have some time?"

"Um. Well, I'm in the studio with these guys for at least the next few days. Why don't you come by?"

"Yeah? Okay, cool."

"What kind of project is it?"

"I need something simple. Like really simple. Maybe just a guitar even. I'll tell you all about it, and you can help me decide."

"Yeah, sure, dude. No sweat."

"Thanks, sweetheart. Nice meeting you all. I'm headed to rehearsal. Gotta run." Kyle kissed Timmy smack on the lips.

"Later, twinkle toes."

"Oh! Timmy! Roulette. Tomorrow night, karaoke and crazy shit. You should come."

"Sounds great, dude."

Kyle disappeared onto the street.

Lord have mercy, that was hot. He knew a few places in the Crescent he could do that, but here? Good to know.

Timmy laughed. "That guy is insane, dude. 'Karaoke and crazy shit' could literally mean anything. Oh. Colt. I meant to ask—you good with a place to stay? I know the studio is putting you up for a couple of days in a hotel, but after that? I got a room if you need one."

"Yeah? I—I gotta call Nathan and find out what happens, but I might could use a real place. Somewhere I can cook." He could spend him a few days in a place not a hotel room.

"Sure. Offer stands, kitchen isn't big, but it's got all the… kitchen stuff. I don't cook."

Mr. Bill and Hank gave them all a shake. "I'm gonna get Hank into a cab and head home. We'll catch y'all tomorrow morning, yeah?"

"I'll be in by eight. Studio is yours whenever you show, bro."

Little Mel was looking at her phone. "No later than nine, boys. I want the full day we're paying for."

He nodded, nibbling on his fries. "I'll be there, ma'am. No worries."

He didn't want to go back to his room and sit.

Timmy patted the table. "How about a drink and a little New York style jazz, dude?"

"Yeah? I'm in, boo." Oh, he liked this guy. He wanted to go and see, hear. Do.

"Birdland, Mellons. You coming?"

"Timothy, if you call me 'Mellons' again…."

"If the shoe fits, sister."

Little Mel grinned at him. "Get out of here before I squash you flat."

Timmy leaned in and kissed her cheek. "Yes, ma'am. I'll see you at eight, I know. Come on, Colt. Mellons means business."

"Timothy!"

Timmy laughed himself silly all the way to the sidewalk.

He followed along, bebopping to the music that seemed to be everywhere. "Thanks for the invite, boo."

"Oh, yeah. Dude, I'm up for music any night, and you don't want to hang out in a stale hotel room when you have this city at your feet, right? Oh, and by the way? Don't change a thing, but up here when someone says *boo*, they mean *honey*. Like 'that's my boo.'" Timmy grinned at him.

"Yeah? 'Kay. Good to know." He knew that it would pop out anyway. He was all about the habits, from chewing toothpicks to falling asleep to *Abbey Road*.

"So I saw the CV Nathan sent, dude. You get around, huh?" Timmy turned a corner, and they headed down a long block.

"I go where the music takes me." It was the best life. His daddy would be damn proud. Prob'ly was looking down and grinning right now.

"You've got sick fingers, dude. I'm glad it brought you around here. You play anything else?"

"Anything you can pick, boo."

He could see the flag that hung outside the club down the block, and the neon in the window drew his eye a second later. There was a line—not a long one; he'd seen worse—but still a line.

"This isn't too bad. We should be golden, dude. Hey, stand with the neon; I'll get a picture for you." Timmy pulled out a phone.

He went to stand, posing like the littlest Cajun dork in history, hooting as he boogied and Timmy laughed.

"That's rad. You got AirDrop? I'll... send it... huh." Timmy glanced up at him and then back at the screen.

"What? My hair weird?"

"No, dude. Kyle is asking about you." Timmy laughed. "He thinks the whole world wants him." Timmy started texting.

"The pretty one?" *For true?* He liked the thought of that, yes he did.

Timmy glanced up at him again and nodded. "The super pretty one. I was about to…. It's cool, I wasn't trying to freak you out, dude. I can tell him to simmer down… unless…?"

"You into him? I ain't no poacher."

"Aw." Timmy laughed, a little embarrassed. "No. I thought maybe I was at first a while back, but no. He's a lot of fun, but he's a buddy, that's all."

"Bon amis are good, yeah? Better than lovers sometimes." He got that. Your friends didn't fall out of your life near as much.

"A lot of times, dude. Totally. So, what do you want me to say? You want me to tell him to chill, or are you interested?"

"I could be interested." His cheeks burned some, but that was okay. A guy needed a little fun in between gigs.

Timmy elbowed him and grinned. "Yeeeeah, dude. That's the way to be. He's a party and a half." He watched Timmy text and speak everything out loud. "Colt… is totally… into hanging out, dude. Yeah? That work?"

When he nodded, Timmy hit Send and waited for a reply.

"Kyle says, 'Great. Bring him to karaoke tomorrow night.'" Timmy looked at him. "Cool? This karaoke thing he does? It's more like open mic night. It's all theater peeps, and it's total talent."

He nodded. Open mic night he understood. He'd spent most his life picking for anyone who would listen. He sang, wrote, played—if it was music, he was there.

"I'm telling him you're in." Timmy texted, grinned at something that popped up on the screen, and put the phone away. "You have a date, *boo*." Timmy winked at him.

"Lookit me!" He gave a holler, and all the folks stared.

Timmy gave him a fist bump and took his arm, steering him into the club.

Chapter Two

"Kyle!"

Tuesday night in the city was slow compared to the weekends, but there was always fun to be had if you knew where to look.

"Hey, Kyle! You're late, man."

It was even more fun when you had a regular crew who were glad to see you whenever you walked through the door.

"Jenny, pour Kyle his usual and put it on my tab."

"On it, moneybags," she shouted back. Kyle was convinced Jennifer was the best bartender in town.

"Aw. Gregory, you're too good to me." He hurried over and gave Greg a kiss.

Ali took his arm. "Why are you late, baby?"

"We had an injury tonight. I had to hang out and make plans to rehearse in a replacement in the morning."

"Oh, that sucks."

"He'll be okay. Back by Friday, I bet. He just needs some rest."

Greg brought him his amaretto sour and put it in his hand. "Now it's a party!"

"Thank you, sweetheart."

The crew was all well and good, but he had one eye on the door. The injury thing was a big fat lie to cover for the fact that he'd actually showered after the show and made himself date worthy. Timmy had texted—they'd been at some other club across town and were on their way.

He'd gotten a good long look at the guitar player with his short, dark curls, bird-black eyes, full lips, and those arms. Colt Boudreaux's arms were pure muscle, made to make music. He'd been enamored of the entire package since the minute they'd met yesterday.

"Are you singing tonight, Kyle?"

"I don't know yet." He could carry a tune, and he wasn't shy, but he did have a date after all, so he needed to leave the evening's plans open.

"Where are we… oh, I see Mig and Trixie. Is there room for a couple more over there?"

"Go pull up some chairs. Ky. There's always room."

"Awesome."

He could have waited another day or two before stopping by and bugging Timmy at the studio about his next project, but he knew Colt would be there working, and he was trying to cause a little stir by showing up there today—before their date. He wasn't above a little drama if it served a purpose, and he'd managed to catch Colt's eye and flirt a couple of times through the soundproof glass.

He hoped Colt would be a little wound up when they arrived.

The little glances, the twinkle in Colt's eyes had reminded him somehow of a curious, quick bird. He was dying to find out what was going on in that mind. He'd find out eventually. At the moment he was more interested in Colt's body. All that rich, tanned skin was calling to him.

He'd just claimed a few seats and was chatting with Mig and Trixie when Timmy showed up. Colt followed behind him, looking around, taking the place in. Timmy, no surprise, headed straight for the bar.

He hung out in his seat, watching, waiting. He'd made his move with the invitation. He wanted to see what Colt's would be. He was pleased when Colt walked right up to him with a warm, open smile, an outstretched hand. "Hey you. Comment ça se roule? You good?"

He stood up and took Colt's hand, returning his smile and digging deep for that high school French. It didn't help him much. "Uh… I'm well. I'm glad you came." He went in for the cheek kiss, figuring that was a good middle ground for a little more than strangers but not quite friends.

"Thanks for the invite. You need a drink?" Colt's fingers burned in his; he could feel each and every fingertip. He wasn't in a hurry to let go.

"Thanks, my buddy Greg hooked me up. But Jennifer's solid. She can make you anything you want. No lie. People try to test her all the time."

"'M a beer man, though I have had a hurricane or hundred, no lie." The cadence of Colt's voice made him want to nod, to bounce along. "Be right back, eh?"

"Sure. I'll keep your seat warm." He opened his fingers, not so much letting go as letting Colt slip free, calluses making his palm tingle. He watched the man walk away, admiring the easy stride, the tight little ass.

Timmy chatted with Colt for a second, then brought some fruit-garnished bright blue concoction over. "I'm here…."

"You are!" God, Timmy would drink literally anything. "Listen, thanks for—"

"Timmy!" Trixie waved, and Mig got up to give Timmy a hug. "Come on and sit."

Timmy gave him a wink and headed off to sit with his buddies. He glanced back at the bar to find Colt smiling and having a conversation with Jenny while she pulled his beer. Friendly guy. He loved that.

Things were going to ramp up pretty soon, and the whole gang was making their way over to the tables they'd pushed together. He took a seat, guarding the one next to him for his date.

Colt came back to him, dancing around the crowd with ease, laughing as he fought not to spill his beer.

Kyle laughed with him. Not Colt's first crowded bar, clearly. "That took some serious talent, mister." He pushed Colt's chair out for him.

"I know some crowds, me. I been working Mardi Gras since I was eight."

"Whoa, really? That's a party I need to go to sometime. I hear some wild shit goes down." He broke out in goose bumps as Colt sat next to him, their thighs brushing together. They were pretty crammed in with so many people around just a few tables.

"It's something else, sure enough. The best party on earth."

"I don't know, we can whoop it up here when we want to." He winked at Colt over the top of his drink and then took a sip that went down just right. "So you're up here for that gig?"

"Yessir. I got me some good work with Little Mel and all. I been jamming my happy ass off."

Mig got up, sat at the piano, and just started playing.

"You sounded smooth. I was watching your fingers fly. It was great. Oh, that's Mig. He does mostly pop and show tunes."

"Mig. Cool." Colt watched for a second with a grin, then turned to him. "You sang?"

Listen to that accent. "I… uh. Well, I sing here sometimes, but no. I dance." *I dance ballet*. Telling another guy that you danced ballet was like coming out. Didn't matter how confident you were or how little it mattered to you what they thought, you were still never sure about how they'd react.

"No shit? That's fucking cool, man." Colt lit up, eyes sparkling. "Like a... like fancy dancing, eh? Not the fais-dodo, but the—" He pursed his lips and snapped his fingers. "—the ballet kind?"

Well, well. That was interesting. He turned to look at Colt, to really look at him and let the man know it mattered to him. "I dance ballet, yes." He had no idea what a "fay-doo-doo" was, though. Except that it apparently wasn't ballet. "You like the ballet?"

"I like anything that has to do with music. Anything. Y'all know how to make y'all's bodies do shit I can't even figure. So friggin' cool." Colt grinned at him, not the slightest bit mocking.

Oh, this one was interesting. *Where are you from? Who are your people? How did you pick up guitar? Do you play anything else?* All good questions, if maybe a bit personal yet. And he didn't feel like asking any of them right now. What does your chest look like under that shirt, was more like it, but it seemed a little early and two drinks shy yet. "How are you liking New York?"

Ali got up and took the mic, singing a pop song he didn't know, but doing it well, as she did everything. Her voice was raspy and all-out rock and roll crammed into a five foot nothing package.

"It's something else, no? Like all sorts of worlds all smashed together. Music everywhere. Lots of folks, not so many gators. It's all good."

"No alligators, plenty of sharks." He laughed. There was music everywhere and actually, that was easy to take for granted when you lived here day in and day out. Street performers, buskers in the subways, musicals, clubs... everywhere. "It is all good. And a lot of times, people don't even look at you funny when you dance down the street." He did that all the time. Most of the time without meaning to.

"There's lot to see. All sorts. Lots of pretty men." Colt winked at him, looked him up and down.

He hoped Colt wouldn't be disappointed that he wasn't the type to blush. "Lots. And I've always got my eyes open. But I'm only looking at one right now."

"Listen to you. I'm just another bayou baby, but I 'preciate it."

Colt apparently was the blushing type. The little dip of his chin and the roll in his dark eyes was lovely.

Kyle decided to push a little harder, see what he got. He laid a hand on Colt's thigh and slid it slowly down over the musician's knee, giving it a squeeze. "I need another drink, bayou baby; you want something?"

"No, sir. I reckon whatever's fixin' to happen, I don't want to be high for it." Colt spread for him, natural as breathing. "I still got me half a beer."

"The night is young." He stood, trailing his hand up a muscled arm and across Colt's strong shoulders on his way to the bar. Mmm. He liked that answer. He didn't plan on being high for it either. Just a little bit loose. It wasn't early at all, except by theater standards. Nothing fun started until at least 11:00 p.m. with this crowd.

He set his empty glass down on the bar. "Jenny! Darling. Hook me up?"

"You got it. Beer too for your friend?"

"No, if you can believe it. Apparently he's not the drinker I am. And he's a date, not a friend. Isn't he lovely?"

"He is. Wild curls and completely new to town, isn't he?"

"New to town, new to me, totally new. I can't wait to get my fingers into those curls." He leaned on the bar and looked over in Colt's direction. "He's here for a studio gig, so I don't get the impression he'll be in town long, but while he's here, I'm hoping to enjoy the hell out of him."

She pushed his drink across the bar. "Go play. Give him something to remember."

"On it! Thank you." He picked up his glass, left her cash and a decent tip. After a sip of his drink, he was wondering if he shouldn't have left her more. It was strong as fuck.

"That's Trixie up there on the guitar, she's fun. And in a second, I bet… yep. That's Greg with his slap-top drum." He sat back down beside Colt and set his glass next to the beer on the table. He dropped a hand onto Colt's knee, but his eyes were on the little stage.

Colt was moving to the music, totally focused on the rhythm, leg and head bobbing, hands drumming on the table.

He's into it. Kyle gave Colt a smile, nodding to the beat of the music. They were just having some after-hours fun here. Colt was probably a much better musician than most people in the room, but the guy was into it anyway. That was cool. After a minute, he recognized the song and started throwing out lyrics, and Ali joined in and sang along with him.

Soon a harmony started up, rich and low, the sound vibrating in his bones.

Ali clapped her hands and moved over to Colt, sitting her petite little butt right in Colt's lap. Kyle leaned in, matching Ali on the melody until she shifted up a third, giving him goose bumps. He wasn't a trained singer at all, but he could carry a tune, and he managed the melody okay. A couple of other people joined in to back him up.

Up onstage Trixie and Greg stepped it up a notch, and the bar just filled up with music.

Lips brushed his ear, Timmy's voice whispering, "You want to see something, man? Hand him a guitar."

The neck of an old battered acoustic pressed into his hand.

He had no idea whose it was, but that hardly mattered; stuff ended up passed around at these things all the time. He took hold of it and gave Timmy a nod, then pushed his chair back to give Colt some room. Ali put her eyes on the guitar and got out of the way, grinning.

Kyle didn't have to make much of an offer. As soon as Colt laid his eyes on the instrument, he pulled it right into his lap.

Colt bent to the guitar and music started pouring out. Kyle had to admit that Colt wasn't trying to outdo Trixie; he wasn't trying to steal the spotlight. Colt was joining the stream of music and… bending it, making it more bluesy, giving it a richness, a soul.

Ali rested a hand on Kyle's shoulder, and he looked up, listening to the way her rock style shifted in tone as well, blending with Colt's harmony. She cocked her head at him and gave him a thumbs-up.

He listened to that guitar and the way it made him want to move, and he realized suddenly that he might have already found the musician he was looking for to help him with his next original project. Assuming he could afford Colt. Someone with this guy's talent wasn't coming cheap.

The longer Colt played, the looser the lean body got, the way Colt moved with the guitar pure, liquid sex. Oh, he intended to turn Colt inside out, see what made the musician tick.

"Fucking hot," Mig mouthed at him across the table and licked his lips.

"Mine," he mouthed back, dead serious, sending Mig into a fit of laughter. *Poach someone else's date*. He'd given up singing—everyone but Ali and Colt had—as the pop song that had started all of this evolved into a jam.

It wasn't long before Trixie bowed out, too, but not because she couldn't keep up. She left her guitar on the stage and perched on the edge of the table barely a foot from Colt just to watch him play, and Greg hung out a few feet away, following Colt's lead on his slap-drum.

They were all beginning to sweat, to move with one another, because this is what they did, wasn't it? This was what they were made for.

"He's new," Trixie said. "Something really new."

"Nah," Timmy argued. "He's old-school."

"Old-school new?" she teased.

Kyle didn't really know one way or the other, but he liked it; the music, the man, it was impossible to separate the two right now. It was definitely the man that had him half-hard, though, mouth watering, hungry for a taste.

Colt lifted his face, eyes boring into him, and the blues dropped a half step, became filthy, an unabashed come-on.

Fuck, yeah. That was his cue. He stood up, leaned right over the guitar, and planted a hard kiss on Colt's lips, bracing one arm on the back of Colt's chair. Colt opened for him, lips hot as liquid fire, not even a hint of nerves. Hungry bayou baby.

He groaned into Colt's mouth, so ready just to tear into this guy. His friends already knew he had no shame, but all the same, someone gave him a firm swat on the ass.

"Let the man breathe, Ky." There was laughter all around them.

Kyle ended the kiss as gracefully as he could manage, running his tongue along the length of Colt's lower lip, and then leaned in to speak into Colt's ear so he was heard over the guitar. "They're jealous. And they should be."

Colt's answer was a deep, low moan. "Oh, cher. That was just fine."

"I don't know." He grinned slyly, falling back into his chair. "I think I could have done better. Did you even miss a beat on that guitar?" Because it sure didn't seem like it. He'd try again another time. It was good to have goals.

Colt gave a wild, happy sound—one that had everyone in the place looking and laughing. "Lawd, lawd. You keep on tryin'. I'll keep on likin' it."

"You're on." He laughed along with everyone else. Colt's energy was contagious.

Colt was well occupied even after he finished off that song. He was mobbed by Trixie and Timmy, who were full of questions about his music and his background, and later by Ali, who chatted with him excitedly too. Colt was just as patient and friendly as could be.

It was maddening.

They did manage to exchange a couple of glances, and Kyle loved the promise that was still in Colt's eyes, hot and steady like burning coals banked for a later fire.

He wasn't patient, though, never had been, and waiting was starting to get to him.

Colt drank two bottles of water before someone—Mig probably, fucker—brought him a second beer, and he drank deep, licking his lips clean, the simple act making the best kind of promises.

"Should I get myself another drink?" he asked, perching on the table near Colt and gracefully planting his toes on the chair between Colt's thighs.

Ali chuckled at him. "How about I get another beer for myself?" She leaned in and kissed him on the cheek before slipping away.

"Mmm. Look at all you, cher. So fine for miles."

Kyle could feel the touch of that gaze like it was a physical thing.

"I can party it up with this crew all night, baby. But I've got a hot new toy I want to take home." Take him home, play with him, blow his fucking mind.

"Yeah? You want to play, cher? I'm over twenty-one and willing."

"That's what I like to hear." *Cher*. How wonderful was that? He dragged his foot along the inside of Colt's thigh and stood up. "You okay with my place, bayou baby? Or would you rather your hotel?"

"Timmy knows you. If I cain't trust you not to try and fuck me up there, I cain't trust you in a hotel room. Take me home." Colt looked around, guitar in hand. "Who this go to?"

Wait. What? "Oh. Uh. Timmy? Guitar?"

"It's one of Trixie's. I got it. Just leave it on the table."

"My place is going to be way more comfortable. And fun. But am I hearing you have ground rules?" He leaned over and nibbled on Colt's earlobe. "Because I have every intention of fucking you, so if that's out, you should probably let me know now."

"Mmm… nah, cher. I catch just fine. I mean no trying to fuck me up, eh? No being evil to me." Colt moved right into him with a happy little groan. "I'm ready to play."

Holy fuck, me too. He looped his arm through Colt's. "I ended up in bed with the last guy I tried to beat up, so you're safe either way." This close, Colt smelled delicious. He didn't know if it was cologne, or hair product, or just something specific to Colt, but it was irresistible.

They got a bunch of cheers and laughter on their way out the door, which was par for the course. He'd have been disappointed not to be teased by that crowd. A cab pulled up almost instantly. "They like you. Get on in, baby."

Colt slipped into the cab, dark eyes staring into him from across the seat, one callused hand held out to him.

He climbed in, closed the door behind him, and gave the cabby his Christopher Street address. Then he took those strong fingers in his and slid close on the seat. "When I first texted Timmy, he thought you were straight."

"Yeah? That ain't my thing. I love women, me, but not in the Biblical way. Played good music with a bunch of them."

"Yeah. He was all, 'Dude, I don't know if he's down with that.'" He laughed. Colt was down with that all right. Colt was so down with it, he didn't dare kiss in the cab for fear the cabby might need a fire hose to get them out of the back seat.

"I'm pretty damn good at going down, cher." That wicked little grin sent a zing through him.

"Oh, beautiful bayou boy, we're going to get along very, very well." Assuming he remembered how to breathe for the rest of the cab ride.

"Number?"

"Huh?" Kyle blinked at the cabbie. *Hello, hormones.*

"The number, Romeo."

"Oh. Thirty-five."

The cabbie whistled. "Damn. Nice."

Yep. It was nice. He paid the driver and let Colt lead him out onto the sidewalk. "That's it." He pointed. "Thirty-five. Come on."

"Yessir. I'm with you." Right with him, hard cock pressed against his thigh.

Inside. Don't get tangled up on the sidewalk. He led Colt up the stairs and through the first door, the breezeway, and then the second, which opened into a bright foyer.

"Now, then." Thank God. "Where did that kiss leave off again?"

"You were promising me more." Colt muscled in, face lifted.

"I was." He gathered all that bunchy muscle close with one arm the way he might support a dance partner and pressed his lips to Colt's, the light, bitter taste of beer answering back first.

Colt tasted every bit as good as he smelled, and Kyle was hungry.

He wanted his dance.

Colt reached up, hands curling around his shoulders, fingers digging in and rubbing in lazy, slowly increasing circles.

"Mm." He swept Colt toward the staircase and led him upstairs, stopping briefly when they reached the landing to kiss and taste Colt's neck. Salty, musky. "You taste so good."

"Do I? Good. That's important." Colt's words were shaky, breathless, the lean body vibrating against his.

He smiled, pleased, and moved toward his bedroom, maneuvering Colt ahead of him gently. Once there, he took Colt's lips again, harder and hungrier, his fingers sliding into those dark curls. They were soft, slick, wrapping around his fingers and tugging them like the curls were encouraging him to hold on.

He reached down with his other hand, getting ahold of a firm, round asscheek and sliding his leg between Colt's thighs. Colt arched, pretty as you please, grinding against him, pushing hard enough Kyle knew he had to be aching so good.

Jesus, the man was lovely. He pulled his shirt off and dropped it, then broke their kiss to concentrate on Colt's. "Off." He lifted the shirt, exposing sumptuous smooth skin. He'd get a taste of all of it, very soon. Once the shirt fell to the floor, he started in on his own belt.

"Look at you, cher. I could worship at your altar for a good bit." Colt eased off his boots, then opened his jeans, shimmying right out of them.

"We've got all night, baby. I'm planning on using it. Starting right here." He reached out and slid his fingers over Colt's belly, the tight muscle under them making his breath come faster. Colt was compact, not an ounce of spare flesh on the lean body, the muscles standing out like they were begging to be played.

He slid past the stiff cock with little more than a brief touch and cupped Colt's balls, tugging them lightly, as he stepped very close. The move won him a low groan, and he smiled again, enjoying the way the man appreciated being touched. He explored the smooth, rich skin around Colt's shoulders with his fingers, and traced the valleys between the muscles with his tongue.

"Fuck." The single word held a whole wealth of pleasure and desire.

"Mmm. Soon. You're delicious." He herded Colt toward his bed.

"I like that. You're about fine, cher. All this pretty." Colt went, following his lead like he was meant for it.

"Thank you." He was holding back. He could rip into Colt right now if he wanted to, but he liked making himself wait. The wanting was nearly as good as the having. And he was really enjoying the way Colt played along. Such patience. He stretched out on his bed. "Come on up here."

Colt crawled up his body, nuzzling and rubbing the whole way. His thigh was explored, then one hip, his abs. He shivered and his belly went hard. He dropped a hand to Colt's head. "Colt." Fuck, that was way needier than he'd meant it to sound.

"Mm-hmm." Colt licked a line up to his nipple, pondering it for a second before drawing a line around it with the tip of his tongue.

He inhaled, air hissing through his teeth. Fucking tease. God, he liked that. He really fucking liked that. "Yes."

Colt drew the circle once more, then leaned back and blew a long, focused breath over him, making his skin draw up.

"Ah!" He shivered and the cool air made him laugh. "Jesus. Come here." He hooked a hand around the back of Colt's neck and pulled him into a kiss.

One biting connection turned into another, and Colt rocked down against him, long cock nudging his belly, leaving tiny burning kisses.

Their sounds filled his ears as they went at each other, panting breaths and muffled moans and the jarring sound of clashing teeth. Finally, he grunted and rolled them, using his raw dancer's strength to his advantage. He bent and tried another kiss, covering Colt's mouth with his own.

Colt cried out, bucking under him, the strong hands cupping his head as Colt demanded more.

He groaned and arched, finding sweet heat against Colt's hip, but that wasn't enough, wasn't what he wanted. He needed more. All he had to do was disrupt a searing kiss that had a fucking will of its own.

Colt wasn't going to make that easy, with the way he poured himself into Kyle, giving it all up.

He made a sound he'd find humiliating anywhere but the bedroom and pulled away, breaking contact and blinking like he'd broken a spell. "Fuck, Colt. Just… just hold that thought." He reached for supplies, winded and breathing hard.

"Want you. Fuck, cher. I ache, huh? For you."

"Yeah. Yes." It didn't take a second to deal with the rubber, and he was looking forward to what a little lube was going to do for Colt. "For you too." He tapped the inside of one smooth thigh, letting Colt open for him, and offered two slippery fingers.

Colt pulled one leg up and out, exposing himself, the sweet, tight balls drawn toward his body, cock bobbing over his belly.

"Mm. Baby, look at you. Best view around." He lined up his fingers, pushing past the rim, and eased them deeper, doing his best to take his time despite the fact that his mind had already raced three steps ahead of him, and his cock right along with it. He ducked and caught Colt's raised knee with his shoulder, focusing in on Colt's need like it was his own.

The tight ring of muscles clamped down on his fingers like a vise, working them, squeezing tight.

He'd take that as a promise. "Jesus, Colt. Easy, baby. Let me slick you up or I'm gonna tear you in two."

"That would be awkward." Colt panted for him, arching into his touch. "Been a few."

"Mm. Can't wait to help you remember." He could go easy. He turned his head and kissed the inside of Colt's thigh. "Deep breaths," he suggested softly. "It'll be so good."

"I ain't scairt. I like a deep touch." Colt reached out for him, stroked his face, his jaw.

"I've got that for you." He twisted his fingers slowly, testing, and pumped them gently before letting them slip free. "There you go, so sweet." He went for a little more slippery stuff, his cock so happy, it practically leaped out of his fingers as he lined up.

Colt watched him with those near-black eyes, not hiding a thing from him.

Letting Colt keep hold of his eyes through that first stretch and burn was so fucking intimate, it was bordering on uncomfortable, but he wanted to give back the energy Colt was giving him. He stopped, though, still shallow, and started to rock into Colt slowly, a little deeper and a little more stretch with every thrust. Fuck, it was so slow, it made him ache down deep. He felt like he might shatter if he didn't stay mindful.

A moan cracked the air, raw and deep, the sound vibrating through him, drawing his abs up with the power of it. "Fuck. Fuck." He leaned into his shoulder, bending Colt farther, and pressed his cheek into Colt's thigh, lungs clawing in air. "Christ, baby."

Colt nodded, the motion desperate, eyes wide as they stared into him. "C'est bon, cher. Good. All good."

"All good? Good. Thank fuck." On his next thrust he sank deep, balls slapping Colt's ass, and then he picked up a powerful rhythm, setting all that tension free and chasing his need.

Colt fought to match him, meet his thrusts, one after another, teeth bared as they moved together. Oh, Colt didn't need to work so hard, but the guy's face was pure sex, and Kyle was totally enjoying it. He took it up a notch, reaching into blow-Colt's-mind territory, and wrapped a firm hand around Colt's erection, feeling it press willingly into his palm, hard and heavy.

For the first time, Colt's eyes rolled up, that laser-focus hiccupping.

"Beautiful." He stroked up the full length, giving Colt the pressure that body was begging for. So fucking hot. He hadn't realized how Colt's intense eye contact had been keeping him grounded, but without it, he slipped right out of his head, finally concentrating on his own undeniable need. That had an intensity all its own. Colt's heat clung to him, making him groan with nearly every stroke.

Colt's sounds joined his, sliding underneath them and lifting them up, the percussion of their skin slapping keeping time. He shifted, ducking out from under Colt's leg and letting it fall, moving over Colt to take those trembling, full lips in a kiss. Colt wrapped around him with the softest cry, tongue tangling with his. So hungry. How could anyone resist this?

He wouldn't know how even if he wanted to, and he didn't try. He sank right into it, letting the rhythm and their strange harmony consume him. "Colt!"

"Yeah, cher. Fill me up." Colt's body tightened, gripping him like a fist.

He grunted and dug in deep, pounding into Colt the way he'd imagined since their first kiss in the bar. He tried to keep himself in check just enough to make sure Colt was with him, though. Fuck, he loved a photo finish, and Colt seemed like he was in total agreement, jerking and grunting out a warning before he shot.

He only got to enjoy the stunned look on Colt's face for a second before his eyes crossed, sound was muffled, and every thought in his mind was yanked down into his balls. His orgasm was both painful and perfect for a long, lovely moment, and then it was all relief as he slowly remembered to breathe again.

"Mmm. So fine, cher. Tore my ass up." Colt's voice was pure postorgasm slur.

"Fuck yeah, I did." He kissed Colt again, still pretty breathless. "You are irresistible." He rolled out of bed for a quick second to clean up, then got back before anything had a chance to get cold. He tangled up with Colt again and looked down at him.

Colt traced his ink, the black shoulder sleeve one tribal animal after another. He watched, the callused finger rough against his skin. "It's a work in progress." He loved it. He loved dreaming up what was going on his skin next. He loved that it set him apart from the purely classical dancers. He loved that it pissed his father off.

"It's fucking hot. I'm scared of needles, me, or I'd get one."

"Thanks. I'm pretty proud of it. I like all your pristine skin, baby, no reason to mark it up if it's not your thing. What would you get if you were into it?"

"Music." That took no time. Someone had thought about this.

Kyle nodded, wondering if there was a reason Colt was afraid of needles or whether it was just a generalized thing. If he'd thought that hard about it, maybe he just needed someone to give him some courage. "Music notes? A particular piece of music? A guitar?"

"Score for 'Hellhound on my Trail,' no question. Robert Johnson makes my soul sing."

"Oh, wow. A whole score would be so cool." He really thought it would, just a blanket of music. "But that's a long project and a lot of ink for someone who doesn't—what's your thing with needles? Just get nervous?" He kind of regretted asking as soon as he'd done it; he barely knew Colt. But then again, Colt had brought it up, right?

"I don't know. I just know that when I went and saw? Lawd, cher, I couldn't do it."

"That's fair. But nothing worth doing is easy, baby. You can do anything if you want it bad enough." He gave Colt a wink and a grin. "But that's not a project you want to start and then find out you don't want it bad enough."

"True that. I do like yours, though. They're fine." Colt's fingers danced over the ink, playing with him.

"Well, if you're ever in town when I'm getting more, I'll invite you along to watch." He hovered over Colt's lips for breath before kissing him.

Colt groaned softly, lips parting again like he was meant to be kissed, like there was nothing on earth Colt wanted more right now.

There was such truth in Colt. He couldn't steal a kiss that was freely given; he wasn't concerned with later when Colt made right now so important. Being with Colt was like familiar steps set to entirely new music.

"Are you staying? I mean, I'd love it if you stayed. If you want to." Colt wasn't his first fly-by-night musician. They always had a gig to be at or a bar calling them. Itchy fingers, itchy feet. He didn't read people well all the time, but it felt like Colt wasn't in a hurry.

"I want." Colt pulled his bottom lip in, sucked gently. "I got to be at the studio in the morning. I got all night."

"Mmm. I'll take it." He'd take the rest of that kiss, too, and whatever else he might get.

Chapter Three

Colt woke up in a rush, sucking in air as he fought to figure out where the fuck he was this time.

Never changed. Never once. Every damn morning it was a whole new world trying to reckon his place in it.

He knew this place was all kinds of fancy. You could smell money in the air.

Money in the air and amaretto on the pillowcase. Music he'd never heard before coming from another room.

The pretty dancer. Kyle. Right. He hunted a bathroom, brushed his teeth with his finger, and washed up. Then he got himself dressed and went hunting the sound of the music and the pretty man who had turned him inside out last night.

Following the music, the smooth male vocals, and the hot slow-dance rhythm, Kyle wasn't hard to find. But he stopped dead in the doorway as Kyle spun by him, one turn after another all the way to the far end of the large, open room.

Kyle stopped to stretch next to a mirrored wall, one long leg coming right up alongside his ear, damp, dark hair plastered to his forehead. "Good morning, music man."

"Mornin', cher. You been workin' hard."

"Every day, baby." Kyle came over, walking with a dancer's bare feet in skintight, black shorts, ink, and nothing else. "Hi." Kyle kissed him like it was what they did every morning. Simple. Affectionate.

"Hey. You taste sweet." He approved. Kyle knew how to kiss a man, how to make it feel good.

"You taste like my toothpaste and beer." Kyle winked at him and kept stretching as they talked—graceful, drawn-out movements with great, long extensions of arms or legs. "Are you hungry? You need to run? It'll take you maybe half an hour to get to the studio."

"They said nine." He hadn't even plugged his phone in last night, and he assumed it wasn't too late. It was unnatural, this waking up and making music before noon.

"Yeah. I know Timmy is there at some ungodly hour every morning. And I can tell you the guy must never sleep, because he closes the bar with us often. I guess studio time is at a premium in the city. Timmy says morning is cheaper." Kyle pulled a towel off the wall nearby. "You've got a little time. Let's make you some breakfast."

"Just coffee, cher. I ain't ready for food, but thank you." He was a pure coffee-until-supper kind, always had been.

Kyle gave him a playfully disapproving look. "Let me guess. No sugar or milk either?"

"Black, though I do love a café au lait, me." Sweet and creamy like early morning sex.

"Hm." Kyle led him back down the hall to the stairway they'd climbed together the night before. It was curved, the steps were wide, and it had a long, brightly polished railing leading down to a flat banister. Kyle perched on it and slid all the way down, landing gracefully after shooting off the end. "Coming?"

"Look at you!" He applauded and headed toward Kyle, walking down the stairs like a man that needed his hands and arms working so he could keep himself in french fries. "That was cool. You're something else, ain't you?"

Like this sparkly magic man. Like Baron Samedi, somehow.

"Thank you." Kyle bowed neatly. "I hope so."

He bowed back. "So do you dance for a company deal?"

He thought that was how it worked, right? In the ballet? They had companies that were like symphonies. He'd played with local symphonies before, when they needed a pinch hitter.

"I do, and I don't." Kyle pulled him into the kitchen and started making coffee. "I choreograph for a modern ballet company. I dance with them as well, and I sometimes dance on my own."

"Yeah?" Fancy. That rocked his socks. He loved to see folks doing what they loved and not starving. "You like it? You must, huh?"

Kyle snorted. "Do you like playing guitar?"

"Not a bit. Dread it." He grinned over, waggling his eyebrows.

"Yeah. I should have been a financial planner like my dad wanted me to be." Kyle laughed. "It's not about like, right? It's… in here." Kyle reached for him, as if trying to claw something out of his chest. "I'm not me without it."

"True. I ain't nothing but a vessel, and thank God for it." He knew that like he knew his own name. Without music, he wouldn't be worth a plug nickel.

"Listen to you." Kyle brought him a mug of coffee and cupped his jaw in one hand, hazel eyes shifting between brown and green in the light. "You really believe that, don't you?"

"It's the truth, cher. It ain't no thing." Lord, look at those pretty eyes. A mind could write a thousand songs about them.

Kyle's look was hard to read, but the kiss that followed was easy enough to understand. "Is your coffee okay?"

"Uh-huh." He was sure it was fine. It wouldn't be like home, but it would be better than Folgers. Kyle didn't seem like the Folgers' type.

"You have your phone on you?" Kyle reached for the counter and pulled his off a charger.

"I do. Thanks." He handed his phone over, then drank deep from his coffee. Oh. Oh, fuck. That was nice. He took another drink and moaned. "That's fine."

Kyle smiled and plugged in his phone. "Coffee needs to be good. What's your number?"

He typed it into Kyle's phone, and Kyle called him. "There. Now you have mine."

"Excellent. I'll use it. I would see you again."

"I would like to see you again too. Do use it. There must be something we didn't try last night." Kyle's tongue ran across a flirty bottom lip.

"I bet there is." He stroked one hand down Kyle's belly. "I bet there's lots."

"Mm." Tight abs grew even tighter under his hand, and Kyle reached out to draw circles on his chest with a long finger. "Well, you think on it. And let me know what you come up with."

"I can do that." His nipples drew up, hard as a rock, the touch making him dizzy.

Kyle leaned in, nuzzled his jaw. "You want an Uber? Or are you going to brave the subway?"

"I'll manage. I don't mind. I'm brave." He liked exploring all these new places. Hell, where he grew up, you couldn't even plant dead bones in the ground before the water pushed them up, much less run a train down there.

"When in New York, right? Good for you. You better get moving, then. Closest station is at Seventh; that's about a ten-minute walk."

"Good deal. Call, eh? I'm playing until six, for sure. Maybe later. I never know." Playing was what he did.

Kyle took his coffee cup, trading it for his phone, and saw him out. "I'll call. How long are you in town?"

"So long as someone wants me here, I'll be here." Or until someone else wanted to pay him more to go somewhere else.

"Works for me." Kyle leaned in the doorway. "Play hard, music man."

"Always." He took another kiss, letting this one mean something. "Bon temps, cher. Roule on."

Kyle smiled at him and gave his hand a squeeze. "Subway's that direction. See you soon." The tall ornate door closed, Kyle disappearing back inside.

Time to get to work.

Lord have mercy, it was gonna be a grand day.

Chapter Four

After the day he'd had, Kyle had needed a shower almost as much as the coffee he was drinking. He sat on his couch and smiled at Colt's number on his phone, wondering if it was easier to play music all day on a couple of hours of sleep than it had been to choreograph. Thirty was staring at him and laughing its ass off.

How totally fucking worth it, though. His bed had been a playground all damn night. Everything about Colt was fun and sexy, right down to "cher." He liked feeling appreciated. If the man was ready for round two, he was game. Honestly, the worst part of his whole day had been waiting for after six to call.

"Let's see if I'm still on your mind, hot stuff." Bouncing a little in his seat, he hit Call.

It took three rings for Colt to pick up, husky laughter sounding before the "Mmm, cher. How you be?"

Seriously? Chills. "Fabulous. How was your session? Or are you still playing? You want to call me back?"

"Everybody just left. I laid down the work today. All the folks here got gigs to run to tonight, but I was looking to hear from you."

"Yeah? You just made my day." He hopped up off the couch, grinning, and headed for his room to get dressed.

"Good deal. Where you want me to meet you?"

"Um." Dinner. And something fun. "You're Midtown, so I'll come up to you. In Duffy Square on the red stairs in about a half an hour. Sound good?"

"Surely do. I'm all yours, cher."

"You're so sweet, Colt." Genuine. It just kept him grinning. "I'll see you soon, okay?"

"Sounds good. I'll be there." There was a musical whistle and then a click.

"Fantastic." He danced around his room, dressing quickly in jeans, a tank, and one of his funky dancer T-shirts with the wide neckline. A little off the shoulder was fun, right?

The subway to Times Square took him no time at all, and the next thing he knew he was headed for the big red stairs. They were a landmark for tourists, but he always thought they were oddly romantic at night when all the lights came on.

Colt was there in his white T-shirt and jeans, dark eyes drinking in everything. He looked so good.

"Colt!" he shouted and waved. He picked up the pace, an extra spring in his already happy feet, and climbed the wide steps. "Hi." He sat down next to Colt, close enough to get an arm around his waist.

"Mmm. Cher." God, that smile lit up the world. "How's you?"

"I'm a little tired. Someone kept me up all night, and I worked hard today." Okay, he'd waited at least thirty seconds. That was plenty. He leaned in and took a quick kiss.

Colt's hand burned where it touched his thigh, all the way through his jeans. "Bad someone. You want I should beat him?"

"Nope." Damn. He covered Colt's hand with his. "I was actually thinking about asking him to do it again." They could skip dinner. Or have dinner and skip drinks after. Or have drinks at his place after.

Or he could just jump Colt right here on the steps in the middle of Times Square.

Jesus. Last night he was hoping for some fun, and it ended up hot. Tonight he was starting hot, and who knew where it was going. What a fucking score this guy was.

"I like that. You. Me. An encore."

"Looking forward to it." *You are not seventeen anymore.* He was perfectly capable of making himself wait at least until after they'd gotten something to eat. Doing the adult thing. Getting to know this lovely, lovely man sitting next to him even if Colt was making his brain short out just by being so close.

"Uh-huh. Does now work for you?" Colt leaned in close, lips near his ear. "I been sitting on that stool picking all day, feeling the ache of your cock inside me."

"Oh fuck, Colt." The air in the city was pretty polluted, but usually there was plenty of it. At the moment, though, none of it was finding its way into his lungs, and his cock pressed right up against his fly. "Yeah. Yeah, now's…. Jesus."

"Mmm. You smell like heaven. I could eat you alive, cher, suck you until you beg for mercy."

"Baby, I could throw you down right here. How close is your hotel, again?" Because he wasn't going to make it all the way to Christopher Street.

"Come on." Colt stood and took his hand, hauling him up. He loved how Colt's fingers burned, how he could feel each individual fingertip.

"That's the plan." He took a deep breath and told his boner to cool it, but it didn't really pay attention, and the walk across the street was pretty awkward. He had the picture in his head now, Colt's tight curls down between his thighs, and it wasn't letting him go.

"Uh-huh." Colt dragged him into a lobby and to an elevator, pushing him right in. "'M on six."

"Six." He focused enough to push what he thought was the right button and then leaned back against the doors as they closed, pulling Colt into him. He was already breathless, puffing out air before taking another kiss. Colt tasted like peppermint and coffee and pure unadulterated need.

He pressed his palm into Colt's groin, pulling it away as the doors opened again. "I've got something for you."

"Mmm. I been hungering for you all day." Colt wiggled, little ass rocking back and forth like a metronome, tempting him.

"I hear that." He gripped Colt's hand tighter. "Room. Go."

Colt managed to get the card to work, after three tries or so, the light finally going green so the door opened. And it was still closing as Kyle tore open his belt and lowered his fly.

"I liked the sound of that whole begging for mercy thing." Fuck, his throat was so dry, he could barely get the words out.

"I got this." Colt hit his knees, fishing Kyle's cock out and sucking it down in a single, breath-taking, soul-stealing move.

"Fuck!" he shouted. Or he thought he did. The sudden shock of Colt's mouth on him made him dizzy, and he reached out to brace a hand on the wall over Colt's head. He groaned, that he was sure of, because he felt it vibrate in him all the way to his toes. "You've so got this. Fuck."

Colt hummed, the sound deep and low, making everything draw up in his balls, his thighs. Then the suction started, steady and fierce and sure.

He wrapped a hand behind Colt's head, his fingers tangling into the curls. Colt's mouth was hot, and the pressure was so perfect, he didn't even bother to hold back or try not to lean right into it like a horny teenager. It felt so fucking good. "Yes! Christ, Colt. Just like that."

Colt was going to send him over the edge, was taking everything he had to give. He'd already been half-gone in the elevator, and there were no brakes on this train. He thrust once, testing, and gently nudged the back of Colt's throat, but the second time he disappeared to an impossible depth, making his eyes cross and his hips tremble. "Fuck. Fuck!"

One more thrust and his climax slammed into him, gripping his spine and driving straight through, everything focused in tight. He bucked and shot, forcing himself to let go of Colt as his knees buckled so he could brace both hands on the wall.

Colt gentled his suction, cleaning Kyle's cock so carefully that his eyes crossed again at the sensations.

"Mmm." Once he was pretty sure his knees would hold him up, he reached down and stroked his fingers across Colt's cheek. "You have an amazing mouth, music man." Colt had to be aching now too, which made all this slow, gentle attention that much sweeter.

Colt nuzzled into his palm, lips swollen and damp. "You taste good, cher."

He hooked a finger under Colt's chin, lifting it so he could see those deep brown eyes and licked his lips. "Does that lovely, long cock of yours want my mouth, or my ass, baby?" He grinned.

Colt grunted, his body humping the air hard for a few hard thrusts. "Dieu! Listen to you."

"Ha!" He laughed. "That, coming from the man that had me by the balls with just a few whispered words in my ear?" He tugged his jeans high enough that they wouldn't trip him up and then reached down to help Colt to his feet. He grabbed Colt's T-shirt and tugged it up and off. Then he stuck his hand into his pocket and pulled out a couple of condoms and lube and tossed them on the little desk by the door—about as far as they'd made it into Colt's hotel room. "You want me? You want to fuck me? Whatever you want, baby. Let's have some fun."

Colt grabbed his waistband and hauled him to the bed, then pushed his jeans down past his ass before stripping his shirts off. Those hot fingers dragged down his ribs, and he looked down, staring, expecting to see marks.

"Hot" was all he managed to say. There was more on his mind, but that was the only coherent bit. He shifted, letting his jeans fall so he could step out of them, and kicked them away.

Colt's lips were still a little swollen and beautiful, and he leaned in to taste them as he went after Colt's belt. Colt pushed into him, bringing them fully together, lean hips pumping against him in short, staccato motions.

"God, and I was worried I'd come off too eager." He laughed, playfully fighting Colt a little as he got those well-worn jeans open.

"I ain't so big on playing games, just gigs."

Okay, then. Just here to fuck. Dinner won't be necessary. Got it.

"You won't get any games from me, baby." He pushed Colt's jeans down over delicious hips, and the heavy cock fell right into his fingers. He gave it a couple of long, slow strokes. "Mm. Hello there, fella."

"Cher...." Colt arched hard. "Christ, I been thinking on you hard all day. You're like a good high."

"I can live up to that, I think. Choose your poison on the table there." He'd brought a few choices. He was picky about his protection, and he'd learned he wasn't alone. A man liked what a man liked.

Colt grabbed a square, then moved over to pull out a little, well-used tube from the bedside table. He grinned over, smile wide. "Didn't want to embarrass the cleaning girl with my… bedtime habits, hmm?"

Damn. He liked the view and watched Colt walk back toward him with real interest. "I don't know, what if it had been a cleaning guy? That might have worked out for you."

"No, sir. I got a certain person that tore my ass up last night. I'm interested in that." Colt winked at him. "Be where you are, huh?"

"Uh-huh. Love the one you're with." He was happy to be with Colt as long as the musician was in town, which he knew wouldn't be long. It never was with Colt's type. But hot, fun, sweet, and talented? He'd take it. And Colt kissed like there was nothing else that mattered in the whole damn world.

He hooked his fingers behind Colt's neck and looked down, watching as Colt stretched and smoothed the condom on over that pretty cock. "Mmm."

"You want, cher?" Colt stroked himself, showing off a little.

"Yeah. I want, Colt." That wasn't a lie—his body was warming up and considering a round two. He caught Colt's eyes and gave him a smoldering look. "I want you."

He backed into the bed, turning and giving Colt a good long look at his ass.

Colt hummed, and then those hands framed his ass, thumbs digging in hard enough to make him shiver.

Oh, this was definitely not going to disappoint. He bent, bracing his arms on the bed, giving Colt an even better view, and looked over his shoulder, pressing back against Colt's hip. "Come on, baby. Let's embarrass the neighbors."

"I can do that, me." Colt muscled up behind him, slick fingers sliding against him, into him. The touch was sure, firm enough that his abs drew up tight. "I reckon I can play you, make you sing real pretty for me."

Oh, holy fuck that felt good. He nodded, which was easier than talking at the moment. "Yeah. I… uhn. Seems like you… fuck." He pressed back into Colt's hand with a groan. Brain, words, not happening.

Colt sang as he touched, the sounds random and wanton as he pressed deep, slicking and stretching him. He answered back with long, needful moans until it just wasn't enough anymore and he couldn't stop himself thrusting back hard. "Please. Colt."

"Fuck, I love to see you move." Colt didn't tease, the heavy prick scraping along his ring of muscles, the pressure enough to make him grunt.

"I love to hear you talk." It wasn't just Colt's sexy accent and the lovely creole lilt in his tone; it was the words Colt used and the way he used them.

Kyle dropped to his elbows to better the angle and arched back toward Colt, groaning as he started to stretch. The burn was so good.

Colt's hand landed on the small of his back, steadying him as the short, slow strokes became long thrusts. The deliberate movement was maddening in just the right way, making him ache, Colt's girth impressive. He rolled his hips back gently, meeting each thrust without pushing Colt at all. "Fuck yes."

"Mm-hmm. No rushing."

No, Colt was playing his body like that guitar, making each long strum vibrate through him, filling him up with each stroke. He relaxed, enjoying the connection. He was aware of his own reawakened erection, but it was only a light distraction at the moment. He was far more interested in Colt's lovely sounds and the searing hot fingers digging into his hips.

"Cher." A line of pure heat slid along his spine as Colt licked him, nice and slow.

He rounded his back, bending into the sensation, showing off his dancer's flexibility in the best of ways. "I love how you say that." And how it felt when Colt said it, meaningful and earnest.

Colt groaned and arched, the angle of the thrusts changing, shifting to light him up inside. He gasped and squeezed his eyes shut as fireworks went off behind his lids. "Colt!"

"Mmm. La. There, hmm? Just so."

Kyle moaned as Colt repeated the thrust again and again, pounding him mercilessly.

"Uhn. Fuck." *Breathe*, he told himself. Colt was way too coherent, way too in control for him to race off on his own. But his balls ached, and he couldn't help the grunting. Colt was strong as fuck. He used the only leverage he had and clenched down hard around Colt's cock.

"Cher!" Colt rocked forward, slamming into him with a deep cry that sounded like it came from the pit of his stomach.

He threw his head back and shouted, he and Colt so perfectly in sync, moving together like they'd rehearsed this a million times together, rather than it being something so wonderfully new. "Colt!"

The tempo sped up, driving them deeper, higher, both of them grunting and crying out as the bedsprings laid out a rhythm.

He closed his eyes again, stopped thinking and started just feeling, the way he would with a complicated piece of music. He followed Colt's strong lead with his whole body, and he began to tremble as a luscious heat spiraled in his belly.

"Soon." The single word of warning rang in his head.

Soon, he thought, *or maybe now*. On Colt's next thrust, he arched back so Colt's cock hit him just right, and then tightened up, making sure Colt felt every spasm and ripple as his climax rolled through him. "Fuck, yes!"

A spate of patois poured out of Colt, low and foreign and filthy as Colt pressed deep and stiffened.

He was caught for a second between afterglow and laughter at Colt's dirty little outburst. It didn't matter that he hadn't understood a word; he didn't need to. He reached back and dug his fingers into Colt's thigh as he fought for a deep breath.

"Damn, cher." Colt leaned hard against his back.

He nodded, loving the weight of that incredible body on his. "Yeah. Damn." That little word kind of said it all.

Colt stroked his belly, petting him with lazy, long strokes. It felt so good, but his knees weren't going to hold him up much longer, let alone Colt too. He shifted, grunting as Colt's cock left him.

"Ditch that and then let's relax for a while together, hm?" He wanted to curl up against Colt, lay his head on Colt's chest. He felt like he needed that, which was something new for him.

"Yeah. Then we can go eat or order pizza. Whatever. I just want to be with you."

Kyle smiled. "I was thinking the same thing, baby." He tugged the covers down and climbed into the sheets while he waited for Colt to get back. Colt grabbed a bottle of water and toweled himself off before crawling into his arms, offering him a drink.

"Oh, thanks." He took a big sip and handed it back. "Mmm. You feel so good." He could just enjoy this for what it was. They were adults; they didn't have to apologize for wanting each other. After their first night together, it hadn't even occurred to Kyle that Colt wouldn't want exactly what he did. They'd connected on some level he didn't have words for yet.

Colt kissed him, humming deep in his chest, one hand sliding over his hip and he returned it, in no hurry, enjoying how Colt's kisses were always so deliberate. Like they were everything. Like Colt could be perfectly happy if that's all he ever got from Kyle. It fascinated him, how this man seemed to be so present, nowhere but right here, right now.

He settled with a sigh, limbs tangled up with Colt's, hands working the muscles gently anywhere they could. "That was off the charts, baby." He chuckled softly. "Way off."

"Mm-hmm. Magic." Colt winked at him, rubbed their noses together. "Good end to a work day."

"That's for sure. How was your session? That band seems like a bunch of characters."

"Good. Good. They know what they need, and they ain't stubborn about other folks coming with ideas."

"I bet you have a lot of ideas. Are you just playing guitar?" Someone with Colt's passion for music had to be creative.

"With them? Mostly. They ain't writers or looking for mandolin or banjo or nothing, but that's cool. They like to jam."

"You also play mandolin and banjo?" He wasn't surprised at all.

"I play piano, mouth harp, guitar—acoustic, electric, and steel. Bass, mandolin, banjo. I pass on a fiddle okay, but it ain't my thing." Colt grinned, rubbing against him nice and slow. "I like to play."

He grinned, letting Colt play all he liked. "Yes, I see that. So you're a session musician. Are they making an album? Is it all blues? How many tracks are they putting down?"

"They are. It's sort of blues, sort of folk, a little ska. Indie stuff, with soul. We've laid down thirteen. I think they want five more, and then I got to find a new place to play. Timmy, the studio guy? He says I can stay with him if I find a longer gig."

"That's cool. You got any nibbles? If you don't, I have a project I'm working on I need a guitar for. It's… it might not be your thing, and it's short-term, but it's work." He shrugged. But if it was Colt's thing? Jesus, it could be incredible.

"Sure." No hesitation, not even a second. "Playing is what I am. I would play for you."

"Yeah? Well, you see what Timmy can hook you up with, and then we can talk money and work out a schedule." *And that'll keep you in town a few more days.* He slid his toes along Colt's calf.

"Okay. I don't love hotels. I don't get to cook here, and that's no fun."

"It's not at all! I cook too. We should make dinner sometime."

"Mm-hmm. I like that. Yes. You say when, I'm there."

"Mmm. Friday night. Think about what you want to make for me, and we'll shop first. After my dance studio, the kitchen is my favorite room in the house. It's laid out just perfectly to get things done. There's a ton of counter space to roll things out, or for prep work or whatever. I cook all kinds of things."

He might be a dancer, but he was every inch an athlete, and he ate like one. Healthy, but he wasn't shy about seconds, and he didn't worry too much about cheating. He danced at minimum two hours a day, and on a regular day he was up around five or six. He could handle dessert with the best of them.

That said, though? With Colt around, the bedroom was quickly making its way to the top of his list of favorite places to be.

"I like it. I cook all the things—gumbo, étouffée, chilis. I can cook a whole pig and a gator, both."

"I don't think I need a whole gator." He laughed. Imagine that? "But thanks for thinking of me."

"Ain't nobody needs one, lest they're starving, cher. It's fishy chickeny tasting."

"So stick with fish or chicken. Fish sounds great. Let's do surf and turf Friday. You do something with fish, and I'll grill us a couple of fat steaks. What do you think?" With roasted potatoes or something. Oh, that sounded so good. Or maybe he was just hungry.

"Surely can. Y'all got a fish market or what?" Colt's belly began to rumble, and he laughed, the sound joyous. "We're making me hungry, cher."

"We're making me hungry too, music man. You want to head out and find some food? Or we could get room service or order a pizza... I'm easy." So easy. "Especially when you're around, it seems." He slid a hand over Colt's chest, tracing the contours.

"What you like? I could be naked with you for hours and just munch and talk and learn all the things."

"Room service, then." He smiled at Colt. "I like the sound of being lazy with you. So something easy to eat in bed, hm? Where's your menu?"

"Hrm. Where'd I put that book deal...." Colt rolled up and started digging through drawers, giving him a view of that tight ass. He could just... mm. Damn. He really could.

"No rush."

Colt looked back and up at him, offering him a huge grin over one shoulder.

"I'm not at all ashamed of myself for looking, baby." Not one little bit.

That earned him a wiggle and a shimmy, then a happy cry sounded. "La! I found it."

He patted the bed. "Let me see. We need some finger foods and stuff, right?"

"Mm-hmm. I like french fries." Colt clicked his teeth together. "I like to crunch."

"French fries, then. Watch those teeth." He grinned and took the book from Colt. "And the cheese platter, yeah? Maybe a bottle of wine?"

"Mmm. Works for me. Something red and rich."

"Yes, perfect." He reached over and picked up the phone to call in the order, adding malt vinegar for the fries and something sweet for dessert.

Colt's hands found his back, the fingers digging in, playing his muscles like a maestro.

"Oh. Oh wow. That feels great. You have the best hands." He let his head hang forward, melting into Colt's touch.

"Merci." Colt hummed softly, singing to him again, searching out little knots of tension.

"De rien." High school French for the win. "But I'm the one who should be—oh, right there—thanking you right now." He groaned as Colt found one of his hot spots. "I have a… ooh. Yep. Right there."

"Mm-hmm. I feel." Colt dug in, rubbing the knot out until he wanted to scream or purr or melt or something.

"Ask me anything right now and I'd say yes. I would. You're magic." He was actually kneading the sheets with one hand.

"Mmm. Good to know. I'll keep that in my pocket." Colt moved down to work on his ass, his legs.

He stretched out, very ready to enjoy all the attention. "The piece I want music for is pretty simple. And it's not all that long really. But I love telling stories with my body, and the music will fill in the gaps, add emotion, tension. We would work it out together, make the pieces fit, you know? And then you'd record it for me for the show."

"I can do that. You show me what you want, I will play it." The confidence in Colt's voice made him smile.

"I have no doubt. I'll show you what I do. I bet you'll figure out what it needs. And I was thinking guitar, but now that I know you play such a huge range, you may have other ideas there too. We can collaborate a little."

There was a knock at the door. "Oh. I can't get up right now." He could, but he was so relaxed. "Will you?"

"Surely do." Colt stood up, grabbed a towel, and wrapped it around his waist before answering the door. "Ooo, that all smells good. How're you?"

The soft back-and-forth, so Southern, so very warm and welcoming, made Kyle smile and made the young server blush. He'd noticed that when Colt asked someone how they were, he actually listened to the answer. He could learn to love a guy like that, he really could. Maybe even a musician. Maybe. Though that might be a bad idea.

When the door closed again, he tossed off the sheet he'd pulled over his ass for modesty and made himself sit up. "So do you try to make people blush, or does that just happen to everyone you talk to?" He grinned.

"Hmm?" Colt settled the little rolling cart close by and started pulling off lids.

He gave Colt a fond smile. Of course Colt would have no idea what he was talking about. He reached for the wine and the bottle opener. "Never mind, baby. What are you feeding me first?"

"It all looks good. You like a certain kind of cheese?"

"If it's cheese, I like it." He leaned toward Colt. "Surprise me. Again." He winked.

Colt explored his options, then carefully made up a bite with cracker and cheese and a dollop of some sort of jelly.

"That's pretty." He opened his mouth to accept the bite and made a little show of holding on to Colt's fingers with his teeth for a second. He poured them each a glass of wine and handed one to Colt. "Yummy."

"Thank you." Colt lifted his glass. "Bon temps, cher."

"Cheers to you, baby." The wine was perfect, rich and dark. He reached for a french fry and held it out. "You have family back home?"

"I got a mamma. My daddy passed when I was ten. He played blues on the Quarter. Mamma, we don't talk much. She got her a fancy husband after I left home at fifteen."

"My mom's fancy husband is also my father." He snorted and took a fry for himself. "Fifteen? Why did you leave so young?"

Colt shrugged, lips twisting. "Lots of things. I mean, don't no one want a queer boy. Don't no one want a dumb queer boy. Don't no one want a dumb queer boy that proves Mamma was fucking a blues man in N'awlins."

"Hm. I'm sorry, baby." He stroked a hand over Colt's back. "But you look like you're doing well for yourself despite her. Nobody wants a queer boy in my family either. My mother wants me to marry one of her friend's debutante daughters." He laughed. "My father says I'm 'really pushing it' dancing."

"Pushing it. That sounds right." Colt took a fry and nibbled on it. "I looked you up on my phone. I could watch you dance for my whole life and then go for seconds."

"You… really?" He felt himself light up, a warmth that came up from his belly and put a blush on his cheeks. He smiled, pleased and touched. "You looked me up?"

"Well, sure. You're something. I like the one with the bed best. It made me sad, but there was a happy ending, I think."

"Bittersweet." He nodded. "A lot of ballet is like that. To die for romance, star-crossed lovers, obstacles keeping lovers apart, broken hearts, lots of drama." He loved the drama of the whole thing; you had to.

"Blues too. It's story, and not normally a happy one."

"Oh, we're going to work so well together. Tell me how you learned to play. Did your dad teach you first?"

"He did. Mamma is a piano teacher, so I learned to read music from her, to score. I learned soul from my daddy. I learned the blues on the streets, I think." Colt made him another perfect bite. "I had lots of help, and I wasn't alone long. There's a tribe of folks that have themselves and no one else."

"A tribe. I like that." He'd never had anything like that. Or, well…. Maybe he had? "I had some school friends I danced with and the companies that cast me—same idea, I guess. Artists, like minds sticking together."

"That's it. We get it. Needing to do what we do." Colt leaned against him and fed him a french fry. "It's a little bit different—the studio and the street. The street is all in the dark, but the studio? Oi, that's anytime."

He munched down the french fry and followed it with a big sip of his wine. "You have an agent now, though, right? How long did you play on the street?"

"I started playing the bars when I was seventeen, got a studio gig about three months later. Christmas music in July. Crazy."

He laughed. "Christmas music. You've come a long way, then." He kissed Colt, just a quick one.

"Oh cher, I felt about eighty foot tall, getting that paycheck." Colt leaned into him, sipping his wine. "Ain't nothing like that first check."

He put an arm around Colt's shoulders. "No shit. Nothing beats that first real paycheck for doing what you love to do. Mine was tiny, but I got to wave it in front of my father and tell him he was wrong."

"When did you start dancing?"

"It's kind of ironic, actually. I started when I was about four, and I went to the same studio as my three older sisters. I was so jealous of them, and my mom stuck me in class just to shut me up. They all quit, and I'm the one that stuck with it."

"That's cool. Three sisters, huh? Y'all close?"

"We keep in touch. Katie comes to my performances every so often; she's still local. I've got an older brother too. He's a super-lawyer. One of those white-collar people. I'm not sure I get what he does."

"Ah. None of those in my woodpile."

"You could take a match to most of mine—that would be okay." He winked and sipped his wine. "I just stay in the city, and they stay over on the Gold Coast, and it's all good."

"It's about making a place—places, I guess—that you're cool."

He smiled, leaning in for another kiss. "I'm cool right here. I know that."

"Yeah." Colt nibbled his bottom lip, playing with him.

"There's more cheese if you're hungry," he teased, reaching out with his tongue and licking Colt's upper lip.

"More french fries too. I like the wine in your mouth."

"I was just going to say I like the salt on your lips." God, how silly. Fun, and true, but silly. He pushed his fingers into Colt's hair and kissed him, his curious tongue slipping past Colt's lips.

The touch of Colt's hand on his hip made him hum, made his hips roll.

"I listened to Robert Johnson this morning after you left. 'Hellhound.'" He pushed Colt back into the pillows. "I like it. I was dancing, trying to work out the reasons it speaks to you."

"You know the myth, eh? That he sold his soul for the music?"

"No. Really? Tell me the story?"

"Robert Johnson went to the crossroads with his guitar, and he met the Devil there, a big old bastard, black as pitch and three times as sticky. The Devil tuned up for him, played a couple three songs, and when the last note disappeared from the earth, Robert sold his soul for the blues."

Oh, he could choreograph that story. "So Johnson's playing the blues for the Devil now?"

"Don't no one know, but if he comes to me in the dark, I'll hide my head and sing."

"Does that make him go away or just make you feel better?" To Kyle, these were children's stories, things you told each other at sleepovers to scare your friends. The Devil wasn't anything more than a spook to him. But Colt sounded so serious. It was strange and fascinating.

Colt gave him a serious look. "I 'spose that depends on what you're askin'. The Devil comes in all sorts of clothes and lies, and he's made of music. The question is, is your soul safe or your body? Your body ain't hardly ever safe, because Lucifer can take hold of that, but your soul? That you got to give."

He watched Colt for a bit, thinking about the things he'd sell his soul for, wondering who he'd give it to. "Would you sell yours for what Johnson had?"

"I got the blues. I pray that if they told me they'd take my hands unless I give my soul, I'd say no and trust that I would learn to play with my feet." Colt sounded so… sure. Like this was something he thought about, worried on.

He stroked Colt's cheek, soothing him.

"I can't say I pray, but I don't know what I'd do if I couldn't dance. I promise you I know that feeling." The idea terrified him, in fact. "Gives me nightmares if I think too hard about it."

"Yeah. It eats the whole world, the need to do this thing we do." Colt leaned into him, resting hard. "And that ain't bad."

He pulled Colt close, let him lean. He took some comfort in Colt's heavy presence. "No, baby. It's not bad at all."

Chapter Five

By Friday night, Colt had put in seventy-five studio hours, spent two long nights making love with Kyle, and was feeling like an empty glove.

One that had been filled with chicory and shook hard.

He waved Timmy off about putting the guitar away. "Nah. I might have need of it. You still renting a room, Timmy?"

"Totally still renting, dude. Lost my roomie to a Texan. You wanna check it out?" Timmy got the last of the cables dressed.

"Yeah. Yeah, I do. I got to make a call about supper around eight and how to get there." And did he need to bring a toothbrush and all?

"Kyle?" Timmy played it off, casual.

"Yeah. I like him. A lot. We're cooking." Although they hadn't shopped. Were they cooking tonight? He thought so.

"Oh yeah? He's a fan-tas-tic cook. He's a good guy too. You see him dance yet?"

"Not officially. I seen him practice and on the phone. He's magic." Watching Kyle move stole his breath clean away. One day he wanted to pick and let Kyle dance, jam together.

"He's something else." Timmy pulled out his keys. "You want to see the room? Make your call on the way?"

"Surely do." He grabbed his phone and dialed. Timmy led him out of the building, locking up the studio and the big safe on the way.

"Hey there." Kyle sounded warm, pleased to hear from him. "You all done?"

"I am. Been a lot of work. I'm fixin' to go see the room to rent, and then I'll head your way, if I can figure out how to find you again." He'd manage, he was sure, but he felt a little like he'd been called up from the dead.

"Wow. You sound tired, baby. Take an Uber. Timmy can call one for you."

"Yeah? Cool enough. I can't wait to see your face." He was addicted to Kyle, finding himself thinking about his new lover, again and again.

"Mm. I can't wait to kiss your face." Kyle had a little growl in his voice. "Don't dawdle, lover."

"No dawdling. Gon' look at this room, say it'll work, and come to you." It was a plan. It was possibly even a good plan.

"I'm waiting." Kyle ended the call.

Timmy was laughing. "Dude, you should see the look on your face."

"Is it a bad look?" He was tired but happy, so that should balance everything out, right?

"No way, man. It's a good look. A lot like that look you get when you're playing and hit a sweet spot."

"He's a sweet spot, all right. Let's do this thing. You said your roommate went to Texas?" He'd played Houston, Dallas, SXSW a lot.

"No. He went with a Texan. They're still here, most of the year. They travel back and forth."

"Ah." They went to a decent enough place with a nice room that he could settle in with his guitar. The kitchen was functional, and the front room was fine. It worked way better than some hotel room. "I want it, me. We work good together."

"We do. I wouldn't have offered if I didn't think we could hang, dude. I work a ton, you work a ton, we get each other. You don't mind a little smoke now and then, do you?"

Colt snorted. Shit, he'd probably done more things in his time than Timmy had even heard of. "I got no issues with the green—smoke or fairy."

"You like that shit, dude? I know a bar for you next time you're interested. And just so you know, if I light up and you're around, you're invited. Just assume. If I didn't want to share, I'd wait."

"Fair enough. So, how you want we should do this? You want me to come after I get done with Kyle?" That could be tomorrow morning, could be Monday. He didn't know. He didn't really care.

"Hang on." Timmy disappeared into the kitchen and came back with a key ring. "The big one is for the foyer doors, and these two are for the apartment. Top lock, bottom lock. There's only a few days left in the month, so we'll call us square until the first. I have to walk the rent over on the last business day of the month, so I'd appreciate your piece in cash a few days early, if that's okay."

"I can do that. I'll bring it when I come back. Kyle said you could call me an Uber?"

"Oh. Yeah. You should get the app on your phone." He watched Timmy call up an app, tap a few things. "All set. He'll text when he gets here. Driver's name is Ray."

"Thanks. I'm still learning this new phone, but I'll figure it. Does he know where to go, or do I need to text Kyle?"

"He knows. I've been to a couple of parties at Kyle's, so I have his address in the app. Oh, man. You should convince him to throw a party. They're… an experience."

"Mmm. I like that. Not today. I'm wore." He was running on fumes and a handful of hard candy.

They talked shop for a while, waiting on the car. When the car arrived, Timmy grabbed the door for him. "Get some rest. Only a few days left next week, but they're going to be long ones. We've got some work to do."

"And then we move on to a whole new band." A whole new sound, a whole new style.

"You moving to a new studio? You're not playing with the group that's coming in next, are you? Or are you?"

"I got a email. It's staying in your place, hmm? Rockabilly? Ring a bell?" He didn't know. He went where he was sent.

"Totally! Ohhh, duuude." Timmy drew the words out ominously. "Those guys… they're friendly and talented and stuff, but they're gonna try your patience. I'm just sayin'. Show up ready to go with the flow. They never start or end on time. They drink. They take crazy breaks to, like, brainstorm over Mongolian barbecue."

"So long as they pay me, huh?" Goodie. Of course, he could be flexible, couldn't he? Hell yeah.

"They always pay me." Timmy winked. "You better run, dude. See you whenever. Or Monday."

"I'll text. Bye." He ran down and looked for the car, so ready to get to Kyle, to somewhere quiet for a minute.

The Uber was anything but quiet. His driver, Ray, had questions. *"Where you from, brother? What brings you this far north? What do you play? You know Peyton Manning was born in New Orleans? Jared Leto? Reese Witherspoon? Great food down there…"* and on, and on, and on.

He answered and laughed, letting himself enjoy the company, the questions, because this was what it was all about, right? Learning stuff about people. Hell, by the time they pulled in front of Kyle's, he felt better, more solid.

Kyle answered the door in a tank top that wasn't clothing so much as decoration, and beat-up, loose jeans that sat low. Colt got a kiss right there in the doorway. "Oh, so good to see you."

"Yes. Lord yes." He was a little dizzy with relief that he was here.

"Come in. Come in, baby." Kyle linked arms with him and led him through the hall and into the kitchen. "Do you want some coffee? You really look exhausted."

"I do, please, and to rest my fingers for a bit."

"You worked like a dog this week." Kyle poured him a strong cup of coffee from a carafe on the counter, then picked up the hand he wasn't drinking with and massaged his palm with what seemed like practiced thumbs.

He stared for a second, his mind trying to understand what he was feeling. Did it hurt? Did it feel like sex? What?

"Hurts? Come on, sit down." Kyle led him over to the little café table and sat him down, then pulled up a chair opposite him.

"I don't know. I don't know what it feels like." He sat. Boom. Okay. "How's you, cher?"

"I'm good. I'm a very satisfied kind of tired." Kyle smiled for him and just kept on working the tendons along his thumb and up the outside of his hand. "This should feel like someone working your worries away. Never had a massage before?"

"No. I knew they were tender, but not so much." His fingers curled as Kyle worked out a sore spot, and he jerked as the tension popped like a sprung guitar string.

Kyle let him go with the sudden movement but went right back to it, more gently as he relaxed. "How hungry are you? You want something?"

"Cher, my belly done forgot eating. Later, hmm?"

"Yeah, I hear that. You want to cook tomorrow? It's later than I expected; we could shop in the morning. I think you should let me work on your shoulders and your back some; they've got to be as tense as your hands."

"I can cook tomorrow. I.... Lord, cher, you make me dizzy." He didn't know if it was selfish to say yes, please, touch me.

Kyle kissed him softly. "Tomorrow, then. Come on, let's get you stretched out." Kyle led him upstairs to the bedroom and started undressing him slowly, fingers moving over buttons, fabric, and skin like he was something precious.

He closed his eyes and inhaled, filling his lungs with Kyle's scent. Lord, that was just right.

"Other than obviously exhausting, did recording go well today?" Kyle voice was soft and had a soothing lilt in it.

"Jus' fine. Lots of good music. I laid down a few solo tracks they could use if they needed them later too."

"You work hard, don't you? No wonder you're so tired." Kyle turned down the bed and gave it a pat. "Stretch out on your tummy, and I'll work on your back a little. You can just rest. Talk if you want, don't if you don't. I'm here either way."

"You had a good couple days, cher?" He rolled over and found himself a comfortable spot.

"I did. We've got a show opening in a couple of weeks, and it's getting serious around the theater now. This is my favorite part of the process—pulling it together, focusing in on the details—but it's real work. We have some amazing dancers, though. Sometime you'll have to come see."

"I would love that." He loved to see people living out their passions.

Kyle's fingers were slippery when they touched his back, and they roamed over his skin for a bit, warming it with just light pressure at first. "Me too. You'll have to let me know if you get some time away from the studio in the next couple of weeks."

"I got time after Tuesday. You let me know." He blinked slowly, mesmerized by the caresses. "Feels good."

"I will. Depending on how rehearsals go, maybe Thursday or Friday." Kyle started in with long strokes with flat hands and heavy pressure. "So, it's great that you're taking a room with Timmy. Does that mean you're in town for a few more weeks?"

"Uh-huh. I like the work, the place. I want to stay about." He liked Kyle. A lot. Enough to stay a bit.

"I probably don't need to tell you I like that you're 'staying about.' But in case there's any question, I'm glad to hear it." Kyle's thumbs dug into the muscle across his shoulders.

He had intended to answer, but all he could do was groan. Damn, that was better than sex.

Kyle chuckled softly, the sound warm. "Good right there, huh?" Kyle kept it up, across his shoulders and slowly up the sides of his neck, working every little knot and every bit of tension those fingers stumbled over.

He might have spoken; he might have just moaned. Hell, he didn't know. He might have told Kyle every one of his secrets.

He was aware of Kyle's hands on him for a while. Working muscles in his arms, his lower back a little later, even his thighs. And then some amount of time must have passed, because the next thing he was really aware of was a dark, quiet room and Kyle lying next to him, hair damp and smelling freshly showered.

"Mmm. Magic man." He had to smile. Had to.

"Mmm. Hi. You don't have to be awake, baby." Kyle moved closer, like gravity had just pulled him in.

"Love how you smell." He let himself snuggle in and enjoy, feeling like a king—happy and melted and comfortable.

"You crashed a long while ago, and I popped in the shower. How do you feel?"

"Like I been taken care of. Thank you. You didn't have to, but you did." He took a long, lazy kiss, pouring his thanks right into it.

"Mmm," Kyle hummed, sounding happy, willingly accepting his kiss. "I wanted to. You didn't seem like yourself. You looked like you needed some love."

"You know how it is—you pour yourself out, and then you pour more and more, and then you're bleeding music."

"I know exactly. You need to think about something else, right? Feed your heart and your mind, and let your soul recover. We'll do something fun tomorrow. Something totally different. Maybe get up high and see the view. You want to? Or go shopping. Or walk in Central Park."

"Yes. Yes, we can explore. Together." He loved that. He loved to hear the beat of somewhere new.

"See? You sound better already." Kyle kissed him, smiling against his lips.

"All you, hmm?" They were basking like gators on the bank.

"I'll take the compliment." Kyle hummed at him again and tightened an arm over his chest. "Sleep, Colt. We both need it, and we don't want to lose the day tomorrow."

"No. No, we don't. I want to be with you." He wanted to go play and know all the new things there were.

"You are with me, baby. We'll get up to some fun tomorrow." Kyle rubbed his chest, soothing him to sleep.

Chapter Six

The next morning was brilliantly sunny, and Kyle pulled open every curtain in his home studio, letting the sunbeams warm the floor. A sunny day called for Santana, yes? He started up his music and let it inspire him, feeling that perfect burn as he stretched his hamstrings and his glutes on the barre.

It took that whole first song and two more before he was warmed up enough to dance, and he marked out the steps to a piece he was performing with two other men in the new program. He obviously didn't need to rehearse the steps, because his mind kept wandering away from what he was working on to the fascination of the man he'd left sleeping in his bed.

That was it. Colt was fascinating. So strange and wonderful, and Kyle was drawn to him in every way. Physically? They could just burn each other down when they wanted to, or Colt could carefully shatter him with one touch and then put him back together piece by piece. He was drawn to the musician, the artist, Colt's creative mind.

A week ago he and Colt had been drinking and singing in a bar. Colt was young and looked it; he was full of energy and wonder at the city he'd landed in. But last night Colt just looked exhausted. Burned out. Granted, they'd kept each other up nearly all night at least twice. But even so, Colt had just allowed himself to be spent, played until his fingers were sore and beyond.

If he ever tried to dance like that, he'd... well, he'd be useless. He'd never allow himself to dance to exhaustion. Colt either didn't know his limits, ignored them, or simply had no perspective when he was working.

He heard Colt's lilting words, spoken even in his mind in that smooth, sexy accent—*Robert Johnson went to the crossroads... and sold his soul for the blues.*

Huh.

Even exhausted, Colt was magical. One might call it intuition or empathy, but there was more to it than that. There were things about art, about creativity, about being human that he just seemed to understand, deeply, as truth. And on top of that, Colt's faith, his spirituality wasn't only surface deep, or habit; it was in his skin. It was a part of his soul.

Kyle didn't understand faith, not like that. He felt as though he could study the man forever and Colt's own truth could still slip right through his fingers if he didn't pay very close attention.

Work, Kyle.

He changed the music and ran through the piece again in his mind, then took up his starting position and cleared his thoughts to focus on telling the story. The story of what is left when a man's true love chooses another.

The dance was everything, emotion running down his spine and out to his extended fingertips and pointed toes. That, combined with the exertion as every muscle fired at once, lifting him off the floor and powering him through turns, was as exhilarating as it was exhausting.

The music was appropriately powerful in parts, soft and subtle in others, and he was easily swept into the drama. He hadn't choreographed this piece, and he was glad about that, because the steps were not his own, but something he'd had to make his own. Still, that didn't stop his heart from breaking every single time.

When it was over and he was panting, his chest aching with emotion, he looked over, finding Colt sitting in the other room where he could see, cross-legged on the floor, guitar in his lap, one tear sliding down his cheek.

"Ain't you something, cher? It'd kill a man, to see you dance to the blues."

"That piece is painful but beautiful, right?" He found he could breathe easier with his own lover, at least of the moment, close by. He walked over, knelt in front of Colt, and kissed him. "You should see it with the other two dancers. One dancing the lover that left me and one his new love interest."

"Mmm. One day. Good morning, cher. How you be?"

"I'm—" How was he? The sun was out; he was dancing, Colt was sitting here with his guitar.... "I'm perfect. Wonderful. You? Did you sleep well?"

"Like a log." Colt began to play, a more sultry version of the song he'd just danced to, the whole vibe less heart-wrenching and more… wicked.

"Mmm. I like that." He stood up and stretched a little, just keeping his muscles warm. The twist on the very familiar piece made him grin, though. It had a groove to it that made him want to move. "I like that a lot. Come in. Come into the studio."

"Yeah?" Colt rolled up to his feet, adorable with his bare chest, bare feet, jeans loose on his hips.

He took Colt by the hand and led him right into the center of the large room. The sun had shifted so it wasn't as bright, but the sky was a brilliant blue. "Can I get you a chair, or are you more comfortable on the floor?" He had a couple of folding chairs against the far wall.

"However you want me, you got me. You want I should play for you?"

"I would; will you? You don't mind the floor?" He waited while Colt got settled. "Just play anything you want for now. I'm…." He waved his hand near his head. "I'm just—I've got something."

"Surely." Colt strummed idly for a few seconds, then found it—Kyle wasn't sure what *it* was, but suddenly there was a hunger in the air, the melody like a stalking tiger that was teasing its prey, taunting it, pushing forward, then easing back.

Kyle nodded and stepped back from Colt slowly, eyes on the floor but focused inward as he worked through the sound of the music, the tempo, the patterns. He moved across the floor in small movements at first, marked turns, small jumps, and then suddenly he had it. He dove toward the floor and rolled, landing in a long, stretched-out pose that he held for a second not a foot away from Colt's guitar. Then he reached back and lifted himself to his feet with one arm and took off across the room.

The tempo changed, the slaps on the acoustic sounding tribal, the deep thumps adding a necessary bass, one that reverberated through the room. He felt the bass in his chest, let it drive his movement.

He didn't think at all after that; he just went with it, moving freely, though he knew some part of his mind was remembering the steps when they were really right. Improv was about staying in the moment, not thinking ahead more than a measure or two.

Colt seemed to get it, seemed to get him, giving him a delicious mixture of tempo and pause, the dark eyes on him, learning him. He was too focused on his form to look back, but he knew. He could feel Colt's eyes track him down the length of the room.

Once he realized how in tune they were, he decided to have some fun, to see how Colt's playing responded to him and his movement instead of the other way around. He pulled out some of his own choreography, a piece he'd been working on largely in silence for lack of the right accompaniment. He made a point of heading off in another direction, stepping off the beat on purpose and hoping Colt would catch on.

The music grew softer for a moment, curious; then it attached itself to his heels like a shadow, finding him unerringly.

The piece started out cautious emotionally, reticent, but took a few small risks that became more frequent as they were rewarded. It was a piece about stepping beyond one's comfort zone, about the process of learning and the things that open up the world of what's possible. Toward the finale of the piece, it exploded with joy, an energy that filled the room to the rafters and echoed off the walls.

By the end the guitar was ringing, the strings bent to Colt's will, the studio reverberating with pure happiness.

Kyle let the last notes dissipate before he moved, and then he spun around and slid across the floor to Colt, still trying to catch his breath. "Woo!"

Colt was sheened with sweat, breathing hard, and he got a grin, a wild kiss. "So fine."

He laughed breathlessly and stretched out on the floor on his back, in front of Colt. "Amazing. Just… fantastic. Stunning. Will you remember any of that? I'd love to get it recorded sometime. You know, I hadn't finished choreographing that piece? The whole last third was just… on the fly. It just kind of happened." He was talking fast, even for a New Yorker. It would be a miracle if Colt actually understood any of that. "God, that was awesome."

"You are. I could do that forever." Colt leaned forward, touched his arm. "Magic, eh?"

"Not me, baby. Us." He covered Colt's hand with his and rolled to face him. "It was magic. That's the only word for it." He sat up then and kissed Colt quickly over the top of the guitar. "You're not going to do that forever, though, because it's our rest day. I'm done dancing; you're done playing. Quick showers, some coffee, and then we have a city to see. Right?"

"Right." Colt grinned at him. "I want to see things, hear the sounds, hmm?"

"Feel the rhythms. Soak up the energy." He stood up, still high on their positive vibe. "Have some fun."

He waited for Colt to stand, and then they made their way back to the bedroom for showers. After that, he made them a pot of strong, dark coffee and some avocado toast.

"What do you want to do first? We could go to Central Park and explore. We could go to the top of the Empire State Building. We could head up to the Botanical Gardens or wander around the West Village…." He was up for anything. He almost never got to be a tourist in his own city.

"Yes. Anything." Colt moved in his kitchen easily, tasting food as he cooked, adding a sprinkle of lime here and cayenne there, surprising him with a little strange spinach salad for the top of the toast. Kyle was glad to see Colt eating instead of insisting on only coffee until dinner. The man needed his strength.

"Mmm. This is delicious. And pretty. We're going to have some fun cooking dinner in here tonight." He took his plate and his coffee to the small round kitchen table and pointed to the other chair for Colt. "We'll start up high, then, get a view of the city, and decide what's next from there." He liked the view from the Empire State. It was a zoo on Saturdays, but he'd been given a couple of passes as an opening night gift that should get them up top fairly quickly.

"Sounds good. This is a different city than I'm used to, but all of them are, I think. Everyone has a different vibe."

"What are you used to? You mean compared to home?" He was so curious. He needed to know more about Colt, more about where he was from and what influenced him.

"I been to Baton Rouge, Nashville, Memphis, Atlanta, Dallas, Houston, Austin. They're all different. I love New Orleans the best, then Austin. It's a music city too. Down to its roots."

He nodded. "New York is heavily rooted in music too. You'll see it everywhere. Jazz clubs and other nightclubs with amazing vocalists, street musicians, buskers in the subway." There was no shortage of music in the city. "What makes New Orleans your favorite? Just because it's home? The kind of music? The vibe?"

"It's home. I grew up in Houma, but my daddy played there. It's a special place—there's magic on the streets, voodoo queens and priests, bluesmen and witches."

Voodoo and witches. Like Johnson and the Devil, he would have considered them little more than spooky stories before he met Colt. He wasn't sure where he stood anymore, if he was honest, but he understood that his lover believed in those things deeply, and he had no intention of insulting Colt. "I don't know if I believe in all of those things, but if I ever go, I want you to be my tour guide."

"I'd be honored." Colt winked over the top of his coffee cup. "And none of them things care a bit whether you believe, honey. You make yourself happy, and they will too."

"I'm pretty good at making myself happy." He leaned closer to Colt, smiling back. "You're pretty good at it too."

"I do try, cher. I do. This is some nice coffee. I like."

"That's my little bit of magic. I make a great cup of coffee." He'd finished his, in fact, and got up to take his things to the sink. "Are you ready?"

"Lemme grab a shirt and my boots. I brought an extra. Shirt, not boots."

"Don't rush, baby. I'm going to clean up here."

"Oh. Oh, I'll help. That ain't right, you washing up alone." Colt jumped right up to help.

"Dishwasher, baby." He pointed. "I'm fine. You go on and get ready. We'll get out of here faster. Don't forget sunglasses and your phone for pictures." The glare was something else from up high.

"I'm on it." Colt kissed him, deep and hard enough that he saw lights for a second, and then Colt was off like a shot.

He licked his lips, the coffee tasting even better with a splash of Colt in it. Fuck, those kisses were never going to get old. His mind could have wandered after Colt all morning, he couldn't help but go over that dance in his mind, Colt playing for him and reading his intention so well. And the way they worked together like they shared—

Whoa.

Okay, so that was crazy.

He was just a little dance-drunk, right? Still caught in the music. In Colt's music. In Colt himself, and he still couldn't understand why. He needed to figure it out, figure out what they were doing. He'd invested before in people who had other places to be, and while Colt was interested in New York now, he knew the type. A gig would come up in Chicago or Austin, and Colt would be off, fascinated by a new place. Whatever that was that had happened this morning in his studio felt real but fragile and rare. He needed to understand it.

Colt came back to him, singing softly in a lilting patois, hands finding him unerringly.

"Oh, look. A shirt." He smiled and let Colt pull him in close, exploring the fabric with his fingers.

"I know. I'm all dressed and pretty for you." Those black-button eyes twinkled for him, wicked and playful. Joyous.

"So pretty I could just eat you up." He kissed Colt's nose. "Let's go play tourist." He wriggled away, actually wriggled like he was four or something. God, those eyes made him giddy.

"Works for me, cher. I'm good at playin', me." Colt shot him a wink and grabbed his hand. "Allez!"

LORD HAVE mercy, they'd done looked and seen and heard, and the sun was shining, and he was having the best time a man could with clothes on.

They went up into shining buildings and down into the earth. They walked a million miles, Kyle laughing and leading him from one fascination to another. This time to Central Park.

"We're here!" From Strawberry Fields, they'd taken a nice walk around the south end of the lake, and now they were looking at Alice, sitting on her toadstool, bronze and bigger than life. Kyle just about looked like he was fixin' to bust with happy. "Oh, the Mad Hatter is wonderful. My favorite of them, I think."

"I seen a play once about Alice being lost in the bayou, and the Queen was Marie Laveau." The hatter had been Baron Samedi, and the hare had been a zombie, jittering about. Best had been M'sieu Lapin as a rougarou, the crazy beast chasing le feu follet into the darkness. He'd loved that, the way the people had been all in black, running with fairy lights to give the monster bunny something to chase.

"Okay, who is Marie Laveau? You've got to be sick of me asking you to explain things all the time. I'm sorry." Kyle rubbed his arm, looking honestly apologetic but interested.

He knew Kyle was curious and liked to know things. "Oh, Lord, Lord. She is a voodoo queen from my neck of the woods. Damn powerful, so the story goes. Some say they saw her walking the day after she died. If you have a wish you need spelled, you can go draw an X on her grave, but you got to sneak in, these days, so it better be a powerful need." Wandering St. Louis No. 1 was taking your life into your own hands, especially after dark.

Kyle listened to every word, looking thoughtful, working something over behind those maybe brown, maybe green eyes. "I love your stories." He took Colt's arm, leading him over to a vendor under a yellow umbrella. "Let's sit and have a drink, and then we'll go shop for dinner."

"Sounds good." One day he would take Kyle to Bourbon Street to the Jean Lafitte, to Marie's House of Voodoo, to Jackson Square and have his palm read. So many things.

Kyle bought them lemonade, and they sat by the Conservatory Water, watching the little model boats sail the pond. "If you kind of tune out the building back there, they look so real."

"They got lots of boats from my home too. Lots. You ever been on any?" He'd been on a bunch—airboats and shrimping boats and riverboats and bass boats.

"Oh yeah. My dad has a couple. A thirty-foot sloop and a forty-eight-foot yacht. I've been on a cruise to the Caribbean and on a bunch of little boats for fishing. Also canoes, kayaks, stuff like that."

"How cool is that?" He couldn't imagine what that meant really, but he knew it sounded important. Sloop sounded like a word in a doo-wop song, sort of like duck shit hitting the water. *Sloop*.

"You like the water?"

"You cain't be a bayou baby and not like the water, I don't think."

"Well, maybe we'll get out on a boat sometime." Kyle finished his lemonade quickly, noisily slurping up the last drops and grinning. "Pardon my Scotchman's whistle, I guess I was thirsty."

"Scotchman's whistle... I like that." He blew across his straw, making a deep, low sound that made him chuckle.

"Always making music." Kyle leaned against him. "You want to shop? Do you know what you're making me?"

"What's that, cher? Happy, I hope."

Kyle laughed. "For dinner, baby."

"Shrimp étouffée, hmm? With a good bread?"

"Sounds perfect. And yes, you're making me happy." Kyle kissed his cheek and took his hand. "I'm having a great day. You?"

"I am. This is a good place, so much to see. I bet you could spend a whole life and not get to it all."

"I basically have, yeah. And the weird thing is, when you live here, you hardly ever see any of it, you know? So busy working and whatever. It's just hanging out right under your nose."

Kyle stood up. "Come on, we'll hop the bus and head home."

"Is there a store to shop at?" He'd need the holy trinity and Gulf shrimps, if he could.

"Yeah, closer to my place. You need a fish market?"

"Ooh, yeah." He loved to see all the fishes, see what was good. Sometimes he would go to the market after his long night playing, walk around with all the cooks in their checkered pants.

Kyle smiled at him. "Okay. We'll start there."

The bus was a long trip, but he got to see lots of this part of the city out the windows. The park was on the right all the way to midtown and on the left were cool old buildings, with details and carvings and most of them had doormen.

The fish market was a big, open space. Busy and chilly, and noisy too. Whole fish on ice, filets in glass display cases, live lobsters and crabs.

He wandered, happy as a pig in shit, looking at all the different seafood. The redfish was gorgeous, and they did have Gulf shrimps, head on. "I need two pounds of them, please, sir, and a redfish."

"Whaddya makin', my man?" The older man behind the counter got to work.

"Étouffée." If the shrimps were nice, next time he'd make barbecue ones. Or gumbo. "The fish, he just wants to come home and be eat up."

"Nice. Fresh clam juice on the end there if you need it." The guy weighed the fish and handed it over.

Kyle leaned around him. "I don't think I've ever had redfish."

"No? We'll have it with…. You got rice?" He needed celery, peppers, onions, some parsley and tomatoes….

"Sure, I have rice."

"Shrimp." The man handed over the wrapped-up package. "Enjoy your dinner."

He nodded and grinned, doing a little impromptu soft shoe. "Merci. Gonna. How about veggies? What all do you have, cher?"

Kyle took his arm as they headed to the register. "Um. Usual prep stuff? Onions, peppers, garlic, celery, spinach, mushrooms... I grow some herbs—parsley, oregano, basil, mint. What do you need?"

"'Sides that? A little bit of spices and some butter and flour to roux it up." Oh, he was fixin' to make Kyle's house smell like home.

"You want me to get that?" Kyle pulled out a leather wallet. "You're a rent-paying New York musician now."

"We split it, hmm? Down the middle." The room had to be cheaper than the hotel, so he had to be better off today than yesterday.

"Sure, baby. Down the middle." Kyle handed him cash. "I think I'll have the spices you need. If I'm missing anything, I can run up the street."

"Works." He found a lemon and grabbed it, then paid for the food. "Feels like forever since I got to cook, cher."

"I'm excited. I can't remember the last time anyone besides me cooked in my kitchen. You'll let me help? I'm an excellent sous-chef." Kyle led him out, a happy little skip in his step.

"'Course. It's way more fun together." Cooking was a joint effort.

"That's what I think."

It was a very quick trip back on the subway. One of these days, he'd figure out why and when you took the bus, or the subway, or an Uber, or your feet in this city. Right now it was all just getting around.

Kyle let him in, then followed him to the kitchen. "I think I need a snack and a glass of wine. You?"

"Surely do." That sounded perfect, in fact. A bite and chopping and drinking.

"Hummus okay?" Kyle started pulling things out and spreading them on the kitchen table—a garlicky hummus and pretzel sticks, a couple of cheeses, crackers, a bunch of grapes. And then a glass of dark red wine appeared in front of his eyes.

"Oh. Oh, I have this at Angeli's. So good." He loved to try new things, taste them. He stole a grape and popped it into his mouth. Uhn.

"Angeli is a person or a place?" Kyle took a bite of the cheese and followed it with a big sip of wine.

"Restaurant. Made it through the storm." So many hadn't.

"Wow. You were there for that, huh? The pictures we saw up here...." Kyle shook his head, and warm fingers touched his arm. "So devastating."

"Yeah." He had been in Houma with his mamma, but his daddy hadn't made it out the other side of it. They'd lost some—less than others, but some.

Kyle watched him, Colt felt the stare, and then leaned in and kissed him. "Whoever they were, they knew you loved them." Kyle patted his shoulder, moved to the refrigerator, and pulled out some peppers.

He nodded. If Daddy hadn't then, he did now. He ate some cheese, then started cleaning shrimps, keeping heads and shells for broth.

"How do you want these veggies cut? Little pieces? Bigger chunks?" Kyle pulled out a cutting board and a good chopping knife, then played with the phone on the counter and music filled the kitchen.

"Mmm. Chop 'em up nice and fine. I'll get the stock going."

"You got it." Kyle set to dicing up the veggies, dancing a little and singing bits of the music. It didn't take long to fill a bowl with onion, celery, and peppers, all diced up nice.

They cooked together, making stock and stirring the roux. They sipped the wine and sang and stole long, lazy kisses.

"It smells so good." Kyle leaned closer to the pot and breathed in. "Mmm. And looks beautiful too."

"It does. We'll cook the fish and the rice, and we'll be eating." He was tickled as all get-out. "Thank you, huh? This is... this is a good thing, a soul-deep thing."

"You're welcome." Kyle nodded, pupils big in his hazel eyes. "This *is* a soul-deep thing, it's true. Thank you for sharing it with me."

"Anytime." He pushed up and grabbed another kiss, loving being able to just make the connection.

Kyle never disappointed him, accepting the kiss and returning it like a promise. Like it mattered to him. "You want a rice cooker?" Damn, Kyle had a lot of gadgets in this kitchen.

"Yeah." How fucking cool. "Show me how to make it work?"

"It's easy." Kyle stretched up tall and pulled a little pot with a plug on it out of the cabinet over the stove. Kyle added water and the rice and pressed a button, and that was it. "And you don't touch it again until it's done. Simple, huh? Do you want to clean the fish, or do you cook it like that?"

"I'll clean it up. We just do it simple, hmm? Because the étouffée has the flavor."

"Yep. Grill pan or sauté pan?" Kyle headed for a cabinet across the kitchen. "God, I'm already hungry. By the time we sit down to eat, I'm going to be ravenous."

"Have a bite of cheese." He took the sauté pan and started heating it up before getting the fish ready. "I like me a crispy skin."

"You eat the skin? I didn't know you could eat fish skin. I'll try it." Kyle went right over, picked up a small hunk of cheese, and waved it at him before eating it.

"I cleaned it up real good. You don't have to. One for me?" He opened his mouth like a baby bird's.

"One for you." Kyle cut him a chunk and put it on his tongue, the sharp taste making his mouth water.

"Uhn. Thanks, cher. So good." He got the pan screaming and put the fish on, then tumped the shrimps in the étouffée to cook real fast.

"You want to eat in here, or we could sit in the dining room? It's a little fancy, but sometimes that's fun." Kyle refilled their wineglasses.

"I'm easy as pie, cher. It'll taste good anywhere."

"Dining room, then. With candles. Why not?" Kyle pulled four tall tapers from a drawer and disappeared into the dining room.

"Ooh. Candles!" *How fancy!*

"I don't use this room a lot, just for parties, mostly," Kyle called from the other room. "It's nice, though. Comfy. Getting close?" Kyle came back in, hooked an arm around his waist.

"Two minutes. You want to grab out the rice?" He craned his neck and kissed the curve of Kyle's jaw.

"Mmm. I like that. Rice. Got it." Kyle slipped away to pull the rice out of the steamer. A few minutes later, serving dishes were passed between them, filled, and set out on the table. Kyle opened another bottle of wine while he got the bread out of the warming oven and sliced it up. In the dining room, Kyle pulled out his chair. "Sit, baby. I can't wait to try this."

He inhaled deep, the world buzzing with the scent of cayenne and bay, parsley and garlic, paprika and thyme.

Kyle paused with a serving spoon in his hand, candlelight dancing across his face. "Do I serve this over the rice or next to it?"

"Over is how we do it. You can sop up with the bread too. It ain't fancy, just good."

"Good is fancy enough for me." Kyle served them each a big helping.

"Ain't it? Sometimes just good is better than fancy."

He watched Kyle try it, grinning at the yummy noises and the nearly orgasmic look on his lover's face.

"Oh, Colt. Oh my God. That is… mmm." Kyle took another bite. "So good."

He took a bite of his own, and a wave of homesickness hit him for a second. Oh, that was good. That was just right.

When he looked up again, Kyle was watching him. "Tastes like home, huh? I can see it in your face. Tastes like your mom's? It's cool how food can do that. This is amazing."

"Tastes like my granny's. Just…. She taught me to cook all the good things." Barbecue shrimps and gumbo and jambalaya and étouffée and shrimp and grits and court bouillon and crab boil. All the good things. "What you like to cook best?"

"Pasta. I love Italian food. I make a mean lasagna. I love shellfish and pasta dishes, sausage and peppers, more pasta… God, I love pasta. And I love to grill. Ribs, chicken, steaks, fish, veggies like peppers and corn, pineapple and peaches."

"Mmm. Yes, please." He could eat all of that.

"Good." Kyle's mouth was full, so Colt had to wait for him to finish. "Next weekend I'll cook. I think. Unless I have crazy rehearsals, because we're opening the following weekend. This is so good." Kyle took another big bite. The man wasn't shy about eating, for sure. He had a good appetite.

"Why're they crazy?" He didn't have to worry about having a staged show or nothing. He showed up, played—hell, being onstage was easier than the studio because you just went with the energy.

Kyle smiled at him. "Well, we don't improvise, music man. It has to be exactly the same every night. We have to get all the steps right, the lighting, the entrances, the sets if there are any, costume changes. It's a lot to put together. And it runs for a long while. Months at least. So there's a lot to perfect."

"Exactly the same? Honest?" He couldn't fathom that. Not at all.

"Honest. Exactly the same. All the same steps, same music, same timing, same stories. Every night. Six times a week. You'll see. You can come to opening night, and then I'll get you tickets a couple of weeks later."

Kyle sipped his wine, the glass reflecting the candlelight.

"That's dedication." And he meant that. His music was very much about improv, but he could lay down tracks when he needed to.

Kyle shrugged. "It's just what I do. But you know, that improvisation we did this… was it just this morning? Wow. That was amazing, wasn't it? I've never really done that before, not like that anyway. The way that just came from deep down, and that energy? I hope we can do that again soon."

"It was wow, and you say when." He glanced over and winked. "After we eat."

"Nothing's interrupting this meal. And I'm so going to have seconds." Kyle laughed, reaching out to take his hand. "I want to get that down, though, if we can. Record it like Timmy did for me the last time. That's the next piece I'm working on, you know. Not for this opening, but my next solo exhibition. The only thing better than recording it would be…." Kyle looked at him, eyes flashing. "Oh, I'm getting a crazy idea."

He was all about the crazy. Hell, he was sort of the definition of crazy. "I'm in."

"The only thing better than asking you to record your original music for me would be to improv it every night. With you. Onstage."

"Sure, honey, if you want. You tell me when and where, and I'll let Nathan know."

"Yeah? Really? I mean, some of the show would be staged, but I'm thinking at least one piece could be improv. We pay and do real contracts and everything. I'd just need to talk to your manager." Kyle took another bite and didn't seem to care about a full mouth this time, just kept on talking. "How cool. Everything is so rehearsed in dance, but this would be, like… spur-of-the-moment. It could reflect our mood or the vibe we're getting from the audience, or just whatever your fingers and my feet… do."

"That's my thing, so I got no worries. I could watch you for years."

Kyle gave him a soft smile. "You are so sweet, baby. I could get lost in your guitar for ages. It's just so real."

He sure hoped so; he didn't know how else to be. That probably wasn't true. There were some dark days where he didn't want to be him or anybody like him, but he wasn't smart enough to turn into a stranger.

"The idea makes me a little nervous, you know? Being unstructured and unscripted. But I felt so open and creative this morning. I think we can pull it off." Kyle kissed his hand and then sipped more wine.

"We'll have to try it again and see what happens." And if that was selfish? So be it. He wanted to play for Kyle.

"We will." Kyle pushed back from the table. "Oh, man. I am stuffed. That was delicious. Thank you."

"You're welcome. Thank you for letting me." It had been the best day in a month of Sundays, between the going and the seeing and the playing and the food.

"I'm mulling over how to properly show my gratitude." Kyle looked at him with hooded eyes and a sly, sexy smile.

"Ooh. Now there are some possibilities there, cher...." That look made him some lovely possibilities.

"Infinite possibilities for creative people." Kyle slid out from behind the table and into his lap smoothly. Almost slithering. "And we are very creative, aren't we?"

"Oh, we is that, cher. We got that making thing down." His hands found Kyle's ass like they had minds of their own.

"M-hm. We do." Kyle kissed him with soft, warm lips that felt like heaven and tasted like wine. He could get drunk on that, no question, and he let himself melt into the sweet, velvet richness that was Kyle.

Kyle lingered over the kiss, his lover's hunger real but simmering under the surface, still, as long fingers slid up under his shirt and dragged across his nipples.

His belly tightened up in anticipation, and his sac did the same. The ball of need in his belly wasn't huge, but it was beginning.

"Ooh, I felt that." Kyle's hand brushed over his abs and tucked just under his waistband. "Why don't we clean this up and digest a bit, and then maybe I'll dance for you. Something naughty."

"You have the best ideas, cher. Near wicked." Eventually he would let Kyle's ass go.
Someday.
Soon.

Chapter Seven

"Hold! Hold up!" Kyle turned away from the stage and waved at Jake. "Reset, please? Top of this piece."

"On it." The stage manager said something low into his headset. The music stopped abruptly, and the lights started changing.

"Danny, come down here. Ali? Come on, baby." Kyle waved the dancers over to the edge of the stage. Neither of them looked happy about it. Danny had attitude in every fucking step. He sighed and patted the stage, and they both sat. "Okay. You two are kicking ass up there. And you're the only two. So, I'm playing a little game here, and you two are going to pretend like I'm reaming you new assholes. And then you're going to get up and out-diva the rest of the company so they'll snap to. Yes? Otherwise we're going to be here all night. Hm?"

Allison got it, gave him a nod, and got right to her feet. God, he loved her. She glared at him, fire shooting out her eyes, and then turned and strutted away, heading right for the rest of the company, who were standing there staring. "I need five minutes. Can we take five minutes?"

Danny stood up. "We're taking five, Kyle. You better cool off too. Asshole." Danny strutted offstage.

Kyle sighed and smacked his clipboard into the back of a chair before plopping down next to Jake.

"Asshole."

"Totally."

Jake snorted. "The things you do for art. Oh, hang on." Jake said a few quiet words into his headset. "Someone named Colt is here for you?"

"Ah!" Kyle popped up out of his seat.

"Oh, so not a critic."

"Nope."

"Or pizza delivery."

"Ha. No. Musician. Here to watch some rehearsal." Kyle made his way up the aisle.

"Lover?"

"That too. So nosy, Jake." He ducked through the doors at the back of house and squinted as he stepped into the bright lobby.

Colt stood there, rocking side to side, looking around, wide-eyed. When those dark eyes landed on him, he got a bright smile. "Hello, you!"

He went right up and pulled Colt into his arms. "Mmm. I've missed you."

They hadn't seen each other since the weekend. Colt had two really long days wrapping up things in the studio, and he'd been slammed on Wednesday with tech. He was tired, Colt looked tired, but it was nice to hold his lover for a minute.

"Oh, cher. You feel so right." Colt leaned into him, inhaling deep. "Thank you for asking me."

"I hope you like what you see. Things are a little nuts just at the moment, but I promise I'm not really as big an ass as I'm about to look." He let Colt go and kissed him quickly, fairly chaste since they were in the middle of the lobby. "Come on. It's only a five-minute break."

"Just show me where to sit and be." Colt bounced on his toes, expression eager as hell.

"You can sit with Jake and get an eyeful." Kyle felt like bouncing himself. It was fun having someone interested in seeing him work. Not just dance, but work. And Colt loved new experiences; he was the perfect audience.

"Jake, this is Colt. Colt, this is my stage manager, Jake."

"Helloooo, *Colt*," Jake said, glancing up from a notebook full of Post-it flags and precisely handwritten notes. Kyle rolled his eyes. "Have a seat."

"Taken, Jake."

"My girlfriend would like him too."

"No." Kyle took Colt's hand and grinned, joking, "If he hits on you, let me know. I'll press charges."

"I got this, cher. No worries." No. No, Kyle had to admit, every time he was in Colt's presence, those dark eyes were focused on him and him alone. It was erotic as fuck.

In fact, Colt's eyes, and that smile he got a few minutes ago, either one alone could make his chest ache. But together, he was done. Hooked. Totally helpless. Fuck, he could really get his heart broken this time.

"Don't you have work to do? Go be an asshole, Kyle."

He snorted and headed for the stage. "Ali, honey?" he shouted. "Put the tears away and let's get to work."

"Don't be a dick, Kyle." Oh, Danny did that so well.

"If the pair of you can't lead this cast, there are a hundred others waiting in line." He felt the bristle run through the company and hid his smile. Sometimes you had to light a fire. They were bored of dancing for him, but they'd back up their principals. This cast was so talented, and so ready for an audience. "Can we take it one more time, then? I'd like to move past this. The next piece is much more complicated."

That was true. They needed to nail this one, or it was going to be a late night.

"Jake, call places."

Jake stood up and shouted places, gave him an eye roll, and then got the music started. "He can be such a queen."

Colt watched the stage, wide-eyed, silent and still like he was afraid to miss a single second.

The stage cleared and Allison and Danny took their places center stage in the near-darkness, arms and legs intertwined and tangled so it was hard to tell where one ended and the other began. They were stunning as the music started and the lights came up on them. They started to move like one creature.

All around them dancers entered the stage, walking, crawling, bent at odd angles, and all of them weaving themselves in, around, and through one another.

Kyle sat beside Colt gingerly, like he might break something if he moved too quickly. "Dan and Ali are friendship and love," he whispered to Colt. "And the dancers around them are everything that threatens it. Jealousy, hate, envy, distance, ideology, family, class, death, that sort of thing."

Colt nodded, lips pursed. "I can see it. They look mean, like they want to bite."

He loved that Colt got it, appreciated it. "Exactly." Oh, and his little scheme was working too, because while the principals floated and tangled with each other, the others jerked and bent and halted, all of them focused. "They've got it, Jake. Look at them."

"Your inner asshole is a genius." Jake's tone was dry as a desert.

"So here they break free and…." Colt was just going to have to interpret the rest for himself, because he was completely blown away by the entire second half of the piece. When it ended—Danny and Allison hand in hand and the company scattered to corners and broken on the floor—the theater went silent.

Danny broke first, grinning. "Fuck, yeah!"

Kyle just nodded. The company hooted and hauled themselves to their feet.

"Take five, guys. That was exactly what we needed today. Nice work!" He turned to Jake. "Set for Rush Hour, Jake."

"On it." Jake spoke low into his headset again, and people in black started moving across the stage.

Kyle was elated and kissed Colt on the cheek impulsively. "That was about as good as you're ever going to see that number."

"That was something, cher." There was a line on Colt's cheek, a single trail from a tear. "You made that all up, huh?"

"I did." He reached out and traced the trail with his thumb. "Love wins, baby. Truth and goodness. Things the heart knows."

"That's right. Love wins. That's the biggest thing under the heavens."

"It is. And you saw them, you saw how good that felt. They just breathe it when they want to. I'm glad you liked it. It's one of my favorite pieces." His second favorite was this adorable story in the second act about a boy who finds a stray dog. Just a simple, happy little piece.

"It's beautiful. You been touched by God, I think. So fine." Colt watched him like he was precious.

He shrugged. "I just love what I do."

"Two minutes, lover boy." Jake threw the words at him with a grin.

"Ha. Thank you."

Over the next two hours, Kyle danced twice. The first time was the piece Colt had seen his bit of the week before, about losing his lover, and the second was a solo piece that Allison choreographed for him that showed off his classical training and was about a man who had grown very old, reliving his youth.

The final number ended, a huge company number that showed off talent more than told a story, and Kyle broke everyone and gave them the following morning off. He sure needed it.

"Jake, tomorrow we'll only do cleanup and we'll keep it short, and then I'm giving everyone Saturday off, but don't tell them."

"So much for being an asshole."

"It's ready, Jake. I don't want them to peak too early." He turned to Colt. "You've been quiet."

"I ain't going to interrupt your working, cher, not for love or money." Colt touched his wrist, the caress enough to draw goose bumps over his arm. "That was cool. I appreciate you letting me see how all this works."

It took as little as that. Wow. "It was nice knowing you were here. It was a long afternoon, but you said you wanted to see the crazy, so… that was pretty crazy."

"Who's this, Kyle?" Danny slid up beside them and leaned against the seats. *God. Danny.*

"Lover." Jake offered helpfully, obviously having no idea what he was doing.

He sighed. "This is Colt. Colt, Danny."

"Lover, huh? You got a new one?" Danny looked Colt up and down, and Kyle just knew Dan was going to be a bitch about this.

Colt held out one hand and smiled. "That he did. Pleased."

Pleased? He looked at Colt. Steam was building up behind his ears, but his lover was playing it cool. Okay.

Danny took Colt's hand and shook it, smiling back in a way that didn't quite reach his eyes. "Nice hands. Musician? Where are you from?"

"N'awlins. Blues man." Oh, that drawl dropped down into third gear, almost, but not quite, offensive.

"Oh, how cute, Kyle. You've found yourself a Southern belle."

"That's enough, Danny. Your pirouette needs work."

"Funny." Danny stood up. "Nice to meet you, Colt. Enjoy him while you've got him. He's not going to keep you."

He stood as well, fingers balled into fists, so ready to give Danny a taste of the carpet. But Danny didn't test him.

"See you tomorrow, Kyle." Danny winked at him and headed for the back of the theater.

"He's a little bitch today, huh?" Jake shook his head. "Sorry, I didn't know you… you know."

"Mm. Yeah. Hell hath no fury…. Jesus. I'm sorry, baby."

"No worries. I ain't got nothin' to prove, and he's been all working and emotional and shit, I'm sure."

"He might be tired. That's no excuse, but you're kind to make them for him." He had no idea things were still that raw for Danny. Or maybe

Colt was right and Danny was just seeing if he could get a rise out of either of them. Either way, he felt like an asshole. Not about Danny, about Colt. "You ready to get out of here?"

"Surely. You all done for the day?" Colt winked at him, all grins.

"God, yes." He reached over and gave Jake a pat on the shoulder. "Noon tomorrow? Ish? I'll text you."

"You're the boss. Night."

Jake, he knew, wouldn't be leaving for another couple of hours at least. But it was better than midnight. "Come on, you. Get me a drink."

"Yessir. My pleasure. What's your poison?" Colt grabbed his guitar and threw it over his shoulder.

"Hm. A shot of Colt, warmed up in the hot tub."

"Ooh. Lucky for you, I got that lined up for you." Every warm, sensual smile relaxed him.

"Aw. So sweet. Always thinking of me." As soon as they'd cleared the stage door, he tugged Colt against him and took a kiss. Colt melted into him, unashamed and eager, one hand creeping up around his head to hold him close.

Something was definitely happening here. Three days apart, busy as hell, and he still missed this man, this kiss, like crazy. And it wasn't about the sex, though that draw was undeniable; he'd felt the pull as soon as he'd seen Colt in the lobby a few hours earlier. Colt just had this kind, gentle, genuine-self thing going on that fascinated him.

This felt like the real deal, or what he thought was the real deal, as insane as that might be.

"You're delicious." He smiled at Colt and let himself sink into those dark eyes.

"I'm sure hungry, so I'll take it. Take me home to love on you, feed you some?"

"Yep. Come on." He led Colt down the alley and out to the street where it was easy enough to get a cab. They might get stuck in a little traffic, but he didn't have the patience for the subway. It didn't take too long to get home, and the first thing he did was open the liquor cabinet. "Margaritas?"

"Works for me." Colt's hands landed on his shoulders, fingers digging in.

Oh, hello. That felt like heaven. He loved what he did, and he really didn't find it that stressful most of the time, but four days of work, dancing, and all the concentration had him pretty tight, and his body was tired. He sighed and let his head drop forward, his hand going slack on the cabinet door. "That feels amazing, baby."

"Good." Colt began to sing for him, soft and low, the words nonsensical.

He let the cabinet door swing closed. He didn't really want a drink now; he just wanted more of this. He swayed into Colt a little and reached back, resting a hand on Colt's hip for balance.

"Come on, cher. Let me love on you before we take our drinks to the tub." Colt led him to the sofa and eased him down before straddling his ass and going back to massaging his shoulders and crooning to him.

He didn't fight any of it, just settled right into the couch with a long sigh and listened to Colt sing. Was it just the other night that his lover wasn't sure how to feel about a simple hand massage? The man learned fast. Not only were those hands strong and sure, but he could feel the affection in them. He relaxed and let Colt take care of him for a bit, it felt like it was doing them both good.

Colt leaned down against him, covering him, lips soft on his nape.

"Mm. Hey." He bent his head forward, offering more skin. "I think my spine's gone to jelly."

"Good deal. You been working hard." Those kisses kept going, one after another.

He nodded, eyes half-lidded, and breathed deep. "Yeah. 'S good, though. The work."

"So good. Love to see it."

He'd invite Colt to see more soon. Maybe final dress. Definitely opening night. He'd ask—when he woke up.

Chapter Eight

Colt sat on the floor of the kitchen and started writing. He did okay in the country music arena and even better with the alt-country guys in Austin.

It paid a chunk of bills, that was for sure. It was easier with a partner, though—someone to bounce ideas off. Maybe Norv and Ryder could come out here for a week. Between the Texan's speed and the Georgia boy's way with a hook, they could bang it out.

He stopped, shot off a couple texts, then set back to his own work. He was thinking love song, but a little dirty, a little wicked and wrong. Something you'd dance to in the corners of the sawdust-covered dance floor where the neon lights didn't reach.

Oh.

Oh.

Where the lights don't reach.

Fucking A.

Hours went by, and the sun went down while he was sitting there. He didn't need to move, though. Kyle had the hall light on some kind of timer, and he found himself in the perfect spot to write in the slice of amber light spilling in through the kitchen door.

"You're in the dark, baby." That was where he was when Kyle sat down beside him, warm hands sliding up under his shirt. "I guess I needed a nap. You must be starving."

"Mmm." His eyes crossed at the heat. "I was having a work. You feel good."

"What is that?" Kyle hugged him close with one arm and looked down at his scribbling. "Are you writing?"

"I am. I sell them pretty good, as a rule." He liked writing songs just fine.

"May I?" Kyle picked up his notebook and looked it over, then kind of bopped his head to a silent beat and hummed a few lines. "I like it. Kind of raunchy too."

"Yeah. It'll play on the radio, not too bad, but enough kids will want to sing it." The guys could help him redneck it up some.

"You're that sure of yourself, huh? I like it." Kyle kissed him lightly behind the ear. "Confidence is sexy as hell."

"Well, I mean, it's a good hook." And a singable melody that didn't require a bunch of yodeling.

"It is a good hook. I can't wait to hear you play it."

"You want I should?" He let his fingers move, singing the first verse and the melody, letting the bluesy smoky feel loose.

Kyle swayed beside him—his lover never could sit still when there was music playing. "Oh. That's got a wicked groove. I love listening to you sing."

Oh, that was sweet to hear. It wasn't his best thing, but he could carry a tune in a bucket. "Thank you, sir."

"You're welcome." Kyle leaned in and kissed his cheek and then stood up. "You keep on, I'll listen and make some pasta for dinner. We can have a soak after." Kyle turned on a couple of lights to work by but left the kitchen mostly dim.

Colt kept on keeping on for a bit, but it seemed more fun to help Kyle and touch and caress.

"You know this is a knife I'm holding, right? Don't distract me. I might chop off a finger." Kyle tossed a bunch of fresh herbs into a pot with some simmering tomatoes, then put the knife down and turned to face him with a smile. "You want to put a big pot on to boil?"

"Surely can." He whistled as he wrestled the pan into the sink and filled her up, and then he hauled it to the stove and got heat under it.

"You okay with chicken sausage? It's pretty good. It's supposed to be Italian-style, but it's spicy as hell." Kyle gave the sauce a stir and then pulled a deli-wrapped package out of the fridge.

"I am. I eat anything. I like food, but spicy's my favorite." He grabbed Kyle's butt and squeezed.

"Yeah? I got something spicy for you right here, my rockin' Cajun lover." Kyle pressed back and rocked his hips like they didn't belong to the rest of his body.

"Uhn." Tell him he shouldn't drop to his knees and just lick.

Kyle laughed and slipped away from him, dancing across the kitchen. "You're so easy, baby."

"Well, what good is playing hard to get?"

"None. None at all." Kyle was still giggling as he tossed the sausages into a frying pan on the stove. "I just haven't ever known anyone like you, Colt. You're just... wonderful. That's what you are. Joy and wonder." Kyle tangled their fingers and smiled at him. "I know, I'm melodramatic, right? I don't care."

"Look at them dance in the pan. I love that sound." Colt leaned and took a quick, hard kiss that Kyle returned, nipping at his lip.

"Water's boiling," Kyle sang to him and gave him a mischievous grin.

"You making noodles? You want something to drink?"

"Yes, penne. You want wine? Something else? I'll have whatever you're drinking."

"Is there something that you think will go?" He liked himself a glass of wine; he loved how it felt on his tongue.

"I always like red wine with a red sauce, myself. There's a pinot noir in the cabinet." Kyle pulled a plastic package from the fridge, cut it open, and carefully dumped the pasta in the boiling water.

"Pee-no." He drawled it out, playing with the word, making himself laugh.

"There's a bottle opener on top of the cabinet, goof. Glasses in the hutch."

"You got it. You shoulda seen the first time I tried to use a corkscrew. I pushed the cork all the way down in the bottle."

Kyle laughed. "You can bring it to me, if you're feeling insecure." Oh, that lilt was dripping sarcasm.

"Shut up, dork. I done opened me a bunch of bottles since." He pinched Kyle's ass on the way by.

"Ow!" Kyle hammed it up, faking injury. "Yeah, that's pretty obvious. I'm not a lightweight, but I don't think I've even seen you tipsy yet. Hm. Maybe that's tonight's goal. Get Colt drunk."

"I'm a silly drunk. It don't happen much, though. You got to watch yourself in a bar." He knew how to pace himself.

"Well, this is not a bar, and I could get into silly. I'm more of an esoteric drunk. Everything becomes very interesting. Deep." Kyle winked at him. "And then I usually end up making out with like, whoever I'm sitting next to."

"Well, then, you'd best sit next to me." Because he wanted that making out done with him.

"Ooh. I like that attitude. I will sit next to you every time, lover." Kyle hovered close, watching him open the wine, and chuckled. "Or if I forget, you can cut in."

"Believe me, cher. I will." He was willing to work for what he wanted.

Kyle leaned in, lips close and offering. "Mm. I love that kind of talk. It's hot."

He took that kiss, letting it wash over him.

Dinner somehow made it to the kitchen table despite all the flirting and wandering hands and the heat between them. Kyle served him up a big plate of pasta and covered it with the garlicky pomodoro that had been simmering on the back burner.

"So, you said your songs do pretty well. How come you don't record them yourself? Or do you?" Kyle slid over the plate of sausages and refilled their wineglasses.

"I ain't much of a singer, and I'm less of a performer. I like getting lost in the music, you see, and a singer has to know the audience is out there." He loved the way music spoke to him, but he didn't need the crowd. He didn't mind them a bit, but it wasn't why he played.

He played because his soul needed it.

Kyle nodded and forked up some noodles. "I get that. I know what you mean because I'm like that, though sometimes I can't completely forget the audience either."

"Do you have to, like, look at them? The audience, I mean."

"Depends on the piece. Most of the time, no. I only have to look out over them, and the lights are so bright, I can't see the mezzanine. But some of the more modern stuff calls for eye contact, or at least breaking the fourth wall."

"What's that mean? Breaking the wall?" It was a neat thought, no matter what it meant.

"Oh! Oh, it's a theater term for stepping out of the show and talking to the audience directly. The three walls are the sides and the back of the stage. The fourth is the invisible one between the audience and the performers. Between the play and reality."

"That's cool." Okay, yeah. That made sense. Sorta like singing right to someone in the crowd when you didn't mean it.

Kyle traced one of his fingers. "You like the pasta okay? I know it was a quick thrown-together thing."

"I love it. It's best all in one bite. This is good sausage."

"Yeah, the sausage and the pasta I get from this wonderful hole-in-the-wall Italian market. I'm glad you like it." Kyle looked pleased and smiled at him. "I like cooking with you. I enjoy the way you appreciate the process as much as the result. You make it fun."

"It ought to be, hmm? It's a good thing." It meant family. Home. Good things.

"It should. I didn't grow up with it, though. How'd you learn to cook?"

"My granny. She was the best cook. She spent all her days behind a stove."

"Oh, that's a nice memory. Was she cooking for the family? Or was she making a living?"

"Six of one, half dozen of another. She had a kitchen that did shrimps and all the gumbos and bread pudding. Oo-la!" He'd sit and play with his blocks while she stirred and the girls took out bowls to the shrimpers.

Kyle laughed. "Mmm. Sounds so good! To Granny." Kyle raised his glass.

"To Granny! God rest her." She was smiling down at him.

Kyle popped up and started clearing food and plates. "We can take our wine out to the tub if you want."

"Surely." Lord have mercy, Kyle was a busy guy. Always moving. Colt got up and started dishwater so he could scrub pots. This he knew how to do.

He scrubbed, and Kyle dried, and everything was put away in no time, and Kyle was all hands after that. Strong arms pulled him into a deep kiss, making him wonder if they'd make it as far as the hot tub.

The wine made the kisses deeper, headier, and he followed Kyle like there was a string tied around his balls.

Kyle pulled away enough to grab the bottle off the counter and his glass. "Come on, beautiful, upstairs with me. I want to get naked. Bring your glass."

"Got it." He snatched his glass up and took a sip, the wine sliding on his tongue.

They went upstairs, up the long staircase and down the hall, only instead of turning right to the bedroom, Kyle led him left out a set of double doors and into a square room with a small bar and a large Jacuzzi. The ceiling had several skylights.

Kyle set the bottle down on the edge of the tub and turned on the jets.

"How cha-cha is this?" He laughed, thinking about the Place d'Armes back home and how they'd sneak into the courtyard to swim.

"I know, right? Thank Mom and Dad. This was their place before they bought the big house across the sound, and then they kept it for weekends in the city. Now they have an apartment they stay at on the Upper West Side, and they gave me this place." Kyle casually stripped off while he was talking, tossing his clothes over the back of a wide white couch. "It's really way too big for one person, but I can throw one hell of a party."

"I bet you can." He didn't care one way or the other, but it was neat to see all the fancy.

Kyle made his way over, the lean, naked body catching the dim lights in all the right ways, showing off his ink. "You're too dressed, music man." His lover reached for him.

He let Kyle work his shirt open, then danced him around for a bit, singing as he enjoyed the feel of Kyle against him.

Kyle laughed softly, following his lead, moving smoothly as they rocked together. Kyle's kiss, falling lightly on his lips, was just another piece of the dance.

"Mmm. Cher." He opened his jeans, stripping off so they could dance in the water.

"That's better." Kyle stepped in, long legs disappearing into bubbling water, and extended a hand. "Look at you. I can't believe you don't get to enjoy this view. Come on, baby. It's lovely in here."

"Mmm. I do like to bubble." He took Kyle's hand and slipped in, then settled in Kyle's lap. Colt laughed as the bubbles got trapped between them, the popping making everything tingle.

Kyle was watching him, listening to him laugh and smiling back. He raised an eyebrow, and Kyle just shrugged at him.

"Thanks for coming today. I liked having you there."

"It was amazing, cher. So many moving parts, so pretty." Kyle's talent made his heart damn happy, if he was honest.

"You see it. You get it, I think. I saw how you were watching. A lot of people think ballet has to be so sophisticated all the time, but it's just dance, you know?"

"It's beautiful to watch. Like a great band sounds."

Kyle was running wet hands over his skin as they talked, stroking them down his back, over his shoulders, drawing lines on his chest.

"You know, the day that I met you and I texted Timmy, all I did was tell him you were hot. Which is true, but I never thought for a second you'd be interested. He totally set us up after that. Did you know? He told me all about how he told you I wanted a date and got you to agree."

"He's a shit." Colt owed Timmy a beer. "I am hot, though. Smokin'." He winked over, waggling his eyebrows madly.

"You are sizzling. On fucking fire. Too damn hot to handle." But Kyle handled him anyway, sliding fingers around his shaft and squeezing gently. "Good thing we're in a tub."

"Uh... uh-huh." Kyle made him dizzy, made him want to sing.

"I think we've got something here, Colt. You know? I think this is more than a maybe. I think I'm falling in pretty deep." Kyle leaned in and kissed him.

Colt reached up, tracing a line around Kyle's ear. He got it. There was something about Kyle that was... bigger than either one of them.

Kyle kissed along Colt's jaw to his ear, sucked in his earlobe and then continued down the line of his neck to his shoulder. Slow and sensual attention, nothing rushed, like they had forever to spend right here. He hummed softly, fireworks firing all under his skin. Oh, he could get used to this—long and slow and easy.

"If you had your guitar right now, tell me about what you'd be playing." Kyle leaned back and reached for the glass of wine on the edge of the tub.

"Mmm. Something slow and lazy, something that feels like giving thanks."

Kyle sipped some wine and then offered him the glass. "Hm. I'm not sure I know quite what giving thanks sounds like."

"You know what it feels like, I know." He could see that in the lines of Kyle's joy.

His lover smiled at him. "I do. This is what it feels like." Kyle went back to tasting him, over his shoulder and across his collarbones, down part of his arm. "Just like this." The hand on his cock pumped slowly, long strokes from hilt to tip where Kyle's thumb circled and swept across the head each time.

He arched, his eyes rolling up into his head. "Uh. Uh-huh. Just like...."

His entire body lit up like the Fourth of July.

"Just like that." Kyle's voice was barely above a whisper. "I've got plenty of gratitude to show you. More than you can handle." His grip grew firmer and the strokes a little faster.

"Cher—" Jesus help him, he wanted that touch to keep on, over and over.

"Love." Kyle didn't let up on the kisses or the contact, and his lover just kept on speaking to him. Soft words, praising words. "You are beautiful, you know that? Everything inside you just shines on the outside. It's irresistible."

"Listen to you." That this fine, fine man thought he was worth a plug nickel made him groan. He was just another picker from the swamp, one of a thousand, but he'd take those sweet, needy words.

Kyle hummed to him, a low appreciative sound, and that hand kept moving, firm and steady like it knew him, knew what he wanted. "Love your sounds. Your moans, that little song you sing to me, the way you call me 'cher.' Feel good, baby?"

"Better than. Better than, cher. You got me, all the way around."

"Good." Kyle kissed him deep, tongue sweeping through his mouth.

Oh, praise Jesus. Kissing Kyle was the closest to God he'd ever been without his fingers bleeding on the strings. He pushed in, offering himself up, heart and soul. Their tongues tangled, amazing sounds trapped between them.

He felt Kyle's chest expand as his lover sucked in air. The kiss grew heated and urgent, and Kyle groaned heavily, then shifted and helped him sit up on the edge of the tub. Kyle's mouth was on him not a second later, drawing him in.

"Cher!" He arched, hands going white-knuckled on the edge. "Please!"

That mouth was heaven on earth.

Kyle's tongue pushed up and dragged along his length as he slid in and out of that luscious heat. His lover hummed and encouraged him, fingers digging into his thighs.

Colt let himself loose, let all his need out as he arched and drove in deep.

Grunting, Kyle opened for him like it was everything he wanted. Wet, warm hands slid around and cupped his ass, squeezing.

"Need you like air." It was the truth as he knew it, swear to God.

He felt Kyle's fingers on his balls, rolling first, then adding pressure, and Kyle swallowed, throat working and rippling over him.

"Gonna," he warned, even though it was damn near too late, because he was sliding over the edge. Kyle swallowed again, fingers bruising into his asscheeks. Pleasure washed over him as he shot, his balls aching as he spent.

Not missing a beat, Kyle sucked until he was empty, hot tongue painting long strokes all the way up his shaft. "Mmm. Good, love." At Kyle's coaxing he slid off the side of the tub and back into Kyle's lap.

"Make me crazy." Colt danced against Kyle's heavy erection, loving on him, pondering whether Kyle would let him ride.

Moaning, Kyle nodded, almost as breathless as he was himself. "Need you, baby. So bad." Kyle's hands flailed for a second, and then he took him by the jaw and kissed him.

"Want you to fuck me, cher. You into that? Me?"

"Yeah. Into that. Fuck."

He nodded, reaching down to stroke that heavy cock, from base to tip. "Gon' feel so good."

Kyle gasped. "Fuck. Already does." He nearly slid off Kyle's lap as his lover's long legs unfolded out of the water, but Kyle caught him. "Couch. Stuff in the glass box on the side table."

"Look at you, bein' all prepared!" He clapped, tickled as shit.

"I'm a fucking Boy Scout. Pick one." Kyle's voice sounded like he'd swallowed gravel.

He grabbed a rubber and a little packet of lube. "I'm drippin' on your floor."

His lover laughed at that. "All-weather couch. Tile floor. And your skin looks great wet." Still, Kyle grabbed a small towel and dried off a little before handing it to Colt while he smoothed on the rubber.

Colt got himself sopped up, then crawled up on the sofa.

Kyle helped him settle on his knees and took his hands, hooking his fingers over the back of the couch. Then his lover leaned over him, opening the lube and whispering in his ear, "Tell me again how good it's going to be?"

"You're gonna open me up and turn my soul inside out, cher. I want it. You. Me."

Cool lube and a slippery finger pressed up against his hole. "Right. Fuck. Just want to disappear in you."

"Mm-hmm. Want to feel you for days." He wasn't averse to a good, hard fuck.

Kyle nodded, and he felt the intrusion of one slippery finger, swirling and stretching him, slicking him up. "I'm going to make you forget your name. Forget yourself. I'm going to make you sing a whole new song, lover." A second finger joined the first, and Kyle groaned behind him. "You feel good already."

All Colt could do was nod and sink into it, trusting Kyle to show him what he wanted.

A few more slow, firm strokes of his fingers, and then Kyle's hand left him and gripped his hip instead. He felt the pressure of Kyle's cock against him, pushing in, sweet and slow, sinking deeper little by little as they breathed together. "Colt. Tight, my God."

"Uh-huh." He groaned, not out of pain, but in desperation. The burn was deep, rich, and he *needed*.

Kyle reached around and gave his cock a tug, caressed his balls, and then suddenly they were there, his ass pressed up against Kyle's hips. "Mmm." Kyle moved behind him, gently at first, fingers holding on to him and keeping things sane. But he could feel Kyle's desire building. His lover's cock jerked inside him, and Kyle groaned loudly. "Want you."

"Cher." He braced himself, ready to take it and ride. Kyle's cock was a solid fire, throbbing inside him and making him breathless. Those fingers pulled at him. Kyle's hips rocked against him a couple of times, then took him suddenly, strong and deep, rhythmic and powerful. "You feel so good, baby."

A bass beat started pounding in the base of his skull, throbbing in a way that promised to take him right over.

Kyle didn't tire and with the control of an athlete, urged that hard cock deeper still, shoving against his ass with every thrust, threatening to slice him right in half.

"Cher!" The sound tore out of him, loud and raw and pure need.

"That's right, baby. Remember me, forget yourself. Sending you right out of your head." Kyle's voice was rough and dark but hardly sounded winded at all. That same relentless rhythm rocked him over and over.

His world spun, tightened to his ass and the pressure of that heavy cock.

Kyle grunted and leaned heavily over his back, bracing one knee on the couch. "Fuck, you're so... oh God." Kyle panted in his ear as the pace grew faster. "Fuck, baby."

He sobbed, humping back onto Kyle, taking every inch, every fucking thing Kyle gave him.

The pace nearing frantic, Kyle whimpered and groaned for him, no sign of the composure he had just a few moments ago. "Want... oh fuck. Colt!"

He could feel Kyle start to tremble, a heavy presence at his back, strong hands grasping his hips and bruising into his flesh.

Colt moaned, the ache from Kyle's fingers enough to shove him over the edge, make him shoot and bear down on Kyle's cock.

Kyle cried out, long and loud, orgasm rocking them both, hips jerking and then finally going still. "Fuck. Fuck, love, so good." Kyle dropped dozens of kisses on his back, and words of praise and love across his skin.

"So good." He sounded broken to his own ears, just cracked.

"Everything." Kyle slipped away for a second and then quietly coaxed Colt back into the hot tub. "You are everything, love."

He sank into the water, floating close. He needed to touch, to be there with Kyle, to connect.

Kyle drew him in, tracing fingers over his skin and through his hair and whispering to him in soft tones, "I'm not going anywhere, love. Settle in. Breathe, baby."

"Sorry. I just...." He needed to be held. Kyle had liked to break him.

"Shh. No. Not sorry. Let me hold you, okay? It's good. It's perfect." Kyle kissed him, gentle and slow. "Let me take care of you."

He put one hand on the center of Kyle's chest, feeling the strong, steady heartbeat. Lord have mercy, he loved this beautiful son of a bitch.

Kyle cupped a hand around his and just stayed quiet, the two of them indulging in the water's warmth and in each other. For a long while the only sound in the room was the music of their breathing and the rhythm of the bubbling water.

He sent a prayer of thanks up, for this moment, for this feeling, for this man.

Finally, Kyle reached over and refilled the wineglass from the bottle on the edge of the tub. After taking a long sip, Kyle offered him the glass. "Have some, love. Share it with me."

"Mmm. Thank you." He sipped, his eyes going heavy at the way the wine coated his tongue.

Kyle watched him, taking the glass back when he was done. "Tired? Should I take you to bed?"

Colt had the sneaking suspicion that he'd follow Kyle anywhere he wanted to go. "I'm easy, cher. I jus' want to be with you."

"Let's sit here awhile, then. Finish the wine. See if you get silly." Kyle winked at him. "And I'll find the closest guy and make out with him."

Chapter Nine

Kyle finished laying out his shoes on his dressing table carefully, in the order that he would use them, heels all lined up in a perfectly straight line. Without needing to think about it at all, he moved on to the next part of his preshow ritual and laid out paper towels and his makeup brushes, also in the order he would use them.

He had his iPod on, his Diet Coke next to the mirror, and was wearing his silver satin robe as he sat down and got to work.

On the far end of the table was a bouquet of flowers from Katie. His sister never forgot an opening night, even when she couldn't be there. She'd be the only one of his siblings—of his entire family—to know or care, but at least he had the one. He wouldn't complain.

But even better than the familiar comfort of Katie's bright gerbera daisies was the exciting, surprise vase of roses from Colt. Jake had hand-delivered them, which meant that Colt had arrived and was somewhere in the theater. Knowing his lover was there made him smile.

He broke ritual long enough to read the card for the third time, touched and grateful that he'd been made that kind of priority. "You got this, cher," the note read, and he smiled. He did. The company was ready, he was ready, but Colt's confident words steadied him and helped the opening-night nerves dissolve to a low simmer.

He put on his makeup, only being interrupted by Jake calling time. Right on schedule he finished his makeup, put the brushes away, and went for his tour of the stage.

He was standing center-center as Jake gave the five-minute call. He touched his fingers to his lips and then bent over, touching them to the mark.

"Merde," he said out loud as the rest of the company joined him onstage and the dance captain gave her opening-night pep talk. Nearly everyone touched the center mark as well on their way to places.

"Merde!" Jake said to him and shook his hand, the last piece of his ritual. Now he had his focus.

The next couple of hours were an intense and wonderful blur of music, dancers, applause, and finally, curtain calls. He realized that he hadn't firmed up with Colt the after-show plans, and he hoped his lover wouldn't wait for him in the lobby but would know to just come backstage. The perk of being a significant other.

When he got back to his dressing room, though, there was a note on his dressing table. He picked it up and opened it. "Son," it read. "Your mother and I saw this evening's performance and are waiting in the lobby to see you. Dad."

Well, the note was signed "Dad" and not "Mr. Alexander," so he wasn't being disowned. Yet. His hands started to shake. His parents were here? They stayed for the whole thing? He picked up a bottle of water and sat down hard in his chair.

His phone buzzed, the vibrations catching his attention, and he grabbed it. There was a text from Colt.

So good. So goddamn good. Tell me how to see you?

Oh, shit. His parents were going to hate Colt. He grinned at that and texted Colt back.

The flowers were inspiring! Hit the stage door. Jake will let you through.

He drank the water down while he waited in the dressing room doorway for Colt, wondering what the hell his parents could possibly want from him and why they didn't tell him they were here before the show. Something was up.

"Oo-ee, cher. That was so good. Are you proud?" Colt's voice preceded his huge, happy smile. He couldn't live under a cloud with that shining on him.

"Come in, baby." Kyle tossed the note on the table and held his dressing room door open. "I am so proud. Crazy proud. You had fun?"

"I had a ball. It was even better today." Colt came to him, offering his lips.

Kyle pulled him right in for a taste and let the door swing closed. "Mmm. Thank you for coming. It means a lot." He knew what it meant that Colt had come. He still wasn't sure about his parents. "My parents are here."

"Yeah?" Colt searched his eyes. "You want I should disappear, cher? I know that some folks ain't pleased."

He sighed. He wanted Colt to stay, for the two of them to stand up to his parents, but he couldn't force that choice on Colt. "I can't even tell you why they're here. They've never come to an opening before. Nothing is going to make them happy. I don't want you to feel—"

He looked up at the knock on the door. "Jake?"

"It's us, Kyle." His father's voice was unmistakable and sounded impatient. "Did you get our note?"

He looked at Colt. "Go or stay, it's up to you. I'm introducing you as my lover if you stay."

"I ain't ashamed of you, cher. I'll stand with you, no worries." Colt squeezed his hand and offered him another one of those smiles, eager, happy.

Kyle smiled and kissed him. "I'm proud of you too. Thank you."

"Kyle?"

Kyle went to the door and opened it. "Mom, Dad. What are you guys doing here? I thought you were waiting in the lobby."

His mother kissed his cheek and then brushed by him. "We got tired of waiting. This is your dressing room?"

"Yes. Did you enjoy the show?"

"Some of it."

His father followed her in. "Some of it was too...."

"Gay?"

His mother looked at him. "Sad."

He sighed and rolled his eyes. "Why are you—"

"Oh. Excuse me, I didn't.... Who is this?"

Who is this. Because heaven forbid the woman say hello before she knew whether Colt was beneath her.

"Ah. Mom, Dad, this is my lover. Colt Boudreaux."

He waited while the room dropped ten degrees. His mother looked Colt over, said absolutely nothing, and then looked back at Kyle. "Your sister gave us her tickets when she found out she couldn't be in town, and she...."

"She asked us to see you dance."

"Wasn't he amazing, y'all? He was stunning." Colt grinned over at his parents, just bold as brass.

Kyle smiled and took Colt's hand, watching his father's face.

"I wish you would at least dance normal ballet, Kyle. Respectable, classical ballet as you were trained."

"You know I don't like that, Kyle."

He shook his head. "What, Mother? Holding hands with my lover?"

"I wish you wouldn't—"

"Where are you from, Mr. Boudreaux? New Orleans, right? What do you want with our son?"

"I like how he cooks, and the way he dances makes me a little stupid." Colt squeezed his fingers. "The sex ain't bad either, to be honest."

"Mmm. That's true." Kyle laughed and wiggled his fingers.

"Ugh! Honestly. We were trying to be kind by coming, but there seems to have been little point." His mother swept out of the room, indignant.

Dad looked at him. "I don't see what your sister sees in… you. This. What a waste of our time. And you." His father turned that look at Colt. "Your kind has no business…. Don't let me see you near my son again."

"Or what, Dad?"

"You are this close, Kyle. Don't tempt me."

He would have argued further, but his father left the room just as abruptly.

"Huh. They ain't real nice, cher. That's a shame. I'm a good guy."

Kyle looked at Colt a little wide-eyed at first, hurt and ashamed, but Colt didn't seem to be blaming him. He just started to laugh. "You are."

Colt cupped his cheek. "You were amazing. I couldn't stop watching you. So proud."

"Thank you, love. It felt good. I really like knowing you're watching. And I love my roses." He leaned in and kissed Colt. "I'm sorry about them. I'm not the least bit proud of them, and as far as they are concerned, I'm just disappointing. I'm not sure what Katie was thinking asking them to come." He might just call her to find out.

"No worries. It ain't no thing."

Yeah, it was a thing. It just wasn't a thing that had anything to do with Colt.

There was another knock at his door. He sighed. *What now?* He opened the door to find a handful of dancers standing there. "Coming out, Kyle? We're headed to the Poet."

"Um, maybe?" He looked back at Colt, grinning. "What do you think?"

"I think that I'm at your convenience, you beautiful son of a bitch."

Someone in the group hooted.

He really couldn't contain his smile; it felt as big as his whole face. "Well, then, we're partying, music man." He grabbed his jacket and Colt's hand, and that was that.

The Purple Poet was a favorite among this crowd. It wasn't touristy. It was close to the theater and always full of performers, music, and lots of like-minded locals. They headed there in a group of energetic dancers and techies high on opening-night adrenaline. Colt was right there, hand in his, thumb rubbing circles around and around. It made him tingle, made things just that much better.

They'd make this work. Colt might have to travel, and he could too at some point, but that was the life of an artist, right? It was about the work; it was who they were. Nobody else was going to understand it better.

"This is Colt?"

"Yep. Colt… this is Joey, Ali, Brian, and Allegra, who we call Tweak, and that's not a drug reference. Then walking over, there is Rob, Mora, and… well, you met Danny. Jake and his stage crew are up ahead there."

Joey stuck his hand out. "Kyle told me all about you the other day. Nice to have a face to go with the brilliant musician reputation."

Colt shook, bowed dramatically. "Pleased, y'all."

Kyle smiled as Colt was showered with a bunch of greetings and handshakes from everyone within earshot except for Danny—*the brat*—then they were all hustling and jostling one another through the narrow door to the Poet.

He pulled Colt right to the bar. "What are you drinking, baby?"

"Beer. Y'all got an Abita or a Shiner?"

The bartender shook his head, obviously picking up on the accent. "Nah, man. No Shiner, and not the Abita you want. I got a Big Easy IPA, same brewery; that do it for you? Or a Yuengling?"

"Big Easy is fine. I appreciate it." Colt nudged him, grinned slow and easy. "What you want, stud?"

"Dry martini, Alan. Extra olives."

"Could set my watch by you."

"Throw him on my tab, okay?"

"Done. Give me a sec." Alan got to work.

"Stud, huh?" He slid his fingers up the side of Colt's neck, loving how Colt just gravitated into his hand. Always. Every time.

"Yessir." God, that smile was electric.

"Big Easy and your martini."

"Thanks, Alan."

"Hey! Kyle!" Joey was waving him over.

"My people are calling. Come on, baby." He made a straight line for Joey and six other dancers all crowded around a table. Two more seats appeared, and he and Colt squeezed in.

"The opening number was smooth tonight, huh?" Mora said, tapping his hand.

"I have very few notes on anything, to be honest. Everybody did a great job. That middle section, the tempo change? I would never know how difficult that switchover is if I hadn't choreographed it myself. You guys made it look easy. Right, Colt? That tempo change right in the middle of the first number?"

"It looked like y'all meant it to be like it was. Just like."

Kyle didn't miss the way Mora stared at Colt, and she wasn't the only one. "Uh. Thanks," she said and exchanged a look with Tweak.

"Exactly," Kyle agreed, breaking the awkward silence. "Totally smooth."

"What about the little jazz section in the carnival piece?" Joey asked, and about three people jumped on that one at the same time.

Kyle reached down and took Colt's hand under the table, giving it a squeeze.

Colt winked at him, leaned back, and drank his beer.

LORD HAVE mercy. He listened with half an ear to the dancers chatting and gnawing on the bones of their performance. So different from a night of jamming, but what he did wasn't so much about his body. They spent hours playing and drinking and playing and drinking.

These folks left all themselves on the stage with sweat and blood.

Thought about shit a lot too.

Him, he played and hoped it worked.

He sipped his third beer. Of course, folks here thought more than his type, he reckoned.

His type. Shit.

Kyle's people had looked at him like he was a piece of dog shit, hadn't they? Bless their hearts. He forced himself not to roll his eyes, because someone'd think it was meant for them, but damn. Uppity folks that thought their shit didn't stink were everywhere, and, fuck, but they hated it when some poor motherfucker like him pointed out they needed some Lysol in their lives.

Maybe shot up their asses.

Oh, wouldn't that be fun as all get-out?

A can of Lysol, a lighter, and a hose.

Sounded like a Saturday night at home, so long as there was a pig roast.

"He's the most talented dancer I have ever seen, you know." The sweet little dark-haired lead dancer was suddenly standing next to him. "Your boyfriend."

"I do. He's magic." He had never doubted that, not once.

"I'm Allison… Ali, remember? And yeah, he is." She put a hand on his. "You look bored to tears, and who could blame you, really? This group." She rolled her eyes. "You want another beer? I was just heading to the bar."

"Do I? I ain't bored. Just listening. I'll come with and help fetch and carry." Dammit. He didn't want to hurt Kyle's feelings. He loved watching and listening; he just wished he could do it with a guitar in his hands.

"All right. Come on, then." Allison led him away from the group and over to the bar where she ordered a round and put it on Kyle's tab. "How'd you two meet? I've only ever seen Kyle with… I mean, it's hard to meet people who aren't also dancers."

"We got us a friend in common. My roommate. He brought us together." He knew mostly musicians, bartenders, and cooks. He reckoned that was normal.

"Oh, that's cool. I keep thinking I need to fish in another pond too." She winked at him. "So, you live up here, then?"

"I do. I have a lot of work, and the hotel was expensive, and there wasn't a kitchen. My roommate works at the studio. It's all good."

"Nice. Too bad you don't have your guitar. I'd love to hear you play. I have to tell you, I never would have put Kyle with a blues musician."

"It would have been awkward as all get-out in the theater." Why would a blues man be weird? He was common as salt.

"Yeah, too bad."

Kyle laughed loudly and bumped shoulders with one of the dancers sitting next to him.

"He's quite a showman, Colt. I'm impressed how you've got him hooked." She smiled. "Actually, it's impressive that I *know* you've got him hooked."

"I just care about him, simple as that." Hooked, like Kyle was a gator on a line. Lord. He looked back at Kyle, smiling. His cher was way finer than anything on the end of a line.

"It's not as simple as that for most people. The rumors make him sound hard to love, but they're just rumors, and with this crew it's usually the whole pot-and-kettle story. I'm happy for you both."

A bunch of beers and a couple of mixed drinks landed on the bar. "You need help with these?"

Allison shook her head. "No, thank you. I've got a buddy." She scooped up what she could carry. "Can you get those? I'm sure you know who the martini is for."

"Yes, ma'am." Rumors? Lord have mercy. He sort of wanted to grab Kyle up and hug him and tell him he was a good guy.

"Thank you." Allison passed out her drinks and then took all but the martini from him.

"Colt! Kyle says you're going to do music for his exhibition?" Jake took his beer from Allison and set it on the table. "Thanks, Ali."

"Yessir." He handed Kyle his drink. "I'm looking forward to it."

"It's going to be amazing." Kyle tucked an arm around him. "Colt is so talented, you guys. I can't wait for you to hear him play."

Jake grinned. "Are we going to get our usual sneak peek sometime?"

"Oh, uh. I don't know. We'll have to see." He looked at Colt, explaining. "Usually I do a sort of mini performance for the company to get some feedback on a couple of pieces, but what we're doing might not really require feedback, you think?"

What did he care? He got to play, one way or the other. "It'll change every time, huh? What we do?"

"Every time," Kyle agreed.

"Change every time?" Jake looked at him. "What are you doing? Like a different ending every time?"

"Improv," Kyle answered for him.

"Whaaaat?" Mora shook her head. "That's crazy."

Kyle looked at Colt and grinned. "Yep."

He winked over. Improv was his life. He just went with it. No big.

The group hung out, talking for a little while longer, but finally started to break up with some folks going home and some just getting drunker as it got late. Kyle was on martini number one-too-many—four maybe?—when he leaned in close to Colt. "Hey there. You're handsome. Wanna make out?" Kyle slurred and planted a kiss on Colt that tasted like vermouth.

He chuckled softly and kissed Kyle back, keeping it light, lazy. He needed to pour them both into a cab and get them home—either to his room or Kyle's house, he didn't care.

"Was your beer good? We should go to a bar that has beer you like." Kyle started to get up and stumbled a step. "Oh. Your lover is a little drunk, baby."

He grabbed ahold of Kyle around the waist. "Mm-hmm. Let's go home, cher. Maybe have a long bath together."

"I'm all yours. Anything you like." Kyle leaned on him as they made their way through the bar. "You liked the show."

"I loved it. It was damned fine. Your place or mine?"

"Let's do you, hm? Way closer. And I can smooch Timmy." Kyle looked at him wide-eyed. "Smooch hello, lover, not smooch smooch. I got you to smooch smooch."

"You so do." Lord have mercy, that was cute as fuck. He got them a car and got them moving before Kyle passed out or puked. A B-12, a Tylenol, and a big glass of water was on order.

"'M not that drunk, you know." He let Kyle lean on him in the cab, full weight against his shoulder. "Sorry I have asshole parents. They want me to marry this girl, Danielle? She's my mom's friend's daughter. I think they're missing something kind of important about me."

"Is that still a thing, cher? I thought that was for princes and all."

Kyle started to laugh, but it wasn't happy or amused; it was rueful and ugly. "I am a prince to them, baby. My father and mother are king and queen of denial."

"Well, you ain't got to do a thing but die and pay taxes, you know?" No one could force someone to get married these days.

"Nope. I keep wondering what they're telling Danielle. Poor woman." Kyle sat up. "Enough of them. Tell me you're ready to start working on Monday."

"You know it. I'm yours." He meant it. He thought they'd have a ball—moving and playing.

"Mmm. So mine." Kyle slid a hand up his shirt.

"Yes. All the way." He let himself kiss Kyle's jaw. "All the way, cher."

"Are we *still* in this damn cab?" Kyle pouted at him and rubbed his belly. "I mean come *on*. Hurry it up, driver!"

Colt chuckled softly. God, drunken Kyle was cute as fuck.

"Jake said there were a couple of critics in the audience tonight. It was good, right? You said you thought it was better than the rehearsal you saw even, right? Those critics can be so mean. But this company is so talented, aren't they? I mean, Ali? She's just smooth as glass. And Danny's a turd, but he moves like he's not even trying. And they usually like me, so…." Kyle grinned. "You're not talking much."

"I loved it. I thought it had the best hoodoo. All y'all."

"Is this your neighborhood? Oh, I love it. It's so, like, real New York, you know?" He let Kyle babble while he paid the driver. "Like, real people live here, not spoiled-brat ballet dancers."

"You're real, cher." He grabbed Kyle's hand. "Come see my room. It's sweet."

He tugged Kyle into the building and up the couple of flights to his apartment, but when he unlocked the door, it wouldn't open. Something was wedged under it.

He grinned. Timmy was smoking.

"Hey, dude! One second, man. Hang on. Okay. Wait, I got it." The door opened a crack, and the second he and Kyle had squeezed through, Timmy slammed it and stuffed the towel back under the door. "Sorry about…. Hey, Kyle!"

"Hello, Timmy, you cutie pie. You're up to no good, hm?"

"Oh dude. You got him drunk."

"He got himself drunk. I was just there to love on him and make sure he was having a good time." He winked over, got Kyle on the sofa, and snagged Timmy's spliff. One long drag was all he needed.

"Finish that up, dude. There's a clip on the coffee table if you need it." Timmy followed them in from the kitchen with a glass of water and handed it to Colt. "I have some Tylenol. Let me grab it."

"I am fine, Timothy. Don't fuss over me. It was just... um... the thing with olives. Martinis."

"There is B-12 too. I'll get him one from the bedroom." Mmm... the green made his eyes cross for half a second.

"Oh, the two of you," he heard Kyle say as he ducked into his room.

"Take both of those and the whole glass of water, twinkle toes."

Kyle sighed loudly. "Come sit with me, Timmy."

"I don't think so, pretty dancer. You're spoken for, and I have a nice buzz on I'm going to go enjoy in my room."

He winked at Timmy as they passed in the hallway. "How you doin', boug?"

"I had a good night, just chillin'. How was the opening? Looks like you two had some fun."

"It was amazing. I could watch that for a lifetime." He'd loved all of it, except maybe meeting the folks. That had been on the suck side.

"Yeah, he's got a hook for sure. I'm hittin' the hay, dude. I'll be out of your hair. Good night." Timmy gave him a friendly slap to the shoulder and headed off for his room.

He wandered back to Kyle, vitamins in hand. "Take these, huh?"

"God, what now? I don't need more pills." Kyle took them anyway, though, and swallowed them down with the rest of his glass of water. "Happy?" Kyle gave him a flirty smile, softening the irritable words.

"I am." He climbed onto Kyle's lap. "Very. You?"

"Understatement. Ecstatic, elated, delirious, over the moon." Kyle kissed him. Drunk Kyle kisses were almost better than sober ones in their abandon.

"Mmm. Like that word." He rubbed Kyle's temples with his thumbs and held on, the kisses dizzying.

Kyle nipped and tugged at his bottom lip and slid eager hands up under his shirt, going right for his nipples. "You taste a little green, lover."

"You want a shotgun, cher?" Oh, hell yeah. He arched into the touch.

"No, baby. Don't you know that old rhyme? Beer then grass, on your ass!" Kyle laughed and pushed his shirt up, replacing mischievous fingers with a clever tongue.

His eyes crossed, that deep buzz making him a little dizzy.

"You want to show me your room, baby? I should probably shower."

"I do. You want company?" He could wash that long body, clean him up.

Kyle tickled his belly. "Your company? Always, always, always."

"Mmm. Good. Come on." He grabbed ahold of Kyle's hands and hauled him up.

Kyle was not nearly as steady as it seemed on the couch and hadn't sobered up at all. He stumbled along, carrying a lot of Kyle's weight down the hall and into his room. "Oh, 's big, huh? Gorgeous tall windows."

"Yeah. I like it. There's a view and a big bed and great acoustics."

Kyle looked at him. "That's my blues man. I love that you just said great acoustics. I love that you notice those things." Kyle started stripping without regard for the windows and tossing his clothing on the bed. "Hot shower time."

"You know it." He got himself naked and then led Kyle to the bathroom, one arm around Kyle's waist. No falling, after all.

"Oh, it's kind of tight in here. We're gonna have to get close, lover boy." Kyle smiled and kissed him.

Such a problem that was. He chuckled and muscled right up, rubbing in the best way.

"Mmm. That's very nice." He had Kyle pretty well pinned, which seemed to suit his lover just fine. Kyle stuck fingers in his hair and tipped his head back under the spray. "That's nice too." He felt a hot tongue run up his neck to just under his ear.

"Yeah...." Oh, this was the best way to end a night—booze and green and a nice fuck.

Kyle got hold of the shampoo and worked it into his hair, taking his time, massaging it into his scalp and down the back of his neck, humming softly something he recognized from the show. Everything began to tingle, his cock filling slowly, steadily as Kyle loved on him.

"I love the smell of your shampoo, baby."

He closed his eyes as Kyle angled him back under the spray, the soapy water slipping over his skin. Kyle rubbed the suds into his chest, down his side and around to his ass, fingers digging in.

"You... I want to know every inch of you." More than that, he'd give up all of himself.

Kyle nodded. "Go ahead. Have every inch." He let Colt go, eyes soft with alcohol and arousal. Colt started washing, making sure to spend time on the little hot spots, the places that made Kyle arch and moan.

Kyle reached down and took a firm hold of his own cock, and Colt watched it fill and stretch in that knowing grip. Kyle groaned and started to stroke, eyes sliding closed.

Lord have mercy, that was enough to make his mouth dry.

"Mmm." Kyle leaned back against the shower wall and swallowed hard, throat working and that Adam's apple bobbing.

"Look at you." He reached out, dragging one finger along the slit.

Kyle hissed. "You look... mm. And then you can have me." That hand sped up, Kyle's breath coming faster too.

He cupped Kyle's balls, rolled them, knowing how good that felt, how his picker's fingers made things wild.

"Baby, your hands are half-satin, half-sandpaper. Fuck." Kyle's measured breaths were shallow but steady, echoing a little against the tile. "Jesus."

He pushed behind, dragging along that sensitive strip of skin. "They love your skin."

"They can... have—" Kyle groaned and those hazel eyes popped open, locking on his and not letting go. "Oh, fuck."

He watched as Kyle's shoulders tensed and that strong chest expanded, veins standing out under Kyle's skin.

"Yeah, cher. Jus' so." He repeated the gesture, dragging good and hard.

With a long moan, Kyle's hand started to fly, and Colt imagined that perfect grip doing everything just right—pressure, speed, heat, everything just the way Kyle needed it. "Yes. Mmm." Kyle's rhythmic breathing faltered, eyes sliding closed again. "Colt. Baby."

"You know it." He leaned in, bit Kyle's earlobe. "Give it up now."

"Fuck!" Kyle's face pressed into his neck, hips jerking, and it wasn't even a second before he was treated to that lovely shiver and sigh. "Colt... fuck."

"Mmm. Yeah. Love how you smell."

Kyle kissed him, leaning into him heavily, breathing hard, tasting like martini and olives and still a little tipsy. "You want me, baby? You can have whatever you want."

"Mmm. There ain't a bit of you I don't want. Let's get your sweet ass to the bed." That way he'd know whether Kyle was wanting or fixin' to pass out. He could use his hand in the latter event. It was no big thing.

But Kyle flirted plenty as they toweled off and led him by the hand to his bed, looking pretty steady on those talented feet. "You've been watching long enough, lover. Don't you think?"

"Yeah. Yeah, I think." He pushed in close, letting himself need all the way. "Shit, I know. I need you, cher."

Like breathing, if he was honest.

"Yours." Kyle kissed him, then turned and stretched out across his bed, lean muscle and inked, pale skin standing out against his sheets.

"God." He moaned as he ran his hands up along Kyle's thighs. The single word was a plea and a blessing and a thank-you.

"Let me ease you, baby. Come on." Kyle reached for him, voice part whisper and part song.

"Yeah." He gloved up with shaking hands. He was so hard just that threatened to make him go over the edge.

"Look at you. I got this." Kyle snatched up the slick and flipped over onto his knees, giving Colt a little show as he got ready.

"Jesus...." He grabbed the base of his cock and squeezed hard as he got the best show of his life.

With a moan, Kyle's hand fell away. "Colt."

"Uh-huh. Now, cher. I got a need. Now." *Please. Say it is time.*

Kyle nodded and arched back toward him. "Now. So ready."

Thank God for small favors. He surged forward, pressing into tight, breathtaking heat. His eyes rolled up in his head, and he grabbed hold of Kyle's hips.

Kyle cried out and reached back with one hand, digging long fingers into his thigh. He wasn't seeing clearly, but he felt Kyle roll back to meet him, taking him even deeper.

Colt had not a bit of grace left in him, not so much as a hint of it. All he could do was push and thrust and rock harder.

It wasn't long before he felt his lover give up trying to find a rhythm too.

"Colt!" Kyle made fists in the covers, bracing and giving him something solid to work against, and together they filled the bedroom with sound—grunts and groans, begging and filthy affirmations.

He stretched up over Kyle's back, his forehead slick as he rested them together, driving in for a few more, restless thrusts before he grunted, the room spinning as he emptied his balls.

Kyle panted out a couple of rough breaths and moaned, shifting under him. "Jesus Christ, baby."

"Uh-huh." Right. No talking. Dizzy.

They lay there for... a long time. Could have been hours, could have been two minutes. How would he know? Finally, he felt Kyle's lips on one arm, dropping light kisses and warm nuzzles. "Okay, music man. You need to let me breathe. Slide over." He thought about trying to move, but Kyle beat him to it, lifting up so he sort of slid off onto the bed. "Oh, I'm going to be deliciously sore in the morning."

"Uhn." That was close to a yes, right?

Kyle laughed and curled around him. "Good night, love."

"Love." Yeah. Yeah, love. He closed his eyes, humming himself to sleep.

Chapter Ten

Kyle woke up slowly, tangled up with Colt and buried under an unfamiliar comforter. It took him a little time to figure out where he was and how he'd gotten there, and that came along with the realization that he was more than a little hungover.

He shifted, stretching and grinning at an ache he was going to enjoy all day. Colt's smooth, warm shoulder was right there, and he gave it a kiss. He'd be happy to stay here forever, but first he needed some water and some Tylenol.

He could smell coffee—which was either good or bad, his stomach wasn't sure. He pushed up, trying not to jostle Colt.

Oh, hello. The windows in this room were tall and gorgeous, but Jesus, they let in a lot of light. He squinted toward the bedroom door, wondering how many steps it would take to get over there, and then slid out of bed, eyes shielded under one hand.

He opened the door, groaning as blessed darkness surrounded him. Better. So much better.

"Tylenol?" Timmy's hand appeared under his nose.

"Oh. Oh, yes. It's the God of stupid dancers that drink too much." He took the pills right out of Timmy's hand. "How did you know?"

"I was up getting caffeinated, dude. I heard you moving around." Timmy looked like the cat with the canary. "You want coffee?"

He hesitated for a second, trying to get his fuzzy mind around the look on Timmy's face. "Yes?" He nodded. "Yes. I need coffee. Colt is still sleeping. He's tired. Do you have water too?" *Do you have water? Really?*

"We do. And orange juice. Hell, I think Colt has a six-pack of Coke."

Just the words "orange juice" made his stomach flip over. "Just water's good." He sat at the kitchen table and let Timmy get him water and coffee. He took the Tylenol and prayed it worked fast, finishing the water with it. "Thanks, Timmy. Sorry. Good morning, by the way. I'll be better in a minute. Why do you keep grinning at me?"

As if he didn't know. He wasn't so drunk last night that he didn't remember that shower, and Colt... God, Colt. He couldn't remember ever being wanted like that before.

"You're smitten."

"Did you honestly just say smitten? What are you? Forty?"

"Dude, that's deflecting. You're totally gone." Timmy just kept grinning.

"I don't know about totally."

Timmy pinned him with a look. "Liar."

"Maybe." He stared right back, but Timmy was either better at this, less hungover, or both. "He's... like no one I've ever met, and we're good together."

Timmy sat with him. "You love him?"

"Oh, Timmy. You know me. I fall in love every day."

"True. He's a good guy. One hell of a picker and a surprisingly good songwriter for a kid that never got past seventh grade."

"Wow. He didn't tell me that." Why would he? And what did it matter, anyway? What Colt had went way past schooling. You couldn't learn what he did, the way he played. You had to be gifted it. Channel it or something. "He is a great guy. He might even be the right guy. *The* guy."

Kyle did fall in love every day. It just so happened that he'd fallen in love with the *same* guy every day since he met Colt.

"Wow. That's cool. I'm jealous. I'm still looking for two blowjobs in a row."

"I don't understand that at all. You're adorable." And sweet. And a great friend. "I wouldn't have met Colt if not for you."

"Adorable doesn't get you fucked, my friend. Jacked off? Sure. Fucked? Not so much."

"That sucks." The surfer-style California transplant wasn't really his type, but it had to be somebody's. "Patience? You can't force this stuff. It'll happen. I know I wasn't expecting a Cajun blues artist to fall into my lap."

"Sort of literally. He's adorable with you, you know."

"You think? He's so interested in everything, it's so much fun. He's hot too, Timmy. Oh my God. I can't believe you set us up and didn't just keep him for yourself."

Timmy grinned at him. "He's intense, bro, and we have to work together. That can get weird, you know?"

"He's intense for sure." Colt had a ton of energy, but it wasn't wild; it was always so focused. "I've hired him to do a live improv performance piece with me for my next exhibition, and also put down some tracks for a couple of the other numbers. You think it will get weird? I'll want to arrange some studio time for him, by the way."

"I don't know, but it sounds like I need to see it."

"I'm sure you'll tell us it's self-indulgent navel-gazing or something." He laughed. It might be. He wasn't sure he cared. Also, as long as Colt was busy, his lover wasn't leaving town.

"I've seen both of you. I'm sure I will." Timmy winked at him and waggled knowing eyebrows.

"He's good here, right? I mean, it seems like he wants to stick around, stay in the city, right?" Oh, hangover head. He wouldn't ask something like that if he had a filter, but he just couldn't stop himself. He glanced over at the kitchen door, to make sure Colt wasn't standing there. Hell, in for a penny…. "Has he said anything?"

"About leaving? Nah. He says he has a couple of songwriter buds that are staying for two weeks and working with him, but he had his manager give me a check for six months' rent."

"Oh. Cool. Good to know." Really good to know, though he kind of felt shitty for asking. Like he was checking up. He could blame the hangover, right? "I'm going to bring him some coffee, okay?" He got up, gingerly as his head swam a little, and found two mugs.

"He likes it sweet and creamy."

Like he didn't know that.

"Really appreciate the Tylenol, Timmy." He picked up both coffees—his black, and Colt's sweet coffee-flavored milk—and gave Timmy a kiss on the cheek. "You're a sweetheart."

Timmy snorted at him. "Yep. That's me. Hope you feel better."

He laughed and headed back to Colt's bedroom. He loved the high ceiling and the window seats; even the sunlight was better now that he'd had a sip of coffee.

Colt was sleeping, tight, tiny ass in the air. Oh, that was a pretty sight. He put the coffee down, then settled in the sheets, running his hand along Colt's butt.

He smoothed his fingers up and over the rise of one cheek and down that perfect little curve to Colt's lower back, then traced a slow line up Colt's spine with one finger, feeling more than just the pull of his lover's beautiful body. "I think I could wake up next to this every day," he whispered, softly. "Next to you."

He really thought he could. Probably. Almost certainly. God, the idea was both stunning and terrifying.

"Mmm." Colt arched in a slow motion that screamed lazy pleasure. He watched the way Colt rippled, as if being drawn up by Kyle's touch. Kyle cataloged that motion; one day he would use it.

He kissed Colt's shoulder, moving his fingers to work in slow, heavy circles over Colt's back. He kept his voice low. "You're something to look at, music man."

"Make me happy, cher, down to the ground." Colt hummed, the sound soft and low, reminding him strangely of what he imagined a great cat would sound like.

"People have told me that before, you know." He smiled, tucking Colt against him. "But you, I believe." Down to the ground, up to the moon. "I have coffee."

"I like coffee." Colt rolled up to settle on his butt. "And I mean it."

He handed Colt the mug full of sugar and cream and watched as Colt took a sip. "Well, thank you, lover. I really do believe you." It would be nice to understand it, but he could accept it as true for now without that. He picked up his coffee and took a sip, the bitter, dark flavor giving him a much-needed kick in the ass. "Ahh."

"Mm-hmm. Very much ahh. Makes me want to lick the air like a dog."

"What?" He laughed and then groaned. "Oh. The head. I'm a little hungover." But getting better.

"You get you some Tylenol? You were happy last night."

He smiled. "I was. I was better than happy. Timmy saved my ass this morning with Tylenol and the coffee, yes." He leaned closer, rubbing shoulders with Colt. "You were on fire last night."

"It was fun, playing with you, watching you work. The after-work part was pretty amazing too, eh, cher? We had the bon temps, oui?" Colt leaned hard, inhaling his coffee.

"Oui. We're getting good at the bon temps." He laughed, pleased to discover he didn't feel so much like razor blades were slicing his brain to bits anymore. "What have you got planned today? Timmy said you have some buddies in town?"

"Fixin' to be, yeah. We're gon' get together and write on some songs, make some money, I hope." Colt snuggled in. "Today I'm pretty free."

"Well, I have a show tonight, so at some point I need to head for my studio and work a little, but I don't see any reason not to stay right here for a while and sip this coffee." He put one arm around Colt's shoulders, keeping his lover close.

"What do you like to read about, cher? What's your favorite kind of book?"

"A cookbook. Who has time to read? I'm too busy being out there living. I want to do the things other people only read about." The last time he tried to actually read a book he fell asleep. "Are you a reader?"

"Sure. I like stories, especially ones about places I ain't seen."

"What kind of stories do you like? Mysteries? Love stories? Stories about real people? I've done a lot of traveling. I talk to people a lot, everywhere I go, and I do like when people tell me a story or something personal about where they live." He sipped his coffee, already getting toward the bottom of the cup.

"Oh, I just pick up ones that look good from the back. I've read all sorts on buses and trains and planes, sitting and waiting for another set. Where's your favorite place to go?"

"Anywhere that has a beach." He grinned. "Bright sun, clear water, and warm sand do it for me. I could listen to the waves all day long. I love St. Barths, but it's a pain to get there."

"I been to the Gulf a lot, all over it, and I been to LA."

"Oh, the Gulf is lovely. I've only been on the Florida side, but I loved it. The clear water, the white sand. Just lovely." And the last resort he'd stayed at had Starbucks delivery in the morning if you ordered it the night before. Starbucks *delivery*. He almost didn't leave.

"Yessir. It makes a man feel small, but in a good way." Colt began to stroke his belly, petting him.

He nodded. "The city is like that too, but in a different way, you know? Waves everywhere. Of people, of light, of sounds—the subway, the traffic, music. Right?"

"Uh-huh. It's just perfect. I think I'm good here."

"Good. I'm not ready to let you go home." He tried to hide how relieved he felt, but he wasn't sure how well he was doing. "And I'm not the long-distance relationship type." The one time he'd tried had been a complete disaster, and he wasn't going to do that again.

"Well, I got good work, so I intend to stay for a while. Timmy told me all about the wintertime here. I want to see the ice skating. I want to see the lights at Christmas." Colt sounded like he was hypnotized, lazy and barely slurred.

He smiled. He loved the city at Christmas. "The big stores do all these elaborate decorations in their windows along Fifth Avenue; they're amazing. And there's a big tree at Rockefeller Center. And the Empire State Building gets lit up red and green." He kissed Colt's temple. "Oh! And the Rockettes!"

"We can see everything. I want to see everything with you."

"You will." Maybe this would be the year he stopped putting himself through Christmas Day with his parents. "We could put a tree up at my place. Decorate it." That would be a first for him.

"Oo-eee! That would be something. I ain't had a tree in a long time."

"Me neither. I've never had one at my place at all." He suddenly could picture them, running strings of lights with classic Christmas carols playing in the background—Nat King Cole, Bing Crosby, Andy Williams. "Where should we put it? The front hall? The den near the fireplace?"

"The front would let other folks see, but we'd see it more near the fire." Colt turned his face, smiled up at him. "Why not?"

"Why not, what? Put it in the den? It's for us, we'll put it there."

"Why not you ain't had a tree? No time? Have you ever had to be the Nutcracker?"

"Oh, no. I've danced in the show, I don't know, four or five times early on in my career. Ensemble parts usually, but I danced Cavalier once, and I was a swing for the Mouse King in another production. But I've never been the enchanted toy himself, no."

He set his empty mug down on the bedside table. He didn't think Colt would let him ignore the question again. "You haven't had a tree in a long time, either, you said? I'd guess our reasons might be about the same. Christmas is beautiful outside the house, out in the city where you can look and enjoy it and celebrate. Inside the house it's just… lonely. I always say I don't have time. I might if it mattered."

Colt nodded. "I been on the street for a while, then I went from that to fancy-assed hotels, huh? Home is where my guitar is."

He never really thought about his place as home, maybe because it used to belong to his parents. For all that it was beautiful and comfortable, it could be a big, lonely place, and he often felt more at home outside the brownstone than in it.

"I'm happy you're keeping that guitar here. We'll make some of our own kind of fun for the holidays this year. What do you make for Christmas dinner in New Orleans? We could each pick a couple of things we like, right?"

"You mean a réveillon, cher? We could have ourselves a wee feasting."

"A wee feasting? I don't feast small, baby." He laughed. "What's a réveillon? Like, a party?"

"Is a lovely supper—turtle soup and turkey, barbecue shrimp and croquembouche. But we can make whatever makes us happy and have candles on the table to wake the light up and welcome the bébé."

"Turtle soup? Oh, you have to make that. I've never had it." The waking the baby part he'd just let his lover have if he wanted it. Hopefully Colt didn't want to go to church or mass or whatever too. He might burst into flames. "Candles sound great, you know I love that stuff. The shrimp sounds fantastic too. I have to have some potatoes, though. And something green. Brussels sprouts or spinach or something."

"You ever had brussels sprouts fried? Oh, that's heaven." Colt hummed softly, then chuckled for him. "Of course, I'd be happy to sit with you and eat corn flakes."

"We are not eating corn flakes on Christmas. But I hear what you're saying." He plucked the coffee mug from Colt's fingers and set it on the table alongside his. "Are you getting hungry, baby? You want to take Timmy out for something greasy?" He leaned in and stole a light kiss.

"Hash browns and eggs."

He loved how Colt said "aigs." Loved it. He nodded. "French toast and sausage. And more coffee. And then we can walk of shame back to my place." He did need to work. Just a little at least, or he wouldn't feel ready to dance tonight.

"No shame. None." Colt swung around onto his lap. "You gon' let me play while you dance?"

He smiled and ran his hands up Colt's sides. "Sure, if you want to. I just need to get a workout in. I'd love that."

Whoever it was that told Colt he was just ordinary hadn't ever seen the view Kyle had right now.

"Me too. I love to see you move. It's like magic."

"It's not magic. Just like your music isn't magic. It's passion. It's obsession and hard work. Nobody else has to know that, but we do. This thing we have going, though? You and me? That is definitely magic. I have no idea how we made this happen."

He pulled Colt's face down closer for a kiss.

Colt smiled at him, dark eyes glistening, so warm.

"Okay, baby. Clothes. I don't guess you have an extra toothbrush? Should I ask Timmy?" He gave Colt a playful little shove to get him moving.

"There's a bunch in packages in my bathroom. I asked if the guy before me was a hoarder, and Timmy just laughed."

"Sounds like he was fond of spontaneous overnight guests to me." He got up, looked around at the floor, and snorted. "My stuff is everywhere. I was pretty drunk. Huh?"

"Just a little. You're a cutie when you're a little around the bend."

He laughed. "Oh God. I've been told I flirt like a fiend. Sorry if I was over-the-top." He remembered most of it. He was way over-the-top. But Colt seemed to enjoy it, so he didn't really feel that bad about it.

He found his jeans on the floor and dug his shirt and scarf out from under the comforter.

"You flirted with me, so I liked it." Colt's fingers trailed over his ass, teasing him, playing him.

"See? You were in the right place at the right time. I told you." He brushed Colt's hand away, laughing. "Get your clothes on, Cajun. Timmy's probably hungry." Timmy was a bit of a stoner. He was always hungry, wasn't he?

"Timmy's always hungry. Him and the green? They are close friends."

Kyle shrugged. "There are worse things." Though you had to wonder why someone as successful as Timmy used so much. He was the studio's head engineer. He had to take home a nice check. He'd be living high on the hog if he wasn't high on the green.

He pulled his jeans on commando and headed into the bathroom to find one of those toothbrushes.

When he came back from the bathroom, Colt was singing to Timmy, teasing him. The sound echoed through the apartment. Okay, that was adorable. He was pleased to find Colt dressed at least. Timmy was blushing, which was even more adorable. He caught Timmy up in his arms and danced him around the living room.

"Kyle!"

"Come on, Timmy." He grinned and winked at Colt.

"Seriously? I don't dance."

"What kind of dancer would I be if I couldn't give you a lead you could follow?" He spun Timmy, moving to Colt's improvised song.

"You goof." Timmy did follow, though, didn't he? And he smiled as they danced.

"Uh-huh. Hey, you're actually pretty light on your feet, Tim. Are you keeping secrets from me?"

"Shut up. Whoa." Timmy laughed and let Kyle dip him right in front of Colt.

Colt pulled a face, the expression silly enough that they all cracked up.

"You want something greasy for breakfast, Timmy? Colt and I want to take you out."

"Yeah? No strings?" Timmy grinned at him.

He laughed. "Hell, no. I'm much too jealous to share."

"You ain't interested in my skinny ass, boo. You like them big and beefy."

"Yeah. They need to be, like, three of you, dude."

Kyle grinned. "Good to know." Not that he knew anyone available that fit that description. But he had eyes. He found his boots and stomped into them. "I don't know this neighborhood. Where are we going?"

Timmy looked at Colt. "Waverly?"

"I'm easy, so long as there's breakfast." Colt wandered up to him and smoothed his shirt down.

"Waverly sounds good." He barely got the last word out before he kissed Colt. "I need more coffee."

Timmy rolled his eyes at them and grabbed a jacket. Kyle hooked an arm around his lover's waist, feeling a need to keep Colt close, and followed the guy out the door.

Chapter Eleven

"Lord, y'all! Welcome!" Colt bounced a little, tickled to death that Norv and Ryder had made it in. He'd told them to meet him over to the studio, because it was easy to find and they'd booked the same hotel he'd used, so it was a quick walk.

Between his studio work, his work with Kyle, and this, he was fixin' to be as busy as a one-legged man in a butt-kicking competition.

Norv grabbed him up, spun him around. "Cajun! I heard you'd got lost up here in this scary place."

"Ain't all that scary, not really."

Ryder shot him a look from under the brim of his cap. "It's damn big."

"Not really, dude. The whole island of Manhattan is only twenty-two square miles." Timmy shook hands all around. "I'm Timmy. I'm your engineer. And these are your badges. They'll get you into the instrument room, the studios, and also the break room. Welcome." Timmy handed them each a little white card on a lanyard that matched the one Colt was already wearing.

Norv flipped the card over and back, frowning at it. "Damn, Cajun. Is this place for real?"

"Fancy-assed, eh? Timmy's cool. One of us. All about the music." And he wanted to get on it, wanted to find that thing that the three of them had together. There was a deep magic that lived where they sat in a triangle.

Timmy gave him a pat on the back and headed for the control room. "I'll be where you need me when you need me."

Ryder looked at the lanyard and shook his head, then put the card in his pocket and pulled out a little notebook. "Let's do it. I started a thing on the plane, maybe got legs. Fingers itch."

"I'll grab my acoustic." He damn near bounced on the way. These guys were a couple of the best, and they let him in like it was nothing, like he belonged.

Norv's chuckle followed him. "Eager to write, huh?"

"You know it. I got a couple things to share." Maybe more than a couple, but a few of them had a real shot to make them money.

Timmy's voice came through the speaker into the studio. "You guys the take-a-break type or the bring-food-in type?"

"We're the forgot-to-eat type." Norv gave Timmy a toothy grin and pulled his guitar out of its case.

"Dude! My favorite. On it."

Norv started tuning by ear, fingers moving over the strings playing scales and patterns. "Leave it raw right now, Tim. We'll tell you if we want a mix. Just make sure you get everything."

"Right on. You're the boss."

Yeah, that was true. Norv was his fucking hero. Ryder was more like him—just a guy who had a knack for this thing. Norv was a cowboy, pure Texas down to the bone, raw and beautiful and completely Ryder's.

Ryder dragged a stool over, sat right next to his shoulder, and leaned in, showing him a couple of rough verses.

"Oh, I like that. I like that a lot." He doodled over the notations, singing low as he worked to pick up the hook.

"Uh-huh." Norv leaned back in his chair and started noodling, light notes here and there that filled out and started to take shape around the rhythm of the lyric. They found their sweet spot, the harmony building itself, the bridge like caramel in coffee.

Ryder's pipes weren't gonna sell a record, but his way with words, his instinct for rhythm and rhyme was magic, and he sang like he knew it. Eventually the words ran out, though, and Norv's fingers went still and quiet too. Colt grinned, knowing they were listening, letting him bring it home.

So he did. He closed his eyes and let the good Lord speak through him, giving thanks as it worked like it had, every time. They all let the last notes of his guitar fade without a twitch, and then Ryder reached out and gave his knee a squeeze.

"Cut it there, Tim, and cue it up?"

Timmy nodded through the glass, and Ryder started scribbling notes.

"That was sweet, Colt. New York's been good to you." Norv stood up and stretched, setting the guitar down in a stand.

"I got me a honey. He does it for me, all the way down."

"What? A Yankee?" Norv laughed, loud. "You're joking."

"Not even. He's a dancer. He moves like… y'all. It's like he's made of music too."

Ryder looked up from the book he'd been scribbling notes in. "A dancer, huh?" He and Norv exchanged a look.

Norv grinned at him. "He must be pretty."

"Where does he dance? Let's get a beer there later."

"Ah-law!" He started laughing, just tickled as a pig in shit. "Y'all don' know. He's like high-dollar fancy dancing, not for dollar bills in his garter. He got him a YouTube. Come see." He pulled up one of Kyle's videos, eager to show his lover off.

About halfway through the video, Norv nodded. "He's good."

"Good?" Ryder gaped at Norv. "He's fucking beautiful. Jesus, Colt."

Norv just shook his head.

"Lucky me, eh? He's like one of them statues, but…." But so alive and fierce and funny and odd and happy.

"But he moves. Wow. Lucky you." Ryder laughed.

"You ready to play that back, Tim?"

Ryder elbowed Colt with a wink and a grin.

"You know it," Timmy came right back. "You want to hear it?"

"Y'all ready to hear this back or what?"

"I'm ready. Bring it on, Timmy." He grabbed his guitar so he could think.

Timmy played the track back, all their ramblings in the beginning leading into something that started to make sense. Ryder bobbed his head along and made notes when he wasn't tapping his pen on his notebook. Norv just did that thing he always did. He leaned back in his chair, arms crossed over his chest, and eyes closed, put his feet up and listened all the way through.

For Norv, this was where the magic happened. He had a knack for taking all their raw creativity and focusing it into something they could sell. The playback had barely ended when he sat up, picked up his guitar and started playing again without letting anyone speak.

"Better get this, Timmy." Ryder gave Timmy a wave and got a thumbs-up in response.

Colt settled on the floor where he was comfortable, and Ryder joined him, both of them listening to Norv, making notes for the next run-through.

They were still deep into work when the lights in the studio started to flash. Timmy pressed a piece of paper against the glass that read "Food and beer in break room" in weird black bubble letters. He grinned at them.

Ryder leaned into Norv. "Can we eat, boss?"

Norv reached down, hand in Ryder's hair. "Always hungry, Georgia Boy."

Lord, wasn't that pretty?

"That's a yes." Ryder grinned, gave Norv a kiss, then popped up off the floor and tucked his little notebook safely into his pocket. Once he was up, though, he stretched, everything creaking. "Oh, man. I'm stiff. Stupid airplane."

"It's a long ways from Austin, huh?"

"Austin to Dallas, Dallas to Atlanta, Atlanta to here." Ryder rolled his eyes. "He's a cheapskate."

Norv snorted. "Thrifty. And you like to fly."

"Not that much. Didn't Timmy's sign say beer?" Ryder was the first one to the break room.

Norv clapped him on the back, chuckling softly. "He's still got a hollow leg."

"Shut up. I'm a growing boy! Ooh. Cheesesteak." Ryder snagged a whole one off the counter.

"There's a couple of subs too. And a bunch of salads. Next time you can look over the menus before you start, and I'll order what you like." Timmy grabbed a container of french fries and a Coke and sat down.

His phone started blowing up in his pocket.

Hey. Your boys get here okay?

Do you have dinner plans?

I hate this rain. What happened to summer?

Helloooooo lover

How's it going?

All from Kyle and all at once. No cell service in the studio, the walls were too thick. He started replying to what he could.

You want to eat with N&R?

It's raining? I ain't seen the outside

Writing hard. I showed u off

Kyle came right back at him. *There u are!* That was followed by four red hearts. *It's pouring rain baby. Water everywhere. Where r N&R staying? Dinner @ my place or out?*

I like raining. I can cook? At that fancy assed hotel I was at. He couldn't stop smiling.

I would love u 2 cook. need me 2 shop text me a list. What do they drink? I have wine

"Is that your Yankee?" Ryder asked, mouth half-full of food.

"It is. Y'all want to have supper at his? I'll make shrimp and grits, if you want."

"Works for me," Norv said. "Ry?"

"I can't wait."

Norv grinned at him. "Sounds like a plan."

you writing good stuff? Am I going to love it?

I hope so. Miss u. Bad. Kind of stupidly bad.

Yeah. See you 2nite. Play hard. Love u.

Timmy interrupted before he could text back. "You guys plan to polish that up today? I've got another group coming in at eight; you'll have to wrap by seven."

"Y'all want to run another or stick with this one?" They could write at the hotel or at his place. The demos were what was important here. In a few days, they could bang out a shit-ton.

"I think we should leave it for now, take it home and shake it out a little. Can we get more studio time maybe late in the week or over the weekend?"

Timmy nodded. "I can slot you in Saturday night, dude."

"What do you think, Cajun?"

He nodded. "Kyle's working then, so I'm all yours, Timmy. Hell, I'm playing for that jazz band, ain't I? That afternoon?"

Timmy nodded. "They're here, uh… eight to five I think. A few hours on Sunday too."

"Damn, you're keeping busy, man." Ryder nodded approvingly. "Folks know what you're worth up here, I hope."

"I've been hooking him up. They know. Colt's not just a guitar keeping a seat warm."

"It's good to be busy. Keeps me in beer and out of trouble." Hell, he knew that he needed to keep himself working so he could stay up here with Kyle. The man was important to him.

Ryder nodded and held up his beer. "Amen to that. Here's to staying busy."

"Got that right." Norv clinked bottles with him.

"So glad y'all are here. I missed you like breathing." They could drive a man buggy, but he loved them to death.

Norv stood up. "All right, y'all. Let's get out of Timmy's hair, huh? I'm just gonna pack up the Gibson and take it with."

Ryder nodded and swallowed down the last bite of his cheesesteak. "Thanks for the grub, Timmy."

"Anytime, dude. Like I said, next time remind me to give you the menu folder."

"Will do. I like choices."

Norv snorted. "He'll eat anything, Timmy. Don't let him kid you."

"Y'all going back to the hotel?" He wasn't sure whether they needed a nap or not.

"Yeah. Ryder was antsy and wanted to get started, but we need to get showers and all. Can we meet you at your Yankee's place? Just text me the address."

"His name is Kyle," Timmy said, helpfully, with just a hint of snark.

Norv glanced over at Timmy and then back at him. "Sorry. Text me *Kyle's* address?"

"Surely can. Y'all have a good afternoon. I'll see you this evening." He texted Norv the address first, then texted Kyle. *Busy?*

"Thanks, Tim. We'll see you Saturday."

"Right on, man."

Just headed home. Walking in the rain. Joy, Kyle texted back.

Done for the day here—can I meet u?

How fast can u get here?

20. He was getting good at this subway thing.

c u soon. This time Kyle followed his text with red lipstick lips.

"I'll text you if anything changes about Saturday with the jazz folks, dude. You enjoy your night."

"Will do." He waved to Timmy, then headed to meet his lover. They could shop or make love or both.

Chapter Twelve

Kyle wandered out of the bathroom, freshly showered, robe tied loosely around his waist. Colt was stretched out on his bed, looking a little muzzy and a lot smug. He leaned over his lover and gave Colt a playful smooch. "Mmm. I should make you miss me more often."

"Uh-uh. You melted my brain, cher. Made me dizzy."

He snorted and smiled. "You're so beautiful, baby. You better get up. Your friends will be here soon." He dropped his robe and stepped into his walk-in closet. "These are, like, blue jean types, right? I don't want to overdress."

"All the way. They're like me, cher. Easy."

Jesus. Hopefully not as easy, or it was going to be an eventful night. "I should have expected that. I'm looking forward to meeting them. It'll be nice to be with some of your people, you know?"

He pulled out some skinny jeans and a long tank top, figuring the kitchen was going to be warm and he could show off his ink.

"They're looking forward to you too." Colt tugged on his jeans and a thin T-shirt. There was something so hot about the sight of Colt's bare feet, the worn-in jeans.

He liked it so much, he decided to go with bare feet too. "I hope they can accept that I'm hopeless when it comes to keeping my hands off of you." To make his point, he ran a hand up one of Colt's arms as he walked by. "You know there's plenty of room if they want to drink and don't feel like Ubering it back to the hotel. Just putting that out there now so you can offer if you want to." He had two empty bedrooms. No problem.

"Thank you, and they're… they're a couple, you know? They're very into each other."

"Oh yeah?" Well, that was wonderful. Kind of a double-date thing. He liked it. "That's…." He looked at Colt. "Was that the doorbell?" He waited another second to see if he heard it again.

"Think so, yeah. Man, I might have to order pizza. Since we… didn't start cooking food." Colt grinned at him, dark eyes dancing.

"How long can shrimp take?" He took Colt's hand and hurried down the stairs. "I'm a little nervous. I know that's stupid, but it's true." He just wanted them to like him. He was a little surprised by how important it was to him.

"It's weird, meeting good friends." Colt leaned into his arm, squeezed his fingers. "You ain't stupid, cher. Not at all."

He nodded. "Yeah. Okay." He took a deep breath. "My house, right? I better get the door." Even if he didn't feel completely confident, he knew he could act it. He made a living at it. He opened the door. It was still pouring rain, but the two of them fit under the little awning over the front door.

Jesus Christ, was his first thought. They really were exactly like Colt. "Hey! Come on in. God, what awful weather."

"Eh, rain's a blessing, I guess. Norv Williamson, pleased." A square, gnarly hand was offered over. "This is Ryder James."

One older, one younger, one in a ball cap, one in a plastic-covered cowboy hat.

"Kyle. Kyle Alexander." He shook hands and closed the door behind them. "I hear you. But in New York City, rain is just a pain in the ass. Do you mind if I ask you to kick your boots off? I've got carpet."

Ryder gave Norv a wide-eyed look, but Norv nodded. "Sure, no problem."

Colt chuckled softly. "Y'all want some help? I know you got your good boots on."

Shit. Southern musicians one, New York dancer zero. And he was probably blushing too. "I'm sorry, guys. They're really nice boots." Jesus. Maybe he should just shut his mouth and let Colt do the talking tonight.

"Ain't they? I met Norv over his boots. You were wearing Luccheses, weren't you?"

"Lord yes. You were drooling over them outside that club on Orleans. Give me a tug, Cajun."

Luccheses. He'd file that away for later. He watched Colt help Norv and looked at Ryder. "You want a hand?" He could do that.

"Oh. Uh."

Ryder looked embarrassed, and he heard Norv's low laugh.

"Oh, come on." He was pretty sure he managed not to make a total fool of himself, and he set Ryder's boots down alongside Norv's.

"Thank you." Ryder's cheeks were the color of cherries. God, he was adorable.

"My pleasure." He looped an arm through Colt's, and they led the way into the kitchen. "Can I get you guys a beer or a glass of wine?"

"Beer, please, for both of us."

Colt chuckled softly. "They ain't all classy like me."

He huffed at Colt. "Seriously? Now you're just trying to make me look like a snob."

Of course, he only had expensive beer, but it was still beer. He gave his lover a little shove and stuck his tongue out, pulling two bottles out of the refrigerator. He popped the tops off them and handed them to Norv and Ryder, giving Ryder a little wink just for fun. The kid hadn't managed to get more than a stutter out since he opened the front door. Norv seemed to have that covered for both of them.

"Thank you, sir." Norv was pure ease, like this stereotypical cowboy, and he made Kyle want to laugh, want to watch him move and use it in a dance.

"Wine for you, baby?" He pulled a new bottle off the rack and fished out the opener. He refrained from asking Colt's guests to take off their hats, even though it made this small part of him itch. That was his mother all over, and he hated it.

He poured himself a glass and hovered the mouth of the bottle over Colt's, asking. Then he fished out some small talk. He was good at that, a more pleasant inheritance from his mother. "Colt said you guys did some great work today."

"We did. Cajun's a hell of a songwriter."

Colt beamed. "You want to give me your hat? I got a safe place for it."

"Please. I swear you'd think nobody'd ever seen a cover."

"Such a Texan. Hand it over."

Ryder folded his hat up and stuck it in his back pocket.

Colt to the rescue. God, could his lover be any more perfect for him? "Thank you, love." He filled Colt's glass and set the bottle down. "We don't see a lot of cowboy hats up here." He grinned, trying out a little flirting to see if that would loosen Norv up a bit. "When we do, it's usually on a handsome cowboy, so we stare. Take it as a compliment."

"Oh, I do, son. No question." Norv smiled at him, the look honest, warm. "So, I got to tell you, the Cajun showed us a video of you dancing. You're something else. It was beautiful."

"Thank you." He smiled and preened. He couldn't help it; he was proud of his work. And even more proud that his lover wanted to show him off. "I love it. I can't imagine doing anything else. Which one did he show you? The outdoor one? That's his favorite, but it's old now. Why don't you bring them to the show while they're in town, Colt? I'll comp you some tickets."

"Yeah?" Colt came to him, gave him an easy kiss. "That would rock. And yeah, I like that one. I like you in the wind, the way you move."

Colt's kisses spoke to him like music, inspired him in the same way. It was impossible not to indulge, not to smile after. It made no difference who was in the room. "You better start dinner, or your guests are going to go hungry."

He gave Colt a swat. "I have some cheese, guys." As he headed for the refrigerator, he caught Ryder writing furiously in a little notebook. A second later the kid was showing it to Norv.

Kyle shot Colt a look, but his lover just shrugged like it was the most normal thing on earth. "We're writers, cher. No stress."

He wasn't stressing. Was he stressing? Maybe he was. He certainly was now. What was the kid writing? Did it matter?

"Colt, come give this a look?" Ryder slid the notebook across the kitchen table.

He let it go and got some snacks together to put on the table, and then he refilled his wineglass.

"Mmm... sweet hook." Colt began to sing, beating out a rhythm on the table.

"Cool."

"I don't guess you have a guitar here?"

Colt? Colt had guitars everywhere. "Up in the studio."

Ryder looked at him. "You have a studio?"

"My dance studio."

"Yeah? Bet the acoustics are awesome."

"We're supposed to eat, y'all...." Colt grabbed the pen from Ryder's hand and jotted a few notes, scribbled some stuff out.

Kyle stepped up behind Colt, wrapped an arm around his middle, and kissed the back of his neck. "Thank you. But if you want to write—if that's what's calling you, baby, it's okay with me. That's why they're up here, right?"

They were artists. Kyle loved a nice sit-down and some good conversation, but if they were inspired, he got it. He had the feeling these two were more "shooting the breeze over late-night beer" types anyway.

"I'll buy pizza," Norv offered. "I hear tell it's better here than anywhere in the country."

Kyle smiled. "No food in my studio." He poked a finger at Norv playfully. "Otherwise, it's yours. I'll join you guys in a few." Maybe he'd listen and dance. Why not? He didn't let Colt go yet, though. He wanted another one of those kisses first. He spun Colt around to face him. "It's okay. Promise."

"You're good to me, cher." Colt gave him what he wanted, a kiss that promised him the world—deep and eager and utterly unashamed.

Who needed dinner? He could just live on that. "Just giving as good as I get. Go on. I'll be up in a few."

Ryder had already disappeared into the hall. Norv gave Colt a clap on the shoulder, and the two of them headed out of the kitchen together.

He looked at the half-full beers left sitting on the kitchen table and Colt's untouched glass of wine.

Was he a little disappointed? Sure. But there was also something wonderful about this. His man, a couple of collaborators making music, creating in his house like they belonged there. Like this was just their normal. He liked it.

He liked pizza too.

Chapter Thirteen

Jesus Christ on a purple sparkly crutch, Colt was tired. Like bone-deep tired enough that if he stopped to think about it, he could see sounds.

Good thing he didn't have a chance to stop and think.

Between rehearsing with Kyle, his studio work, writing with the guys, and trying to get to all the places to do all the things, he was running on seven seconds of sleep and blistered fingers.

Lord have mercy.

He finished his gig and sat there as everyone packed up. Midnight. Lord have mercy.

"Hey, nice work, guys."

This jazz band was a bunch of nice folks, talented, but a little less easygoing. They had a budget and needed to wrap on time, so they pushed pretty hard in the studio.

Timmy came in and pressed a little metal tin into his palm, then started dressing cables and putting away microphones. "Caffeine mints. Two will do you for a couple of hours."

Timmy set three microphones on the chair next to him and went to gather the others.

"Thanks." He took four, breathing fire out of his nose for a second.

The folks in the band gave him nods and handshakes on their way out.

"Catch you tomorrow, Colt."

"Get some rest, man. You look like you need it."

"You need a ride anywhere?"

"I got him," Timmy said, following them to the studio door. "I'll be in at noon tomorrow. Studio is yours at two."

"Right on. Night, Timmy."

He sat there, trying to decide if he could just sleep here and get up and head to Kyle's in the morning.

"Dude, I'm taking you home. Put your guitar away. And leave it here." Timmy started stacking the neatly rolled-up cables into a crate.

"Are you?" He was so fucking tired. "Okay, boo."

He just sat there like a lump.

"Okay, then." Timmy didn't say another word, but the next thing he knew, his guitar was gone and Timmy was turning the lights out. "I called an Uber. But I think I'm even skinnier than you are. I'm not carrying your ass, bro." Timmy did at least offer him a hand up and pulled him to his feet. "Come on."

"I don' need carryin', boo. I just tired, eh?" He was still doing good work.

"You're not just tired, *boo*." Timmy led him out to the car and pulled him inside. "You didn't stand up to see the band out. You didn't even stand up when I told you you should get moving. I just totally put your baby away for you, and you didn't even tell me to be careful with it. You're exhausted."

"True dat." He knew, but he knew it had to be done. Hell, more than that, he wanted it. He wanted it all.

He just didn't know how to.

"When's your next day off?"

He shrugged. Did he have those? He didn't think so. Those were for people who didn't have the music riding them hard.

His cell phone buzzed with a text message from Kyle. It was a picture of Kyle and another dancer with Alan, the bartender at the Purple Poet. Kyle had his arm around the dancer—was it Rob?—and was kissing him on the cheek.

Alan misses you. Aren't you done yet? Come have a drink, baby.

Oh….

He sighed and leaned forward to speak to the driver. "Can you take me to the Purple Poet after you drop my friend off?"

He needed some uppers in the worst way. Just a little chemical boost.

"Is that Kyle? Come on, dude. Tell him you need to sleep. I'll get you some green and you can relax. You gotta work tomorrow."

"I'll work. I swear." Timmy didn't understand, not really. It was hard to be everything he needed to be. Kyle was special. He had to try harder than everyone else, just to keep up. He wasn't as shiny as everyone else in Kyle's life.

Hell, what shine he had was from rubbing hard, not because he was made from gold.

"I know, dude. You work your ass off, I know. But...." The car pulled up to the curb, and Timmy sighed. "You gotta pace yourself or you're not going to be any good, you know? And I'm not talking about the music." Timmy slid out of the car. "I'll see you tomorrow."

"Night, boo. You're good to me, swear to God."

"Night, man." Timmy shook his head, closed the car door, and gave him a wave.

"Thanks for doubling up, friend. I appreciate it." He leaned his head back and watched the light trails dance in the rear window.

"No problem." The driver got him there fine, but it took a while. It was late, but on Saturday night the traffic was as bad as rush hour. The bar was hopping too; a small crowd was hanging out outside smoking, and light and music spilled out into the street.

Kyle wasn't hard to spot, which didn't surprise him. His lover, in skinny jeans and a tight black sweater, was at the bar with a martini, sitting very close to that guy, Rob, who was in the picture Kyle texted. Rob had an arm across the back of Kyle's chair.

Stop it. You're shit-tired and feeling teeth on your bones. He headed over, offering Rob a toothy smile before touching Kyle with his aching fingers. "'Lo, cher."

"There you are!" Kyle gave him a smile that lit up the bar and a kiss that stopped time.

"Mmm. Hey, how you been?" *You been missing me?*

"Move over, Rob, would you?" Kyle made scooty hands at Rob to make the guy slide over a stool, and then pulled him onto the warmed seat.

See? Nothing to get twisted up about after all.

"I had a long day. I needed to see you tonight. Are you okay? Are you sick? You don't look good, baby."

"Just tired. It ain't no thing." He leaned his cheek against Kyle's arm. "I need to get me a coffee IV is all."

"Aw. How was your session tonight?" Kyle took one of his hands and started rubbing like before, dragging warm thumbs over his tired, aching palm.

"Good. They're fierce. They know what they want." His eyelids fell closed at the massage.

"Is that easier or harder for you? Or... maybe that's not the right question. You like to collaborate more, don't you? Do you feel less creative when a group knows what they want?" Kyle let that hand relax and switched to the other one.

"You don't have to think on it. You just give up the notes. You know, like a dance you've done for a lifetime."

Kyle nodded. "Like the show I'm in now. I still love it, but I don't think that hard about the choreography. I just get out there and dance. I really enjoy what we're doing, though, the way we work together—oh! I got them to let us into the theater tomorrow morning. I thought it would be good for you to be in the space for a little while, feel it out for sound. I've danced there lots of times."

"Sounds perfect." This was why he'd come out, not because he was jealous of that picture. "You know how I love to see you dance."

Lord, he needed a cup of coffee.

"We'll just do a couple of hours. I know you have a gig after lunch." His lover slithered off the stool suddenly. "Oh God. I have to pee. Watch my martini." Kyle leaned in for another quick kiss. "Back in a sec."

He watched Kyle go, his lover's walk seeming pretty steady despite the drink on the bar.

Rob looked at him sideways, the uneven bar light casting shadows on the angular lines of the dancer's face. "He is totally into you, man."

"Good." Because he was in love—balls to bones. "I like to hear that."

"He says you're working with him on his next show? He's tough to keep up with. Works all the time. Heard you talking. You want a couple Adderall? You look like you need it."

"What are them?" He didn't want to lose his mind or wake up in three days mostly dead.

"ADHD meds. Stimulants. You know, uppers." Rob pulled a little vial out of his coat pocket. "There's a couple days' worth in here if you want 'em."

"Thanks. Been... been a long week, ain't it?" Gigs and practice and writing and loving and touristing and—he was on his last drop of gasoline.

Rob nodded. "Yeah, man. It's hard to keep up sometimes, right? My number is in there if you want more. Just give me a shout."

It was good to know a dealer. Always. It was also good to know who they were. He had to wonder what Kyle got from Rob. Eh, it was none of his. "Thanks, man. I appreciate it."

"I'm looking forward to hearing you play. He has a lot to say about your talent."

"I do my best." God gave him the talent; he was born to use it, he figured.

Kyle came back to the bar, this time with an arm around Jake. "Jake thinks I should go home."

Jake kind of rolled his eyes. "Not that you ever listen to me."

"You want to take me home, lover?"

"I can do that." He smiled at Kyle, admiring him, top to bottom. Jesus, so fine. He was a little stupid with loving his man. "Come on, cher. Let me help you find the bed."

"Oh, I'm not that drunk. Not like I was the other night. Whoa."

"You're not that sober either."

"Shut up, Robbie." But Kyle was playing, stuck out his tongue.

"You're fine and I ain't even had one, so you're in good hands." He wrapped one arm around his own dancer. "C'mon."

Kyle pressed close and let him lead the way out of the bar. His lover might be a flirt, but they were leaving no doubt for anyone looking on who Kyle was going home with.

"Glad you texted me. I was headed to the apartment, but I hadn't made it."

"It's been a long day. I know you're crazy busy right now, but I needed to see you. I'm really... I don't know. I'm not looking for an all-nighter, I just wanted you with me."

"I'm here, cher. All yours." He had this, no worries.

Kyle got them a cab and was pretty quiet until they got home. "The show was rough tonight. We had some tech problems, and the energy was off. I'm not sure what was up."

"That sucks. What do you do? Jus' let it work itself out?" They started with their shoes, leaving them at the door, and then he put his cap on the hook. The hat tree by the door was new since Norv and Ryder visited.

"At first. I'll start Tuesday's show with a pep talk, and if we're still off that night, then we'll do some pickup rehearsals and figure out what we're running up against." Kyle threaded their fingers together and left the house dark, leading him up the staircase by the light from the street. "Most of the numbers are fine. It was more the energy thing. I reminded everyone tonight to get a good night's sleep. Sometimes that's all it takes."

"Sometimes." He burned for one of those, a long night of dreams. "I'm sorry, cher."

He imagined Norv's pep talk and coughed out a laugh. Yeah, no.

Kyle stopped at the top of the stairs and kissed him. "Thank you. I don't know how to explain to you how it makes me feel that you care about this. It's not even whether or not you get it, just that you understand what it means to me."

He wasn't even sure what that meant, but he was pleased that he was helping and not hurting. Sometimes that was all a man could do.

He let Kyle pull him into the bedroom, the neatly made bed and fluffy pillows calling to him like a siren. Like a muse. *Come to me.* Kyle gave him another quick smooch, then started puttering around the room undressing and turning down the sheets.

"We'll get a little rest, and then tomorrow we'll work for a while at the theater. Tomorrow will be a better day. Do your hands hurt, baby? Do you want me to rub them some more?"

He didn't even have the words to answer. His fingertips had blisters so deep under his calluses that he didn't think they could be fixed. It was okay. He got it. He stripped himself down and went to the bathroom to wash up real quick.

Kyle was sitting on the bed when he got back from the bathroom, and he felt his lover's eyes on him. "Hey. Are you okay?"

"Just tired, you know?" He'd been working on no sleep. He just needed to lay his burdens down for a second.

"Come on, baby." Kyle's arms opened, calling to him. "Come rest."

For a weird, awful second he thought he was going to cry, but he didn't, and that was okay.

Kyle hunkered down with him in soft pillows and under that fat, fluffy comforter and pulled him close. "Oh, you are just what I needed tonight. Thank you."

"Merci, cher." He knew all about need. All about. He laid his head down, the blackness sucking him in.

Chapter Fourteen

Friday. How did it get to be Friday already?

Taking last Sunday off hadn't been the end of the world. Colt had been so damned tired, Kyle hadn't had the heart to wake his lover to rehearse and had let Colt sleep in instead. It hadn't set them back much. He had plenty of rehearsing of his own to do, so he'd just canceled the theater space and spent the morning in his studio, working on the numbers that Colt wasn't playing for.

But Colt had promised him two original recorded tracks that he didn't have in hand yet, and that definitely was holding him back. Despite having some great ideas, he couldn't choreograph to music he didn't have.

The last they'd talked, which had been Tuesday night while Colt was on a break, they'd agreed to meet at the theater this morning. They hadn't spoken much since then because their schedules just weren't matching up at all. Colt had even been sleeping at his own apartment because his hours were so scattered around. Mostly they'd been sending text messages back and forth full of hearts and apologies.

Truthfully, he wondered whether Colt would even remember they'd planned to meet this morning. His lover was already twenty minutes late.

It wasn't wasted time. It was never wasted time if Kyle had somewhere to dance, so he marked out a couple of pieces while he was waiting. He texted, waited, checked his phone, and texted again, but if Colt was in the studio, he wouldn't get the texts until he was out. If Colt was writing with Norv and Ryder, he might not get them at all. Norv and Ryder brought out amazing creativity in Colt, but they were as much of a problem for Colt as anything else.

He looked at his phone and wondered if he should worry. Maybe he should call again. Maybe he should call Timmy. Or maybe he shouldn't treat Colt like he was twelve, let him be an adult and take responsibility for not showing up.

He didn't call.

Colt came squealing in finally, pale as a ghost, eyes like holes burned in the snow. "Lawd, I'm late. I know. I been late all day."

Kyle stared at Colt from where he'd been working out some choreography and didn't move a step closer. "Hello to you too."

"I'm sorry. I misjudged traffic stuff. I ain't used to thinking about cities being busy in the morning. I worked to six, and I wanted a nap, so I slept in the studio. I got your tracks laid down for you."

He wanted to be angry. He wanted to be indignant and raise his voice and say something like "What were you thinking?" or "How could you keep me waiting?" But looking into Colt's eyes, all he could think was *What are you doing to yourself?*

He relented and went over, took that pale face in his hands. "Thank you."

"I'm sorry, cher. I know your time is important." Colt pushed into his hands, cheeks burning up.

"It is. So are you." Colt's eyes were just big, dark pupils. "You shouldn't be laying down tracks for me until six in the morning. You should be getting some sleep. You're overcommitted."

It wasn't rocket science. Colt was high. He'd seen it way too often as a dancer not to know. He let it go for now, though. If he could make Colt cope, maybe nothing would ever have to be said.

"I keep waiting for Ryder to take Norv away or for there to be some time where someone don't need my happy ass in the studio."

He kissed Colt lightly and smiled, then started asking leading questions. "You're in demand, huh? People want to work with you? You need to start telling them no."

"Seems like everyone does, don't it?" Colt stroked his fingers, the touch blisteringly hot.

Kyle took one of Colt's hands in his and kissed the palm, closing his eyes against that heat and steeling himself. He'd missed it; he wanted it. But he needed to do this, first. He'd given it a lot of thought, caught between his love for his man and his love for his work.

It was breaking Kyle's heart, but seeing Colt in the state he was in, looking like he did… it was one thing personally, but professionally….

"Thank you so much for these tracks. I can't wait to use them. But, baby, I… I've decided to cut our live improv piece from the show."

"Oh." There was a pause, like Colt had stopped breathing for a second, and then he nodded, once, and eased his hand away. "Okay. I guess I better let you get back to work, then. You'll call when you need me?"

"Colt." Fuck. Okay, he'd expected something like that, but that didn't mean it wasn't killing him. "I always need you. It's not about us; it's about the work."

"Sure. It ain't no thing. I'm gon' go get some writing done, then make my rent." Colt leaned in, kissed his cheek. "Have a good day, cher."

Colt put up that wall so fast it left him breathless. "Yep." He watched Colt turn and leave, taking the rest of the oxygen in the room with him.

He couldn't have Colt onstage looking like that. He couldn't wonder every night if Colt was stuck in a session and might not show up on time. He couldn't count on someone so overextended that setting their own priorities was out of their hands. He'd have done the same with any dancer with similar issues, and had.

It wasn't personal. It was business. Colt had to get that, if they were going to be a thing.

There was a difference.

Kyle sighed and hopped back up onstage. Time to get to work.

"WHAT'S WRONG with you, son?" Norv asked him, eyebrows frowning like a hound dog's. "Ain't you got to work with your man?"

"Lost the gig. Y'all want to write or not?" He didn't want to talk on it, not really. He didn't want to have to say that he wasn't good enough for Kyle to dance for. Not out loud. That could just be his dirty little secret.

"Why for?" Ryder stared at him, head tilting like a dog hearing a whistle.

"I was late."

"Dude."

"Yeah. My bad. He'll find someone else. Come on. Work, huh? I got to be in the studio at five. This gives us a whole day." He'd be off at midnight, and then he could go home and... well, he'd probably have a beer or three, play some sad songs, and then sleep.

"But...."

Norv touched Ryder's shoulder. "It ain't no thing, right? Let's write some amazing shit. How about a revenge song? Something with bullets and tears?"

"Bullets are tricky, babe," Ryder pointed out. "How about something where we drown someone in the bayou. I bet we could sell that."

"Hm. Not sure we'd find a lot of folks wanting to pick that one up." Norv tapped his fingers on his guitar. "Jealousy. That green-eyed monster sells a lot of music."

"Ooh. Been there. I can get into that. What do you think, Colt?" Ryder leaned right over that little notebook and put pen to paper.

He started doodling, eyes closed, letting himself pour all his hurting into his fingers. He was a blues man, wasn't he? He was born to turn his own pain into song.

"Maybe we need a beer to get us thinking right, Norv. I heard they got barbecue and cowboy bars in this city. How about that?"

"Sure. I read that Chris Shivers and a bunch of bull riders came up here and got into a fight at a bar. Did ten thousand smackeroos of damage to a guy's mouth." Norv rolled his eyes. "I didn't know you could do that much damage to a single mouth."

"I don't want to go to that bar." Truth be told, he didn't need a beer, but he didn't want to be a butthead, either.

"We don't gotta go, Colt. I was just thinking you.... We don't gotta go. I'm good for a pizza too. You wanna play something for me and I'll pick it up from you?"

"We ain't broke up yet, I don't think. He's high-dollar and I'm broke-dick. Y'all seen his house." He wasn't stupid. At some point they would separate out into oil and water. "I just want to enjoy knowing him while I can."

"You ain't that broke. I see the writing part of your paycheck, at least, and you work your ass off. You're worth something." Norv swatted him. "If he makes you feel that way, it's time to let it go. Hell, come to us. We'll let you stay in the guest room for as long as you want. You want to come now? We'll go. Right now."

Colt laughed. "Y'all are good to me."

"That's it! Come stay with us. You seen Norv's studio yet? And he's got a sweet boat. We can go fishin'." Ryder lit up like it was Christmas. Norv sure was good to him.

"Maybe once I've done the gigs I have booked, huh? I don't got to stick around for Kyle's show no more." He wasn't one hundred percent sure he'd be invited to see it.

Now stop it, he told himself. *Even though Kyle was mad you was late and don't want to work with you no more, you're still worth having sex with. Y'all haven't broke up. He'll prob'ly ask you to come see so you can admire.*

Still, he could tell Timmy not to book him no more new gigs, head out to Austin, spend some time writing and fishing and sleeping in the sunshine.

"All right, y'all. Let's focus." That was Norv. He only had so much talking in him. They were here to work, and as soon as Norv said so, Ryder went right back to it.

"Give me… one… okay. No wait."

They started laughing, all of them together, just as goofy as they could be.

Time flew by, and they did write a song, and then they went back and polished another, and by the time they were done, they had two songs ready to cut the next time they were at the studio.

Ryder leaned on Norv, looking every bit like he'd just had good sex. Or wanted some. "That was good work, right?"

"It was. Damn fine." He clapped Ryder on the arm. "Y'all going home, yeah?"

"Yeah. You'll come?"

"As soon as I finish these gigs, I will. I promised Kyle we'd Christmas together."

"You think he'll still want to?" Ryder asked.

He shrugged. "If he don't, someone will." Hell, he'd still have a room at Timmy's bought.

"If he don't, we will, okay, son?"

Ryder reached over and took Colt's hand. "He will, though. I bet he will. I don't get what happened, but he seems like a good guy, and I bet y'all figure it out. I hope you do. He makes you happy."

"He does." Colt wasn't going to worry on it. He couldn't be more than God made him. He hugged them both, missing them already. "Love y'all. All the way."

"You too, Cajun." Norv gave him a nod and saw him out.

He took his guitar and headed to the studio. Everything seemed uglier today, but it didn't matter. The music mattered. Even his music.

Chapter Fifteen

Kyle could have gone to the bar. He'd been invited half a dozen times by various people after the show. He just didn't feel like being social.

He felt like calling Colt and asking him to drop everything else and come over and talk. He'd done the best thing he knew to do, after all, for his show and for his lover. He needed consistent and reliable, and Colt needed variety and flexibility. Colt's calling wasn't theater. It wasn't showing up seven or eight times a week to do the same thing over and over on cue. But dammit, the show wasn't going to be the same without him.

And Colt had looked just awful. Crazy-eyed and pale-skinned. The man that came wheeling into the theater that morning wasn't anything like the easygoing, free-spirited musician Kyle had fallen for at all. If Colt couldn't manage to get out from under his commitments on his own, the best thing Kyle could think to do to help him was lift a commitment for him.

Colt's face when he'd told him had been… fuck. He didn't regret his decision, but he regretted having to make it. No, he wasn't going out. He needed to go home. He needed to be sober. He needed to call Colt.

He tried to text in the car on the way but deleted every single one without sending it. He went inside and showered, trying to figure out what to say. None of that did him one bit of good either, so he finally picked up his phone to make the call. He dialed, hoping to hell something came to him before Colt answered.

If he answered.

"Hey, cher. How you be?"

He couldn't hear anything from where Colt was. Nothing at all. "I've had better days. Where are you?"

"Here at Timmy's. I jus' got off work."

"How… uh. How'd it go? Did you get something good down?" *Are you okay? Do you hate me? Do you want to come over?*

"Ain't nobody complained tonight, so I must have done okay. Norv and Ryder said to tell you goodbye. They went on home."

"They did? You didn't tell me they were leaving." He didn't know whether that would have changed anything, but he wished he'd known. "Where are they headed?"

Small-talking around everything, searching for normal, wasn't working for him.

"Home, I reckon. They just decided to go. It was time. Norv don't do chilly weather." Colt chuckled softly. "He'll holler when he figures out what all we did that might sell."

"Do you want to come over?"

There. If Colt turned him down, at least he could say he tried.

There was a long pause, then, "Sure, cher. Give me a bit to get over there. I'll text when I get close, 'kay?"

"Yeah. Good. Okay. I'll be waiting." Happily. So much better than this awkward phone call. He needed to look at those eyes.

He let Colt hang up first, then pulled on a pair of PJ bottoms and headed down to the kitchen to wait. God, he was terrible at waiting. He pulled out a couple of wineglasses and poured himself half a glass.

It took a while for the text to come, but it did, and soon Colt tapped on the door. Colt stood there in a dark hoodie and a pair of worn jeans. "Evenin', cher. How goes?"

"I'm...." He just couldn't play along. He sighed and shook his head. "You look so tired, baby."

"Been working some hours. You gon' let me in, or we gon' visit on your porch?" Colt smiled for him, the look quiet, not quite right.

"Oh. What am I thinking? Come in. Sorry. You want some wine?" He stepped out of Colt's way and let him in, heading for the kitchen. He wanted a kiss. He wanted to put his arms around Colt and make this okay.

"Sure." Colt took his shoes off, hung his hoodie by the door, the sounds normal, easy. "You have a decent show?"

"It was good. We're in a nice rhythm now. It feels great." He poured a glass of wine for Colt and refilled his. "Are you hungry for anything?"

He found himself second-guessing everything he did. Would he normally have kissed Colt by now? Should he? Was he asking the right questions? This was torture. What was the matter with him?

"I ain't, no. I had pizza for supper." Colt sat, watching him. "Sit, cher. You as nervous as a long-tailed cat in a room full of rockin' chairs. I ain't gon' bite."

"I am a little." He set Colt's wine down and leaned in for a quick kiss. "I'm glad you're here. Do you have to be somewhere in the morning? I listened to your tracks today. They're wonderful. Perfect. You didn't name them, you know. You should. I spent a bunch of time with the first one, the really upbeat one? I thought you might be interested in seeing what I've got so far."

That was good, right? Make sure Colt knew he liked them. They were everything he'd asked for. Both of them.

Colt shrugged and took his hand, tracing his fingers. "They ain't got names, so call them what you will, and I'm working from noon to ten tomorrow, but I know you're up and out before that."

That felt good, more real than anything else between them right now. The touch continued, even if the words didn't. Colt seemed willing to just sit there with him.

He lifted Colt's hand and kissed every one of the callused fingers. "Maybe another time, then. I want you to get some rest, baby. Let's take our wine up and turn in."

"Sounds good." Colt stood and helped him up, then led him to the bedroom.

So Colt was there, but he wasn't... Colt. The look in his eyes wasn't his Colt. His energy wasn't right. He was making the right moves, seemed fine about being there, but he was unmistakably different.

Once they were through the bedroom door, Kyle tugged Colt close and kissed him, trying to remind him what he meant, how important he still was.

How much he still wanted this.

Colt opened for him, hands warm and solid on his hips, holding him carefully, thumbs drawing lazy circles. He tested a little, not sure which Colt wanted more. Sleep, or... this. Him. He ran his hands under Colt's shirt and up his chest.

"Come to bed, hmm? I'll love on you." Colt let Kyle pull his shirt up and off.

He smiled and relaxed a little. That was good, right? They'd figure this out. "Yeah. I'd like that." He slid fingers under Colt's waistband and gave his jeans a tug, then slipped out of his PJs and climbed into bed.

Colt stripped the rest of the way down, slid in next to him, warm and close, lips hot on his throat.

"Mmm. That's nice, baby." He ran his hands over Colt's warm skin and let himself smile, arching his neck for Colt. This was always right between them, wasn't it? Good days, bad days, it was always magic when they were together like this.

"I got you." Colt petted him, stroking him in long, slow motions that aroused and soothed all at once.

He pulled Colt into another kiss. Their tongues tangled, Colt touched him just right, and what could have been a slow burn instead sent Kyle up in flames.

Colt grabbed their cocks, holding them in one perfectly callused hand, finding a rhythm and tugging them, nice and steady.

Jesus, those hands. "Yes." He licked across the line of Colt's jaw, listening to the breath between them grow heavy. He found one of Colt's nipples with his fingers, rolling and tugging on it.

Colt bent his head, resting his forehead on Kyle's shoulder, panting hard as they rubbed together.

"Does that feel good? Is that what you want? God." He fed Colt encouraging words and moans, and tucked a hand behind Colt's neck, his own breath growing shallow. "You like that? Yeah?"

"C'est bon, cher. I got you." Colt arched, teeth teasing the curve of his throat, fingers dancing over his ink, tracing the patterns.

He dropped his hand down between them and curled his fingers around Colt's, adding a little more pressure and shifting their angle just… so. He gasped. "Yeah, baby. Right there." His eyes slammed shut, and he arched his head back, balls drawing up tight. "Fuck."

"Mmm…." Colt rolled his free hand over the tips of their cocks, making the world go bright white as the friction sent him over the edge.

"Colt!" He grunted and rode it out, enjoying the high for a moment, loving the feel of those fingers scraping over his skin. But as soon as he could pull his mind back together, he pushed Colt's hand out of the way, slid down on the bed, and took hold of his lover's cock himself, closing his mouth around the ruddy head.

Colt groaned, the sound deep and raw, rough as hell and wonderful, musical.

He moaned around that thick erection and took it in deep, letting Colt rub and grind against the roof of his mouth.

"Fuck! Cher!" Colt curled around his head, humping a few desperate times before spunk filled his mouth, the bitter and salt so Colt it made him groan.

"Mmm." He took his time releasing Colt, teasing him gently with teeth and tongue as he slowly climbed back up into the pillows. "You're so beautiful, baby. I love doing that for you. You're so free."

"Feels like heaven, cher. Thank you." Colt curled in close to him, cheek on his chest.

He tucked an arm around Colt's back and kissed his lover on the forehead. He was tired too, now. Colt had to be just wiped out. But it felt so good to hold Colt close. "Thank you. You have magic hands."

"We got this. Rest, cher. Morning will come soon."

He intended to. He thought maybe he might even sleep well. But he waited for Colt to fall asleep first.

Chapter Sixteen

"You want to order a pizza, Colt?" Timmy was surrounded in a cloud of green smoke as he came out from his shower.

"Sure, boo. What kind you want?" He had about two hours before Kyle texted, wanting him to come over. They'd found a rhythm over the last few weeks, him and Kyle. He worked from noon to ten or so, he showed up at Kyle's a little after midnight, and then he got up with Kyle and headed out around seven to go home and write before he went back to play. Sometimes he goofed off, sometimes he headed down and played for tips because it made him feel alive.

"Something with mushrooms. And whatever else you want. I have a craving for mushrooms. And maybe a beer." Timmy stuck his arm out, offering the joint between his fingers.

He shook his head. He didn't need to fall asleep now. "You got it." Sausage, onions, and mushrooms it was. He called and ordered, then plopped down next to Timmy. "You get your vacation planned out? You going to Hawaii?" The studio was basically closed between Thanksgiving and New Year's, most folks taking time at the holidays for family. Timmy said he always went away for that month.

"Nope. We talked about that, but we've done Oahu a bunch of times, and the guys wanted to do something different. My buddy got us a sweet place in Puerto Escondido. Big surf, awesome beach. It's gonna be off the Richter. Probably work up a sweat too."

"Good deal. I'm gon' eat turkey with Kyle for Thanksgiving and then go to Texas." Norv and Ryder wanted him there, and there wasn't work for him here. Not only that, but he did love him some Christmas carols, so they'd all play together, make some music. He could be back here at Timmy's in time for Christmas proper to cook Kyle supper.

Lord have mercy, he was going to have to figure what to get a man who had anything he could want. Maybe he'd find something in Texas. "What you want for Christmas?"

"Company." He looked over at Colt and grinned. "Company would be pretty boss. Also, candy canes. You?"

"I got all I need. Maybe I'll get some gloves down in Texas." It would be colder here than there.

"Gloves are a good idea. A scarf. Maybe some warm boots." Timmy nodded. "Your buddies are putting you up? Is it all vacation, or are you gonna record?"

"We'll record a lot." What was he if he wasn't playing? Nothing at all. "And we'll just fuck off and jam. It's Austin, you know? There's music everywhere, and there's always somewhere to join in."

"Sounds like fun. I could totally get into that. Bet you're gonna miss Kyle, though, huh?"

"Yessir." But he'd miss Kyle if he stayed here too. The man was booked solid, and he... well, he had lost his chance to be. At least in Texas he'd be among friends.

"Thanksgiving will be good. Kyle throws an amazing party. That townhouse he has is built for it." Timmy licked his fingers and put out his joint, then leaned forward and set it in an ashtray. "Are you gonna play at it? You should. His friends should hear you play."

"I don't think so, no. I'm gonna just enjoy the day." He didn't play around Kyle no more. He didn't know how to explain, really, so he didn't bother. Kyle didn't believe his gift was worth having, so Colt wasn't going to waste it. It wasn't no big thing. Lots of folks needed him to do what he did. Kyle needed him in the bed, needed him to talk to. Someone else could jam with him.

Timmy had taken that on pretty good. You could look at Timmy and just see a stoner who worked at a recording studio. But kind of like Norv, kind of like a lot of artists Colt knew, if you sat with him on a couch for five minutes, you learned a lot more. Timmy got it. Maybe even better than most because he knew tons of musicians from all over. He knew how to turn a rough studio session around. He knew when to interrupt and feed people and when to step back and let the magic happen.

So he knew what Timmy was thinking. Looked like the guy knew how to cut through bullshit too.

"Dude. You just told me you're going to spend your vacation playing. I don't see you 'enjoying the day' without your guitar. What's up? You and twinkle toes are the real deal, man. It's time those dancer friends of Kyle's got it, don't you think?"

He shook his head. "What I do ain't theirs."

He sort of reckoned it was like lots of stuff. It was just fine to enjoy things that made up more than where you came from, but it was trashy for it to go the other way. His mamma had been that way. He'd been okay until she married money. Then he wasn't. His music had been okay until Kyle was fixin' to have to show it; then it had taken one late morning to be enough of an excuse. It was the way shit worked, he guessed.

"I guess. I mean, you're right. But don't you ever want to show off a little? I'd love to see their faces."

"Oh, boo. If that was what got me what I needed, I'd be on a stage and be someone famous. I need to share my music—on a street, in a studio, with someone else having it." He shrugged. "I got my pride, huh? At least a little of it."

And he knew he was cracked a little and not all the way back to healed. It wouldn't take much to break him bad. Soon he would be back to patched, and the scar left behind would be stronger than ever, but not quite yet.

Soon.

"Dude. You're gifted. Scary gifted, and you have everything to be proud of. Man, I'm proud of you. I love telling people I know this guitarist that absolutely will not let them down. I can keep you in session work forever, if it's what you want to do. I just think you're a lot more than that."

"You're good to me, boo. Feels good to have your faith." He didn't know what else to say. He hadn't tried to let Kyle down, but he had. That was that. Sometimes, no matter how hard you tried, you couldn't be enough. C'est la vie.

"Rock solid, bro. Rock solid." Timmy clapped him on the knee as the door buzzer went off. "Ooh. Pizza's here!"

"I got it. You sit. We'll feast." He had time 'til he got called up to see Kyle. Time enough to relax and breathe easy, eat pizza and have a beer.

Chapter Seventeen

Just looking at the buffet table for his Thanksgiving party made Kyle happy. There was barely any food on it yet; it was just starting to come out of the kitchen, but it looked like fall—the oranges and reds and browns. The paper leaves and the tall taper candles gave off just enough "wow" without going overboard.

It was technically a casual party, but as much as he loved to show off his ink, he got a little dressed up—slacks and a luxuriously soft button-down shirt that he actually tucked in, even a belt.

The house smelled divine too. Colt was up early this morning, starting something amazing, and now the caterers were here too. Guests would be arriving any minute, but first he ducked into the kitchen to see how things were going and to just watch the carefully orchestrated chaos.

"Y'all put them shrimps out with your trays, and the boudin. I'll get on the potatoes and eggs." Colt was in a T-shirt and jeans, his hair all pulled back, directing with a wooden spoon.

Jesus. Colt looked every bit as appetizing as the food. The party hadn't even started and his lover was already on the dessert menu. "There is nothing hotter than a man in the kitchen." He moved toward Colt, smiling. "Unless the man is you."

"Ain't you fine?" Colt smiled for him, warm and easy. "You excited about all your people coming to feast and give thanks?"

"I am. I love a nice party, and this is the perfect day for one. Good food, nice wine, good company." He hooked a finger in Colt's belt loop and tugged on it. "You're working hard in here."

"It's a good working, though. Careful with your pretty shirt. You don't want it ruint." Colt lifted his face for a kiss.

"Mmm." Colt's kiss was sweet and easy as anything.

Things seemed good between them now. Colt was over regularly, and that part of their relationship was wonderful. There was something still a little off, something he hoped they could rebuild if he could just figure out what it was. They didn't go out a lot, and Colt hadn't been back to see him dance, but Colt was easily as busy as he was. He was starting to think maybe he was just oversensitive. He was a dancer after all.

Colt's bag was in his room. His lover was flying out to Texas tomorrow for a writing vacation while he was swamped. It was going to suck, but he got it. There wasn't any work for Colt here with Timmy heading off to the ocean, and Colt wasn't happy unless he was… unless he was playing.

He looked at Colt for a second, but the doorbell rang, and he didn't have time to think too hard about that.

"Excuse me, baby." He smiled and gave Colt another quick kiss. "You'll come out and play soon, yes? Everything smells so good!" He hurried over to the door and started letting people in. With a soft laugh, he thought about Norv and Ryder as he pointedly did not make anyone take off their shoes. He had the carpet cleaners coming on Monday.

It was gorgeous, music low and easy, the bar set up and attended by a lovely man with a wide grin and a deft hand. The trays of appetizers started coming around, filled with a mixture of the expected canapes and some wonderful, spicy, rich offerings from his lover.

He was on his second glass of wine before he really had a moment to stop and actually have a conversation. He looked up from straightening out a tray on the buffet table to find Timmy at his elbow.

"Dude! The food is fantastic."

"Hey, Timmy!" He offered a hug that was returned with enthusiasm. "Thank you. A lot of it is Colt, you know. He's been cooking."

"I wondered. Some of this isn't your usual New York party eats."

"It's great, right?"

"It's fab. Seriously. It's classy with spice. Totally the two of you on a little plate."

He laughed at that. "I like it. I am so jealous that the two of you are going away, can I tell you? I am already looking at a trip somewhere after my solo exhibition closes. It's good timing now, I guess, since that opens in a couple of weeks, but sun and warm sounds so good." It was a short run this time, just long enough to get his real fans in and maybe a few new ones. "I'm not sure what I'm doing after that, so that will be a good time to break free for a bit." Hopefully Colt could join him. Truthfully he was really planning it for the two of them anyway.

He almost never traveled alone, which meant he almost never traveled at all.

Huh. He realized, now that he was thinking about it, that Colt probably wouldn't be around for closing night of his current show. That was... disappointing.

"I know, doesn't it? I know Colt's planning a busman's holiday, though. Mostly writing and playing small venues out there with his buddies. We'll be dead at the studio until after the New Year."

"Yeah, he said he'd be writing. I guess those guys are putting him up. I didn't know they were going to play also." That was disappointing too, to miss that. He'd love to hear those guys play together live. This show-business thing was often all or nothing. "If the studio is dead until after New Year's, do you think Colt will come back for Christmas?" Why he was asking Timmy that question, he didn't know. He wasn't really, as much as just wondering out loud.

"He said you were spending it together, but... I mean, he's going to be flying back like the twentieth, but I.... Whoa. You don't know, man?"

His stomach twisted. "What don't I know, Timmy?"

"Whether he's coming home? When he's coming home? If you two are spending Christmas together? He asked me what I wanted, for fuck's sake. I know he needs gloves." Timmy blinked at him. "You need to pay attention, huh? A little bit?"

"Excuse me? He didn't tell me, Timmy. I would listen if he told me." He gave it real thought, tried to figure out what he'd missed. "We haven't had a conversation about Christmas since—" Since before he'd.... "In a while." Now that he thought about it, he wasn't sure they'd had a conversation about much of anything in a while.

"Ah, well, you should. He's thinking presents." Timmy winked at him. "He needs warmer boots and a coat, if you're asking."

"Thanks." Why wouldn't Colt tell him the plan?

Why hadn't he asked?

Truthfully, he didn't want to know the answer to either of those questions.

"Did you get some wine?"

"I had a glass. But I'm eating now. I'm not so good with juggling plates and drinks, you know?"

"No one is. Timmy, I'm going to go check on Colt. You okay if I leave you?"

"Totally. I'm going to go chat with the little blond over there."

"Oh. Be careful." He winked.

Timmy nodded. "Ah. I will. No worries."

Kyle grabbed a glass of red wine and headed for the kitchen.

Colt was singing softly, getting soup into a tureen. He was covered in grease and shining with sweat, working easily with the caterer.

"Hey, baby." He went in, holding out the wine. "I brought you something."

"Thank you!" Colt grinned at him and took the glass. He drank a healthy sip, then hummed, deep in his throat. "Ain't that nice? Y'all all having fun?"

"I am. Will you be done here soon?" *Are you going to come out and talk to me?*

"You done with me here, Miss Susan?"

"You've been an amazing help, Colt. Thank you, but we have it handled from here."

"Okay, then. Holler if you need me." He looked down at himself. "I'm gon' jump in the shower and all. I'm filthy."

"Probably a good idea." He smiled at Colt. "Take your wine with you, loosen up a little."

"I'll see you back down here in a while and see all your company. Go eat shrimp. You like them." Colt waved and disappeared out the back stairs.

Go eat shrimp. He could do that. If he could manage to not get into it with Danny, who was hovering over them.

"Your new boyfriend made these, huh?"

Oh, good grief. "He did. And he's not new."

"Newer than me."

"Mm. Better in bed than you too." He grinned to soften that a little.

"Butthead. He's a good cook. No one's seen him around in weeks. We thought he was gone."

We? Theater folk did love their gossip. He nodded. "He's in high demand, and he's been working a lot. It's all good. Better that we're not in each other's back pockets all the time, right?"

That sounded good.

"Right on." Danny shot him an arch look. "Are you keeping him in the kitchen with the staff, or does he get to come out to play with us?"

"He just went up to shower, asshole. And he liked the idea when I asked him if he would cook. He's not hired help." Oh. That came out defensive, dammit. Colt wouldn't think of it like that. Would he?

"Whoa." Danny's hands went up. "Kyle, I was just screwing with you. He's one hell of a cook. The shrimp are stunning."

"Sorry. Low blood sugar. You know I haven't eaten a thing yet?" Low blood sugar. Please. He felt like someone had lifted a screen and behind it he suddenly was able to see reality.

Not now. He was hosting a party. He'd talk with Colt later and they'd fix it. He reached for a shrimp, tasting it. "Oh. Oh, wow."

"Keeping this one?"

"Shut up. Yes." Yes. If it was up to him, yes. But the dawning realization that some of the best parts of what they were together had already fallen apart was starting to make him doubt.

"Good deal. Tell him the food is worth paying for." Danny gave him a wink.

"You are such an ass, Danny." To be honest, he'd kind of been the ass. It wasn't a big tragedy, but Danny probably deserved better.

"Kyle!"

He could tell it was getting into the drinking part of the evening as a handful of the younger dancers came over to gush about his house.

"You have a hot tub!"

"Did you guys see the glass ceiling in there?"

"I swear, Kyle, that studio is amazing."

"Please tell me you didn't go in." He'd locked the door. There was a window in it, but he was pretty sure he'd locked it up. A giant open studio room was better than an orgy to a bunch of tipsy dancers.

"Spoilsport. The door is locked."

"God, it's amazing. Seriously."

"So jelly."

Jelly. Good God. He decided not to tell them about the rooftop patio. It was freezing out, and they had to dance tomorrow. He wasn't that much older than they were, but he sometimes felt like "Dad" had been tattooed on him somewhere.

"Are you guys having a good time?"

He was good and surrounded when he caught sight of Colt slipping into the dining room all squeaky clean and shiny-looking. He gave a wave but wasn't sure whether Colt saw it.

Timmy had hold of Colt the next time Kyle saw him, walking him around and introducing him to people. Every so often Colt would look at him, smile at him, dark eyes rolling.

Not long after that, when the caterers had gone and the buffet was pretty thin, the music got loud, and the civilized Thanksgiving celebration turned into more of a house party. He found himself dancing with pretty much everyone but Colt. Jake cut in on Danny, Allison cut in on Jake, Rob stole Allison when Mig stepped in.

At some point, he even danced with Timmy, the guy pressing close. "I'm going to head out soon. I have an early flight. It's been a great party."

He was good with that; Timmy was special. "Thanks, Timmy. For… a lot of things." He hooked an arm around Timmy's back and gave him a practiced turn around the back sunroom, which was serving as the dance floor. "Did you see where Colt got off to?"

"He's sitting in that cushy chair in the foyer, watching people go in and out and making sure if they leave tipsy, they make it to a cab." Timmy chuckled. "I'm not sure he knows what to do without a guitar."

"I'm not sure why he doesn't have one." He let Timmy go. "You have an Uber? You need one?" He walked Timmy to the door, spotting Colt and giving him a wink.

"You going, boo?"

"I am. My Uber is here. I'll send pictures from the beach!"

Colt laughed as he hugged Timmy tight. "You do that. I want to see everything."

"Ugh. Send pictures, but expect swear words in response." He laughed and sent Timmy on his way. "Hope he doesn't try to fly with green. I'm not going to have time tomorrow to make his bail." He grinned and leaned against Colt.

"He's smarter than that… I hope." Colt's arm snaked around his waist. "You having a good time, cher? Did you get good food?"

"Oh, your shrimp was so good. Everybody said so. Thank you so much for doing that. I'm sorry you got stuck in the kitchen, though. I didn't mean for that to happen." He was having a good time. He was so ready for everyone to go home now, though.

"I like to cook, and Susan is a hoot. I'm glad all y'all liked the shrimps." Colt rested hard against him, looking lovely in jeans and a white button-down, black hair curling every which way.

He reached out and twisted a finger into one of the curls, lazily swirling it around his finger. "So we have two choices, baby. Join them, or kick them out." He laughed. There were only a handful of people left, and he'd bet that once one got the hint, they all would. He gave the bartender a wave and the guy faded the music out.

Colt laughed for him. "No more music. Guess they have to go."

Sure enough, people appeared from upstairs, from the kitchen, and from the sunroom.

"You guys have cabs? All good? Thank you for coming." By the time he tipped the bartender and closed the front door, he was pretty done.

"Do you want help cleaning up tonight? I only have until about noon tomorrow."

"No, baby. It can wait. I'm greedy and I want to spend the time with you. Let's just get the lights." He couldn't let Colt leave without.... They needed time to talk.

They did end up cleaning up a little as they went from room to room, turning lights out. Kyle grabbed an open bottle of wine and two glasses to take upstairs with them. He did the rounds up there too and was relieved not to find someone in the hot tub or sleeping off a buzz in one of the guest rooms.

"All clear."

"Good deal, cher. Good party, hmm? Sit and I'll rub on your shoulders. You look tired."

"I'm a little tired." He sat just where Colt told him to. He wasn't half as tired as he was worried. He didn't know how to start the conversation he wanted to have.

Colt started working on his shoulders, fingers digging in, working in sure, strong circles, searching out his sore spots unerringly.

"Danny told me tonight that the dance company thought we'd broken up because you haven't been out to the theater in a while."

"You ain't been keeping them busy enough, they got time to gossip."

"Maybe. I was surprised they noticed. To be honest, I really hadn't. I just seem to have in my mind how busy you are all the time, so I hadn't given it any thought." He sighed. "You know what else I just noticed? You don't keep a guitar here anymore."

Colt found a spot on his neck, working it. "Don't let them make you sore, cher. You busy. I'm busy. If you just noticed, then it ain't no thing."

Colt's fingers felt so good but completely out of line with what the rest of him was feeling. He shifted away, trying to hold those dark eyes with his. "It's a thing, Colt. It's a big thing. I don't understand the game you're playing, honestly."

Colt had just been pulling away, little by little, not telling him things just to see if he'd notice? Subtly removing the things that mattered most, like he didn't deserve them?

One raven wing dark eyebrow flew up. "I ain't playing no games with you, cher. Don't I come when you call, every time? No matter what? Ain't I here for you, whenever you need?"

He sat back like he'd been stung. Is that all this was anymore? A really hot booty call? "Yeah, Colt. You do. You come every time I call. I can't remember you ever saying no. I didn't understand that was all I was to you anymore. You don't call *me*. These days, even Timmy knows more about you than I do, for God's sake."

The expression on Colt's face was pure confusion. "Timmy sets up my gigs. You ain't making no sense, cher. You want I should not come to see you?"

He just stared at Colt, trying to understand what was happening. "What do *you* want?"

"Right now to figure out why you're pissed at me. Is this about your people asking questions about me? I can't be the only asshole that has to work another job for a living. It can't be all that weird." Colt went to sit next to him, hands in his lap. "Is this 'cause I'm heading to Texas? You told me you was super busy for the weeks up to Christmas, and I can get some work in."

"I'm not angry. I'm... I don't know. Confused? Hurt? It's not about my friends, or Timmy, but if it hadn't been for talking with them, I wouldn't have noticed how much distance there is between us these days. And I don't know what's worse, really. That you've deliberately taken your music, your soul out of my life, or that I've been too busy to notice. But we don't have that connection anymore, and I don't know what we have, what this is, without it."

He knew what he didn't want, though. He didn't want someone he could snap his fingers at, who was okay with being treated that way. And he didn't want for Colt to become that person. He meant too much.

"You fired me, cher, not the other way 'round."

Wait a minute. "Okay, I did fire you. I pulled our number from my show because you were overcommitted, late with the recordings, late to meet me, and totally *amped*. I don't work like that. That was business, Colt. Work. Not our personal lives." Okay, now he was a little irritated.

"Once. I was late on you once, and you ain't my boss or my daddy, but you sure took that on, didn't you? I ain't worth talking to. You just took it on and told me what was what." Colt shook his head, looking at him, a deep frown on his face. "Maybe it ain't personal to you, because you're used to fucking the cast and they jump when you say. Me, I ain't cast. You don' want my music, okay. You don' think I'm good enough to speak to like I'm over twenty-one and legal, okay. But then you gonna fuss at me for loving on you anyway? Come on, man."

Whoa. He had to respect the way Colt just stood up for himself, but now he was pissed.

"It's arguable whether I was your boss at the time, but either way, you walked out of there and sobered right up, didn't you? I don't regret that at all. As for not being worth talking to? Timmy told me you were asking him about fucking Christmas presents when I didn't even know if you planned on coming back from Texas. I wasn't worth sharing your plans with?"

He stood up and paced away a few steps, needing a little breathing room. "And don't you ever accuse me of taking advantage of my position and chasing after my company members like a fucking whore. How *dare* you."

"La. I know me a lot of whores, cher. Good folks, for the most part, selling what's theirs, just like we do." Colt snorted. "And like you got to chase anyone. Like you ain't so fine that anyone don't want you. Ain't never been better, and don't we all know it? Shit, you're being a lot stupid. We talked on Christmassing together—on a tree and on food. I can't do that if you here and I'm in Texas on the day."

"I know we talked about it, but that was before—and I…."

Was he wrong? This wasn't all him. Maybe he did fuck up, but he still couldn't put a finger on exactly where, and even if he figured that out, it was pretty damn obvious that Colt was more than capable of speaking up and just… hadn't. He was more disturbed by why it was so easy to just let all of that go than the fact that they had. Did he want it back? Did Colt?

You didn't build Christmas on booty calls and not being honest with each other.

He sighed. "I need a shower."

"Okay." Colt stood up, stepped toward him, and then he backed up, the motion instinctive, immediate. Colt stopped, then smiled at him, the look bittersweet and knowing. "Your body always tells the truth, jus' like my guitar don't know how to lie. Love you, cher. Talk at you later."

Colt grabbed his backpack from where it was sitting at the bedroom door and headed out of the room, leaving a void there.

He didn't go after Colt. Instead he just let the air in the room settle, took a deep breath, and got in the shower, thankful at least for the passion he understood. Colt was right about that; his body didn't lie, and dancing brought him the most joy. Lovers came and went, but there was always his work, and he was going to be busy.

Chapter Eighteen

Kyle sat in the chilly theater, halfway back in the orchestra seats, exhausted and hurting. He had an elbow on the armrest, his chin in his hand, and his left foot out in the aisle, wrapped and elevated, packed in ice, and resting on a folding chair.

The X-rays had shown a stress fracture. It was a common, ordinary dance injury, and one that common, ordinary dancers dealt with all the time. But he wasn't common or ordinary, and he'd known better. The injury was his own goddamn fault. He hadn't paid attention to his own advice, to the first rule of performing onstage—keep your head in the fucking game.

Black Friday, indeed.

Colt hadn't been gone twenty-four hours when Kyle was due to go back onstage. The show must go on, he'd told himself, and he needed to dance. It was what he did. He'd needed the audience, and the applause, to remind him where he belonged. To remind him of the only true passion he'd ever known before he met Colt.

Instead he was dealing with so much pain from all directions.

"Hey, Kyle? Kyle!"

He blinked and lifted his head, looking back at the stage. "Yes. Sorry."

"Where do you enter from?"

They were rehearsing in his understudy for tonight's performance. As dance captain, that was Danny's job. Kyle was only there to help with the details. But just as his thoughts had been with a beautiful dark-eyed Cajun the night before, his heart wasn't in this either. "Right. Sorry. For which number?"

Last night he shouldn't have been dancing at all. Today, it was the only thing he wanted to do, and he couldn't.

Ali squinted at him from the stage. "Kyle... are you all right?"

"Hey, let's take five everybody, okay? No, ten. Take ten."

Kyle sighed as Danny made his way up the aisle toward him. "Dammit."

"Kyle, I really need your attention, or I'll never get through this."

"I'm sorry. I know."

"What's going on?"

He shook his head. He couldn't find the words to explain that Colt had left him. Even if he could, Danny wasn't the one to share his love life with. He couldn't face "I told you so."

Danny sat on the armrest of the seat in front of him. "It's just a fracture. It's not a big deal. It will heal up good as new, and you'll be on it full-time in a few weeks."

"That's easy to say, isn't it?" God, he was whining like a fucking baby.

"You've been pushing hard lately. Maybe your body is telling you it's time for a rest."

It wasn't time for a rest. His own exhibition was supposed to open next week. "I'm going to have to pull the plug on my exhibition."

"Oh. Fuck."

"Yeah."

It was more than disappointing; it was irony. It was karma.

"I'm sorry, Kyle. I was focused on—"

"Stop. You have a job to do."

Danny nodded. "I do. And they do." Standing up, Danny pointed to the stage, his empathetic expression suddenly neutral, all business. "Don't let them down, and don't waste their time."

He blinked at Danny a few times, those words hitting him like being zapped with electric current, his brain just needed to sort itself out a second.

"Right."

Of course, Danny was right. It was about the work. It was always about the work; it had to be. Whether he was onstage or not, people were counting on him. There was a show tonight.

"Yes, right. Of course, Danny. I apologize and I'm ready to work."

Danny squinted at him, gave him a nod and a smile. "That's more like it."

He missed Colt deeply, in ways only his heart understood. But he had to get back to work.

RYDER PICKED Colt's happy ass up at the airport, eyes going wide as saucers at the sight of him. His friend didn't say a word about it, though. Just unlocked the truck and headed straight for the east side of Austin and one of the dive bars.

They went in and lined up three tequila shots, the lime, the salt.

The first one burned, the second one tasted fine, and the third one was like water.

"Better?" Ryder asked.

He shook his head. "Ask me again after a couple more, oui?"

"You're on." Ryder flagged down the bartender, ordered three more shots and a Coke. "I can't stand flying. I'm all white-knuckled the whole time. Good thing Norv is steady. But… this seems like more than travel anxiety, huh?"

"I—I ain't got words. I let him break me, I think. I ain't made to understand all this mess, and I didn't do it right, trying to fix it. I be tired and raw, like I'm rotted inside."

"Shit." Ryder pulled out his phone. "I better let Norv know where we're at."

"I want to go home so bad." But he didn't know where that was, didn't know that he ever would.

"The dancer? That who you mean? He was pretty, but I don't know, Colt. Who makes a man take his boots off? I don't know if he got it."

"That's a fancy-folk thing maybe? Shit if I know. Thing is, boo, I fucking love him, but he don't want my music and that's like…."

"Not wanting you. I get that." Ryder slid another shot under his nose. "Are you sure, though? He seemed into it when we met him."

"I ain't sure of dick." He took the shot. Enough of this and he wouldn't care no more. He got it, why a man would let drink take him over forever. Sometimes the hurting was awful bad to bear.

"If the dancer can't be clear with you, then he don't deserve you anyhow. Or your music. You save that for folks like us that know how to hear it."

Colt reached out blindly, needing a friend so bad. Ryder grabbed his hand, held on.

"Fuck this asshole. Fuck all the goddamn Yankees, man. Come home. Me and Norv would take you in a split second."

"I know, boo." And he did. He knew. So why didn't he just say yes?

"You hang with us for a few days. We'll make some music, grill some steaks, catch a few fish. Right? It'll be good. You'll see." Ryder looked at his phone. "Norv says don't let you puke."

"Tell Norv to suck it. I be a Cajun. I was born to drink."

"Far be it from me, man." Ryder held the phone where he could see it and shut it off with a grin.

He grinned back, letting the company and the booze ease him. "You got money for the jukebox?"

"Yessir. Money and time. Come on."

COLT SAT in Norv's studio, guitar in his hand. "What if I can't?"

"Don't be stupid, boy. You are music. What? You can't you?" Sometimes Norv said the things a man needed to hear. Sometimes Norv was just a fucker.

"Maybe. Probably not. Who knows? Let's just play." He started with the classics, because that was their thing. Christmas carols and blues, Fats Domino and Willie.

Ryder sat on the floor, leaning against Norv's hip, eyes closed as he sang for them. There was the way Norv stared down, eyes warm, heated. They didn't have to be careful here, they didn't have to pretend, and Colt was honored that they trusted him, but damn, it hurt. Bad.

After a bit, Ryder made his way over and sat cross-legged at Colt's feet, grinning. "Give me something, man. Something I can play with."

He blew Ryder a kiss. "Something sultry, hmm? Something rocking and bluesy?"

Ryder nodded and braced his arms behind him. "Whatever your fingers do, I'm in."

He wanted to rock it, wanted it to sing, but what came out was... pissed off. The guitar snarled, the chords raw and almost discordant.

Ryder just stared at him and slid closer to Norv, as if his music had teeth and Ryder was afraid of being bitten.

"Let him get it out, baby. He hurts." Norv's guitar answered his, giving him something to struggle against.

Ryder didn't join in. He understood that; Ryder didn't have these words in him. You couldn't possibly unless you'd been to this dark place, and the kid just didn't understand dark.

Norv, though. Norv had danced with the Devil close, had laid with dogs and come back from it.

Tears began to fall, so filled with rage that he expected his guitar to burn.

It didn't matter, though, how raw and real the tears were or how much pain he poured into his instrument. None of it pushed the pictures from his mind. Images of Kyle so sharp they could cut him into pieces.

"Norv...."

"Let him alone, Ry. This is a safe place."

"La! I cain't... I gotta take a walk." He wasn't going to be able to breathe no more like this.

He needed out.

Ryder hopped to his feet. "How about some blues, Colt? You're feeling bad? That's the way to go, ain't it?"

"I don't know which way to go, boo. I don't understand what I did wrong! I don' know how to fix it a bit."

"Maybe you didn't do nothing wrong. Maybe it's just he don't appreciate you. You tell him, Norv. You can't change what you are even if someone you love don't like it."

"That's true, son. You are who you are. What did he say?"

"That he was pissed about me not playing for him no more. That he was pissed that I was pissed over getting fired. That he didn't want me to come over when he called for me."

"Whut?" Norv looked confused. "That don't make no sense."

"I know! I just...." He just had to admit it. He was a high-school dropout worthless piece of shit who couldn't figure out a high-dollar man like Kyle. He stopped and sighed, collapsing in on himself. "La. I'm broke, me."

Ryder stepped closer. For all Colt wasn't a big man, Ryder was even smaller. "You're a good man. He's a fool to let you go. If he was closer, I'd tell him so to his face."

"I'd prob'ly let you, just to watch him be all shocked." Colt put his guitar down and hugged Ryder hard. "Y'all are my good friends."

"We are." Ryder's hug was deep and warm, offering up whatever Colt needed.

He heard Norv putting things away, and then the man's big hand landed on his shoulder. "We're going to all cook supper together. We're all going to eat and listen to good music and smoke a little weed."

"Norv went shopping. The fridge is busting!" Ryder's grin was huge. The man was always hungry. Colt had never seen anyone so small eat so much.

"Yessir." Norv didn't ask, just turned and expected that they'd follow, and follow they did, like a row of mismatched ducklings.

"How about we catch some fish tomorrow, Colt? Want to? Get some sun, have a beer? I mean it won't be crazy warm, but fresh air is good, right?"

"Works for me, boo." He knew better. He knew that he couldn't stay here, taint their Christmas.

He was poison right now.

"Dammit."

He really needed to remember to keep his phone with him. Hobbling as he was, Kyle never managed to get to the damn thing before whoever was calling hung up. He looked at his missed calls on the way back to his recliner, and was just about to call Timmy back when it rang in his hand.

"Hello?"

"Dude! I got your message, man. Are you okay? That sucks!"

He sighed, settling back in his chair and propping up his foot again. It was good to hear Timmy's voice. "Hey, Timmy. Yeah. I'll be okay. How's Mexico?"

"Rad, man. We're all super stoked about the waves and the weather. We just came in for some lunch. Are you hurt bad? Can you dance?"

"No, I can't dance. They rehearsed in an understudy who will cover me for a few shows, and I had to cancel my exhibition."

Timmy sighed. "Oh, man. I'm sorry. You've been working hard on the solo thing, I know."

"Yeah." It broke his heart, really. It was nice that Timmy understood that without him having to explain.

"You need to cheer up. Make some popcorn and hot cocoa and watch *It's a Wonderful Life*."

He didn't have the stomach for popcorn or the heart to tell Timmy he wasn't into a movie.

"Hello, you there?"

"Sorry, yes. I was just thinking about when I was eight and my pet rabbit died—"

"Oh, I'm sorry dude. What was his name?"

He grinned. Timmy's sympathy was a hundred years late but still adorable. "Really, Timmy?"

"Heh. Sorry."

"His name was Oreo. He was black and white."

"Clever."

"Anyway, I got up one morning, and he had died overnight." He waited on Timmy, but the line was quiet. "No comments?"

Timmy was chewing on something. "Nope. 'M good."

"Okay, well. Oreo died, and I was very upset, but I had rehearsal and I had to go because it was tech week. I didn't want to be there, I didn't feel like dancing, but I knew I had to. My dancing has always been everything. I missed birthday parties, school events, weddings. I missed my grandmother's funeral because it was opening night. I didn't learn to ride a bike. I didn't date. I never stayed up late and watched David Letterman. It was always dance. Always the work."

"Wow."

"I loved it anyway, Timmy. I still love it. But I can't do it halfway."

"Okay. So don't. Is this about Colt, man?"

"I… I don't know. Maybe." Was it about Colt? Or was it about him? He shook his head. "Everything, all of it, was about that exhibition. It was going to be ours. But he just kept… he couldn't say no to anyone. He couldn't make the show his priority, and I don't know how to work that way. I shouldn't have expected him to…. I shouldn't have asked it of him in the first place. If I hadn't asked…."

"Wait. Wait. What are you saying, man?"

"He doesn't even like being in front of an audience. I knew that. I shouldn't have asked him to work with me. He couldn't do it all."

Timmy went silent for a long few seconds. "He wanted to do that show with you. More than anything."

"Then he shouldn't have been doing so many other things at the same time! I thought I was helping him out by taking something off his plate for him when he couldn't manage it himself. You had to see him all wild-eyed and…. Jesus."

"Huh."

"What?"

"He said working with you was magic."

He sighed, the words stinging him, making him ache. "Okay, so firing him wasn't the right call. Fine. I didn't understand…. I didn't think it meant as much to him as it did to me. Firing him was impulsive. Yes, maybe." He sighed. "But nothing he did after that was right either."

Colt was upset. Angry. He got that. And yes, probably rightfully upset. Upset enough to say some things that Kyle hoped Colt regretted, but that was a two-way street for sure. He hadn't exactly been polite either.

But he wasn't anyone's booty call. Why would Colt punish him like that? His work was work; it wasn't… them. They were heart and soul, rhythm and music, but all Colt wanted anymore was sex? That hurt the most. He could get that from anyone. That he didn't understand at all.

"He cooked for your party."

He had. Colt hadn't just cooked—he'd rolled his sleeves up and worked his ass off. "His shrimp was amazing. I don't know what to do, Timmy. But I love him. Maybe it was just too intense to keep up. He *is* his music. I'm my dancing. Maybe we're not meant to spend our energy on other people."

But Colt had inspired him, energized him. So how could that be true? Maybe he was just a selfish asshole.

"Am I an asshole, Timmy?" He dropped his head back in his chair.

"Everybody's an asshole, man. Colt can't be someone he's not. He works harder and cleaner than anyone I know. He's a machine. You know he never finished school, that he was homeless for, like, years? Maybe he… shit, what do I know?"

"I knew about school." He'd assumed the rest, but Colt hadn't spoken specifically about that. "You're saying maybe he thinks I'm a snob? Maybe. I don't know, either, Timmy. I just miss him."

"He thinks you're magical. Special. He believes in that."

"Not enough to be honest with me. Not enough to stay and work it out." He sighed. He was more confused now than he'd been before he'd started talking. He got it. He'd fucked up. Fine. Didn't it take both of them to want to make things work? And he still didn't understand how he could have done differently. He didn't know how to put anything ahead of his dancing. Not even himself. He never had in his whole life. "I think I'm going to put that movie on like you suggested."

He wasn't, but he felt like crap and needed to get Timmy off the phone so he could cry about it.

"Okay, dude. Listen, I'll check in with you again soon. Take care, okay? Don't forget to eat."

"No worries. Hit those waves hard. Thanks for calling, Timmy."

He hung up the phone and stared at the dark screen sitting in his hand. God, he wanted to call Colt. He wished he had it in him to do it, but not today. Maybe he'd call tomorrow.

"COLT? WHERE the ever-loving fuck are you?" Nathan's voice ripped through his eardrum, and he winced, jerking away from the sound. He blinked up, trying to remember where he was. He never worried when he woke up with Kyle, but that was all gone.

"Why you care?"

"Young man, you are frightening me. Where are you? I'll come pick you up. I'll buy you a plane ticket, anything you need."

"I'm in a shelter. I've been playing." He'd left the boys and hitchhiked to Houston. From there, the church bus brought him to Shreveport.

Now he was back in Louisiana, and....

"A shelter. What the actual fuck? You live like you're desperate, honey. Why? You need more than what's in your cash account? You got it. You work like a damn dog. I'm coming to get you. Now."

"You don't know where I am." He smiled, though, because Nathan's straightforward shit was familiar, direct. Family.

There was a long sigh on Nathan's end of the phone. "Fine. You win. What's the plan? Austin? Nashville? Back to New York?"

"I don't know. I kinda... I think I fucked up bad, huh? I fell in love."

"Oh, Colt! That's lovely. In New York? Is that why you asked to stay so long? Wait... wait, honey. How is that fucking up? Are you not there? Oh, Colt. What happened?"

"I'm not made right." That was the only answer he had. "He's so fine, and I'm not."

"Bullshit. You get your head out of your ass, right now."

"What?"

"Not made right. You're the finest musician I've ever known. You will never run out of work. The line to get to you would wrap around New York twenty times."

"Then what did I do wrong? I did everything I thought he wanted."

"Shit, who knows? Who knows why shit goes bad? People break up. Where *are* you?"

"Shreveport. I want a car. A fast one. A convertible."

"Sure thing, honey. Nothing fixes a broken heart like a fast car. And get into a hotel. Quit living like you're a pauper." Nathan chuckled softly. "Promise me. Promise me you'll get a cab to the Eldorado. I'll get you a room for a few days, book you a massage."

Colt looked at his guitar in its beat-up, well-traveled case and his worn-in jeans and wondered what the hell he would do with himself at a high-dollar spot like the Eldorado.

"Promise me, Colt. I'll take care of things for you, okay?"

"You got my word. Me. The Eldorado. A car." A couple days' nap, right? A drink or three.

"I'll check in with you again in a few days. Until then you just rest. Relax. Fall in love with someone else for a night or two."

"Rest. Relax. I hear you." He didn't have his heart back to give it to someone else, so he couldn't promise that.

Hell, maybe he'd never get it back again.

Chapter Nineteen

COLT PAID cash for a Mustang convertible and headed south, driving along the backways, singing along with the radio, flipping stations when one grayed out. Gospel, country, R&B—he didn't care none.

His heart was broke, his soul had a tear, and he needed to play for a few days or until he was lost. He didn't bother to take the exit for Houma as he drove. His mamma was about as lost to him as his daddy.

There was about a thousand missed calls—from the boys, from Timmy, his management, a dozen bands—but none from anyone he wanted to talk to right now.

Right now he wanted rum and blues and a whiskey-soaked voice singing with him, the wail drowning out the rejoicing of the carols. Satan rode with him right now, not the good Lord.

He pulled into the French Quarter, heading straight for the Place d'Armes. They had good parking, rooms with no windows, and enough haints to make him feel at home. He crossed their palms with silver enough to keep him out of the weather until Christmas at least. Then he went two blocks over and two down to Sydney's and bought him the first one of a line of bottles that were needed to help him forget how Kyle had pulled away from him, had proven he wasn't worth a hill of shat beans.

"Lawd, that you, Boudreaux? You Laird's boy?"

"C'est bon. Is."

He didn't have to look to see who it was; it didn't matter.

It was good to be home.

These were his own people.

COLT'S PHONE rang, shut off, then rang again for the eighty millionth time in a row. Goddamn. He didn't even have to look to see who it was.

Timmy.

The man was relentless as a hurricane.

"You drivin' me bugshit, boo."

"Dude! You're freakin' alive! I totally thought maybe the morgue-guy, the uh, coroner dude was gonna pick up. I have called you forty-two-gazillion times! Are you okay? Where the hell are you?"

"N'awlins. I been playing the blues. How was the beach?" He sat up and lit a cigarette, the pure blackness of the windowless room making the flame seem like a beacon.

"Good. First couple days were challenging. Then it was heaven. What happened to Austin? Your boys decide to head south?"

"I didn't want to fuck with their holiday, and I ain't feeling jolly. I went traveling."

"What's the matter? Did you change your flight? When do you get in? I got a session request for the twenty-seventh. You want it?"

"I didn't make a flight back. What kind of booking?" He could go in to spend Christmas with Timmy, do the gig, and get his stuff. New York was always going to be Kyle for him, big as it was, and there wasn't a thing of Kyle here. Not a whisper that didn't live in his own heart.

"It's Fivers—the jazz group you worked with before. But wait. What did I miss? Is this because of Kyle's exhibition? Is he coming down there?"

Coming down here. Shit no. "Me and Kyle…. Things went bad Thanksgiving. I spent the night at the airport before my flight. I'll come to you Christmas Eve, okay? We'll have a couple days, and then I'll do that gig." He took a deep drag, letting the smoke burn his lungs.

"Oh. I… didn't know, dude. I'm sorry. So you haven't talked to him, huh? Wow. Well, I wanted company for Christmas, so thanks for that."

"You my good friend, boo. I'm sorry too. He was my love, but… you know how it is." He wasn't even sure why Kyle was so down on him, not really. Colt had been late, had taken something to help him wake up that bad, bad morning. If that had been all of it for real? Then Kyle wanted more perfect than him, that was for sure. He was a man, not Jesus. Not even a saint.

Hell, he wasn't even in the running for a good man. He was just hoping for Heaven.

"I guess I don't know how it is, actually. I totally would have bet the farm on you two, dude. He had to cancel his exhibition, did you know?"

"Is he sick?" He sat up and swung his legs over the bed, hand flailing for the light. "I call you back, boo." He hung up and slammed his finger on Kyle's name, his heart banging hard. Shit, was Kyle hurt? Was it bad? "Answer your phone, butthead. Now."

It rang a bunch of times, but someone did answer. It just wasn't Kyle. "Hey, Colt. It's Jake. Don't panic. He's coming. He asked me to pick it up because he's gimpy. He lets everyone else go to voicemail, you know."

"Shut up! Give me that." There was some rustling, and then Kyle's voice was clearer. "Colt?"

"You hurt, cher? You okay?" Gimpy? That wasn't right.

Kyle's sigh and the pause that followed held a world of trouble. "Well? I'm hoping I will be. How's Austin?"

"I couldn't stay. I went for a ride. You need anything?" *Me?*

"This call is nice. I could use more of these. Where are you? I miss you."

"I came home for a bit. Been busking all over. You can call anytime, cher. I always answer for you." He took another drag. Shit, he didn't even know what time it was. "What you do to you?"

"Stress fracture in my foot, on, uh… well. It was on Black Friday, the same day you left town. My head wasn't in the right place to dance. It sucks. I was out of the show that weekend and most of the next week. I can dance on it some if it's taped up right, but I couldn't… a ninety-minute show was too much, so…."

"Lord have mercy. I'm sorry." And he was. He knew what all this meant for Kyle. "I didn't know 'til just now. I been living low."

"I know. I didn't want to make a thing of it because of when it happened, and I didn't know when or if you'd be ready to hear from me or not. But I was going to call soon. I just keep thinking, if I only knew someone that could sit with me and sing me the blues."

"La, cher. You got some fair ones in that big city of yours." Not good. Not like here. Not like him. But fair.

Kyle snorted. "Seriously, music man? I need the real deal. I need magic."

"Thought you didn't believe in magic." He grinned, leaned back a little. "I miss you bad. I keep wandering, looking for a place to light."

"I didn't realize how much I believed until you left. Then I figured out what magic really is and I miss it. Will you wander back here?"

"I got to see if Norv wants the Mustang." But he would, because he was an idiot who loved him a dancer. "What day is it?"

"It's Tuesday, baby. Are you okay? Wait. You have a Mustang?"

"I bought one. A convertible. If you were here, I'd take you for a ride."

"How the hell did you… you can afford a Mustang? Garage it with Norv, and take me for a ride after Christmas. I don't have a show, and I need a vacation."

He'd figure it out.

Should he figure it out?

He wanted to. He wanted to figure shit out.

"I'll get myself up to your area of the woods as soon as I can." God help him, he wanted to figure this out.

"I have so much I need to say to you. But I want to say it in person. I want to hold you. Be safe. Love you."

Love you.

Yeah, he did too. With all his heart.

"I love you, cher. You take care of that foot 'til I can."

"I'm on it. I need it to heal right."

"Call if you need me." He hung up and sat there, finishing his cigarette. Lord have mercy, he guessed he had stuff to do.

First of all, he called Nathan. He needed someone to send a Christmas supper and a tree to a fancy-assed house in New York. Then he needed someone to get him up East and find a good place for his 'Stang.

Then he needed to go see whether Kyle could mean it, wanting him, believing in him.

Loving him.

Chapter Twenty

Good morning, music man. I can't stop thinking about you, I'm so relieved you're coming back. Drive safe. Send me a pic of your mustang!

Colt blinked at his phone, wondering how long ago the text had come in. Lord. He'd just gotten out of bed, and Kyle was probably already in his studio. Such an early bird.

Except his bird had a bit of wing clipping happening, didn't he? Poor cher.

He needed to see Kyle. He knew it was probably stupid, but, Lord, he hadn't never once let stupidity stop him.

He slid from the bed and started packing his things.

Heading out now. Miss your face.

His phone rang immediately. "Good morning, lover."

Colt blinked a little. Was he? Kyle's lover? "Mornin', cher. How you be?"

"Impatient to see you. And I'm cursing this fucking foot. I feel optimistic for the first time in weeks, and I need to dance. How... how are you?"

He put his earphone deal in and his phone in his pocket so he could pack. "It's been a weird few weeks, huh? I can't seem to sleep enough."

"I haven't been sleeping at all. You must be making up for me." Kyle laughed, but it sounded off somehow, forced.

"I miss you." The words slipped from him. "Bad."

Kyle huffed out a breath. "I miss you so much. Drive carefully but drive fast, baby."

The line went silent for a long stretch, neither one of them quite ready to hang up, but they didn't seem to know what to say either.

"Colt?" Kyle said at last. "If I apologize, you'll forgive me, won't you? If I figure out how to... once I figure out how to put it all into the right words? You won't just tell me it's okay. You'll really forgive me, won't you?"

"Oh cher, you got all my forgives. Don't you know that?"

"No, I don't know right now. I don't know anything. I need to see you. I want your music back."

"I tried to—I don't know what I did so bad. I want to touch you." He shoved his drawers in his bag, his notebooks.

"I... I'm afraid we just got too busy to communicate. But... but I know...." Kyle sighed. "I don't want to say the wrong thing over the phone. If I'm going to fuck it up, I want to at least do it where you can see I'm trying. I better go. Drive fast?"

"Uh-huh. Can I call from the road?"

"Please. I want to know where you are. How you are. I love you."

Colt stopped short. Then he smiled. "I love you, cher. I'm coming to you."

NEVER, EVER, ever had Kyle sat by the phone waiting for a man to call. Not once in his whole damn life. But with doctor's orders to rest his foot, all he was doing was binge-watching shows on Netflix, napping accidentally, and playing games on his phone. He was bored.

He was bored, and it was four in the afternoon, and he hadn't heard from Colt today. Didn't Colt say he wanted to call?

God, was he okay? If he was driving too fast and got into an accident or something, Kyle would never forgive himself.

Ring, dammit.

His phone rang, the blues sounding, and he grabbed it.

"'Lo, cher! I got me a hands-free deal. Like one without a cord even. How you?" Colt was laughing.

Well, shit, his man was having fun. "Oh, fine. Super busy day watching Netflix, you know. What's going on?"

"I'm tickled as a pig in shit. I got this damn thing working so I can talk with you!"

"Hands-free and you figured out how to make a phone call too! I'm impressed." He smiled. "Where are you right now?"

"Outside of Spartanburg. I'm making time. Gon' have to spend the night here in a bit. I'm ready to see you, huh? Get a hug."

"I've got a couple waiting for you, baby." Where the hell was Spartanburg? He'd have to google it when they got off the phone. "I hope you packed some long undies. It's cold up here."

"I didn't. I'll get some when I get there. I talked to my manager about money stuff."

"Yeah? What did he say? Are you going to have to sell the Mustang?"

"He said stop living like I ain't got a pot to piss in or a window to pour it out of, to get a massage, and pay cash for my car."

Kyle laughed. "Pay up front for a Mustang! You've got a little cash, huh? I don't want to hear any more moaning about how I'm too fancy for you."

"I let Nathan deal with my money. I ain't good with it. I just try to be careful." He heard Colt sigh. "I never had nothing. Sometimes I forget."

"I'm not asking you to live any differently. It's just good to know you don't have to worry about it, right?" Hell, even he couldn't pay for a Mustang outright.

"Lord yes. It's good to know I don't have to take every gig. That I can breathe some, me."

He liked that idea. Not that he expected Colt would breathe much. But maybe they could arrange to catch a breath at the same time once in a while.

"How's your foot, cher? You hurting bad?"

"It's sore. It's better when I wear the boot they gave me. I've only got two more shows, tonight and tomorrow night, and then I can rest it for a while."

"Poor foot. I hate it for you. It's gon' be all better, though, right?"

"With rest and a little more time, it should be good as ever. I'll have to work back up into shape, but that won't take long. Have you talked to Timmy? He told me he has work for you."

"Sorta. He told me you canceled your show, and I hung up on him to call you. I needed to hear your voice."

It was such a relief to know they both wanted to figure this out. He could hear it in Colt's voice, in the honesty in his lover's concern for him. It might be hard at first, but if they were honest, they'd find that magic again.

"I'm okay, love. I'll be just fine. Even better when you get here."

Chapter Twenty-One

COLT HAD sent him a Christmas tree. He didn't know you could send people Christmas trees, but he'd opened the door this morning and in it came. Some hunky guys set it up and turned on the lights, and a tiny little girl decorated it with colored balls and a sweet felt tree skirt. They'd swept out the way they'd come in, leaving him with a festive sunroom.

How cool was that? And how sweet was his music man?

Kyle had his foot up high and the stereo up higher, bags of frozen peas packed around his toes. He'd been on total rest except for the one show he did a night, but tonight's show had been the last one. Closing night. They'd put that baby to bed.

He'd overdone it. It wasn't a conscious thing. It just kind of happened with the energy of the last performance. It was worth it, but he was paying for it now.

He lay there in his recliner, taking in the tree and allowing it to cheer him up while he relaxed and let the painkillers kick in. In his head, he was dancing. Choreographing. Making the best use of this mess that he could and trying to be okay with the fact that the whole cast was out celebrating without him.

Colt was on the road somewhere. They'd talked before the show, and at some point when he found a good place to stop again, Kyle knew he'd call to say good night.

Timmy had been at the show and had made sure he got home okay, but he'd sent Timmy home after that, saying he was tired, but mostly he just didn't want anyone fussing over him for a little while. It was time he figured this out for himself.

It had been all of half an hour. So far so good.

His phone rang, a low bluesy sound filling the air. Colt.

"Hello, lover. Are you driving safe?" Baby, lover—maybe he didn't really have the right to use those again yet, but so far Colt hadn't complained.

"Sort of. How you, cher?"

"I'm… well? I'm going to miss that show, and I'm kind of glad it's over at the same time. I don't know if that makes sense."

"Surely. I'm sorry you're hurt. What you doing tonight?"

"Not a thing. I'm sitting in my reclining chair in the sunroom, listening to music and dancing in my head. Totally serious. I'm pathetic. And tired."

"You want to share a pizza?"

He laughed. "Wouldn't that be wonderful? Soon, right? How long? Where are you?"

"Standing on your stoop with a pepperoni and mushroom."

"What?" He sat up. "What? Oh my God. I…. Okay, I'm coming. Hang on. I just… be patient. I gotta put the phone down." He hung up. He hauled himself out of his chair, letting the ice packs fall to the floor, scooped up his crutch, and hobbled his way across the house to the front door. Fucking pizza was probably cold, and Colt was probably colder waiting on him. At least the pizza was from New York.

He unlocked the door and pulled it partway open, as far as he could manage with his crutch in the way.

"Hey, cher. I brought supper." Colt eased his way in, shut the door behind him. "Let me put this down, and I'll help you settle, hmm?"

He didn't want to settle, he wanted a kiss.

Colt looked… thin. Not bad, really, just a little drawn in the face, and his tiny butt seemed even skinnier. Nothing that some beer and five or six more pizzas couldn't fix.

He followed Colt toward the kitchen, though a lot more slowly. "This is a lovely surprise. Did you know when we talked before the show that you'd be here tonight?"

"I hoped. I didn't want to disappoint you if I was wrong." Colt came back to him, helped him sit down. "What you want to drink?"

"Just water is fine. Thank you." He watched Colt move around his kitchen, smiling slightly just because he liked it so much. He'd been thinking about this moment for a couple of days, but he didn't know Colt would be here so soon, and he hadn't decided how he needed to handle it. The only thing he knew for sure is he'd done a lot of talking and not enough listening. "Pizza smells so good."

"It does. It's good here." Colt got his foot propped up, got him a plate and a glass of water.

"I'm okay. You don't have to fuss over me. You've had such a long drive. You must be tired. Sit and eat something. Grab a beer if you want one. Come tell me about home."

"I am. Eat your pizza." Colt leaned against the counter, watching him. "It was weird, being home. I did a lot of busking in Houston, Shreveport, N'awlins."

"You enjoy that? Busking?" He absolutely refused to read too much into Colt's careful distance. The man was here, right? He'd let it be on Colt's terms. He picked up his pizza and took a bite, the pepperoni rich and spicy on his tongue. "Mmm. So good. Thanks for bringing this."

"Sometimes? Every so often it's good to play for tips, just so you remember how. I like to watch you eat." Colt grinned suddenly. "I swear to God, cher. My ass hurts so damn bad. I never want to sit down again."

That made him laugh, grinning right back. Of course that's why Colt was standing. God, he was such an idiot. He tried to just stay in the moment. "Right? I know just how you feel." He'd been sitting on his ass for two weeks except for a few numbers a night. "I can't believe you bought a Mustang." Like, really couldn't believe it. He didn't understand Colt's finances at all, but he obviously was doing better than he let on. "So were you able to record anything with Norv and Ryder or…?"

Colt shook his head. "I stayed a couple of days. Then I hitched to Houston. I needed to be out of my head, you know? I needed to drive with the Devil a while. The Mustang was at the right place, so I grabbed it. It's a blast to drive."

He nodded. He did know. He hadn't been able to make it through one show. He let himself dance in a bad state of mind. His concentration was off, he wasn't focused, and he got injured. Totally his own damn fault.

"I'm sorry." He put his pizza down. That came out because it needed to be said, but it wasn't enough. "For not trusting you could handle things, deal with your own shit. For not giving you enough credit."

"I'll take that." Colt came to him, close enough to touch his hand. "I don't need a boss or a daddy. I.… Next time, if you think I can't do something, talk with me. I ain't book learned like you, cher, but I ain't too stupid to live."

"Too stupid? Oh, baby. I was honestly trying to help. You were so tired, and you were trying to be everything for everybody all at once, and I thought your energy was better spent on what you do best, instead of on a theater show that was going to tie you down seven nights a week. I was wrong. That was your decision to make, not mine. But I never once thought you were stupid. Jesus, Colt. You're brilliant. You don't have anything to prove to me, or to anyone. You shine so bright, it's blinding sometimes. I am so incredibly proud of you."

"It was being with you, making music with you." Colt stepped closer to him, and Kyle grabbed his lover, reeled him in. "Well, hello, cher. Don't let me hurt you."

"That's the magic, right? Making music together? That's what we need to find again." He let that hang between them a minute and then grinned slightly. "And I want to tell you one more thing." He hooked a hand behind Colt's neck and pulled his Cajun even closer. "I don't care who you think wants me. I don't care if you're right. I want you."

Colt rested their foreheads together and closed his eyes. "I could set my burdens down here, with you."

Yes. Yes, please. "I'll take yours if you'll take mine." He brushed his lips against Colt's. "May I kiss you?"

Colt laughed for him, the sound merry, warm. "You'd better. I need it like breathing."

"More important than breathing." He took a light kiss, and then another, just for a taste and maybe for the sake of being polite, but that didn't last long. He felt Colt's hot breath and took advantage of Colt opening for him, claiming more of what he really wanted. Colt's hands were heavy on his thighs, the kiss going molten, his Cajun holding nothing from him.

He leaned back in his chair, twisted his fingers into Colt's T-shirt, and tangled his good leg around Colt's thigh. Being stuck in this chair was bullshit. If he had two good feet, he'd have Colt on his kitchen table or up against the wall in the foyer by now. He groaned, kind of loving the tease of that image. "Colt."

"Need you, cher. Can we? I need… fuck!"

Didn't that feel good? Knowing Colt was right there with him.

"Fuck, yeah. We… ah, shit." He shoved the heel of his hand against the base of his cock through the thin fabric of his sweatpants. "Christ.

We totally can if...." He wrapped a hand under Colt's bicep. "Not in this goddamn chair."

"No. I won't risk you. Bed? Sofa? Where do you want to be?"

"Bed. If I can dance on it, baby, I can walk ten feet." Okay, it was a little more than ten feet and up the stairs, but… semantics. And the little twinge in his foot that cut through the pain meds was worth it. He could stay in bed all damn day tomorrow, Colt along with him.

Colt looked apprehensive, but once he was up, it was all good. He threw an arm over his lover's shoulders and found a grin somewhere. "See? You're the perfect height."

"Good. I'm gon' get you upstairs. Then I got to get my guitar and all from the car, just real quick."

He nodded. "Yeah. That'll cool us off a minute." It would cool Colt off for sure. It was something like twenty-five degrees out. "Take my coat."

"I'll be quick as a bunny. I swear."

He was laughing before Colt got his butt down on the end of the bed. "Go on. Tell me you packed some patience in your suitcase? I could use some with the heat you're giving off."

"I packed olive salad, pralines, and chicory coffee from the Café du Monde." Colt kissed him again, hard and fast.

He grinned and slapped Colt on the ass. "Kiss me again and your shit is staying in the car, baby. You better run."

"I did miss your smile, cher." Colt disappeared in a rush, leaving the echo of his laugh behind him.

He flopped on the bed, smiling at the ceiling. Something brought his music man back. There was no question Colt wanted to be there with him. Really *with* him. Whatever they still had to work through, they would. They had this.

Chapter Twenty-Two

Colt slept some, but his days and nights were broken, so he ended up eating cold pizza and slipping into Kyle's kitchen to play at the crack of dawn.

He started with the blues, but as the sun began to fill the air with light, the Christmas carols wanted out, so he let them come. The good Lord wanted what He wanted, and this morning He wanted Colt to give praise.

Colt needed to call Timmy, the guys, let them know where he was and that he was… trying. Kyle had said his sorries, and he'd said his piece. He knew he ought to apologize too, but he wasn't sure what he was sorry for. He needed to think on that.

What should he have done? Should he have told Kyle to fuck off about the show? Should he have never said yes?

Colt wanted to say yes. He liked for things to be easy. Everything was always so damn hard, all the time. For once, things were going good, but they weren't at the same time.

The only good thing he had was this gift that God had blessed him with, this magic. There wasn't a single other thing about him that was real or right. Kyle saw that, got it. Hell, without the music, even Kyle knew he wasn't anything.

Except God had blessed him. For whatever reason, this was his, and there was joy in it. All the way.

Maybe it wasn't none of his—why things were the way they were. Maybe he just needed to play his music, love his man, and be thankful for it.

"Venite adoramus…." He heard Kyle singing long before his lover made an appearance in the kitchen. In fact, the chorus was over, and he was on to the last verse before Kyle hobbled in, wearing green leggings, a big red flannel shirt, a Santa hat and a big black boot-contraption on his foot.

Kyle stuck a matching hat on his head and pulled up a chair, still singing with a big Merry Christmas grin.

"Mornin', cher. How goes?" That smile damn near lit the room.

"Merry Christmas!" Kyle kissed him right over top of his guitar before taking a load off. "Let me see. It's Christmas Day, the sun is out, you're here, and I woke up to the sound of your guitar in my kitchen. It really can't go any better."

"When I make you pancakes and bacon, then that will be better." Their supper ought to come tonight. "You okay with me inviting Timmy to supper? He ain't got no one."

"Mmm. Bacon sounds like nirvana. And Timmy's welcome anytime. He's so sweet. He needs a someone."

"He does." He put his guitar away, grabbed his phone to text Timmy, and then started the bacon, stealing kisses between each thing.

"I'm sorry this place is so unfestive. I mean apart from your beautiful tree. I couldn't deal with all the hobbling around to decorate. The doc wanted me off my feet except for the show."

"It's just fine. I got supper coming, we got Timmy, and we're together. That's festive."

"It is."

Every time he looked over, Kyle's eyes were on him, following him, watching.

"You happy, cher?" He hoped so. He wanted them to be.

"Yeah. I've been a little... off. No, that's not even fair. I've been very off since Thanksgiving. I knew I missed you. I was telling myself I'd get over it, but I knew I wouldn't. Having to cancel my exhibition felt like karma. I had a lot of time to think about how if I were you, I probably wouldn't come back, so I didn't feel like I should call. I don't know. It's been a bad few weeks. Today, I'm beyond happy. I'm just trying to appreciate it."

"I wanted to be a part of your show. Bad." He kept his eyes on the bacon. "I want to be good enough for you to dance to. I really thought I was; then I didn't. Now, I think I should have told you that you were wrong and I could do it, even if I had to lose some gigs at the studio."

Norv and Ryder? They were his big money, so they would have worked, but he could have said no to Timmy. Timmy would have heard him.

Arms slipped around him from behind. He hadn't even heard Kyle get up. "There's a space we lived in for a while where we just trusted. It's like you said, my body, your guitar, they always tell the truth. I'm hopeful we can find that again. And then we have to extend that trust to everything else."

His lover took a deep breath and hugged him close. "God, Colt. You're so much more than good enough. I try so hard to do your music justice when I dance."

Colt leaned back into Kyle's arms. He wasn't sure if he understood, but he wasn't sure he didn't, really. What he did know was music—Kyle's music, his music—and when that got caught up, so did everything else.

"I love you. And this feels right. That's all I know for sure right now, but it's making me happy. Oh! That, and I have presents for you."

"You do?" He had one for Kyle too, a mask from home—there was a man painted on the white emptiness, a dancer arching over the eye socket.

"I do. Bought them on hope. Turned out to be a good call." Kyle kissed his neck and let him go, heading for the coffeepot.

"You sit, cher. Rest that foot. I'll fix you up."

Kyle looked at him and then went back to his seat. "I'll let you do that today, but I'm not dancing right now. I can walk. And while I can, tonight after dinner we should go see things. Skating and the big tree."

"So long as you don't hurt. You'd pet me, if I was sore, huh? I know that. I seen it with your dancers."

Kyle waggled long fingers at him. "I would. I do try. You like my hand massages."

"Love." Hell, they were magic all on their own. "You want eggs?"

"Not if you're really making pancakes." Kyle sipped his coffee.

"I'm really making pancakes. Spoiled man."

"So spoiled. So lucky. Did you have good Christmases, growing up?"

Colt shrugged. "I guess. Some. I left home at fifteen, so...."

He'd had some fun ones as a grown-up, that was for sure.

"Yeah, me too. Some. I was just thinking this is already one of the better ones. It's not snowing, though. I wish it was snowing."

"Maybe it's waiting. It's sure fixin' to come up a cloud." He started his pancake batter, humming gently.

"I'll take a sniff outside next time I get up."

The kitchen went quiet for a bit, and Kyle sipped his coffee. He sang while he worked, going through "Silent Night" and "Baby, It's Cold Outside," "Blue Christmas," and "All I Want for Christmas Is You." When Kyle jumped in with a slightly jazzy version of "The Christmas Song" and forgot the words, he picked those up easily enough too.

And then it was piles of pancakes and bacon and Kyle telling him stories about why he should never, ever go ice skating.

"It's fun to watch, though. I mean, if you want to try, you go right ahead, but I'm a complete disaster." Kyle stuffed in another bite of pancake. He'd figured Kyle was up to six or seven and wondered where his lover was putting them all. "And don't tell me that just because I'm a dancer I should be good at ice skating. I wonder if Timmy skates?"

"I haven't the foggiest." He didn't think he would be good at that, and ice was slickery and hard.

"These are really good, baby. I haven't had pancakes in forever." Kyle picked up a piece of bacon and offered him a bite. "What's your tradition? Midday dinner, food coma, and then a late-night snack? Or do you like dinner at dinnertime?"

"They gon' bring supper at three. You watch football?" He didn't care one way or the other. He sort of loved all the Christmas cartoons.

"That is amazing. You are amazing. Thank you again." Kyle grinned and slid a hand under his and tickled his palm. "Nah. The Grinch doesn't play football. Oh, but if that's what you and Timmy want to do, that's okay."

"I like *The Grinch*, a lot. And *Charlie Brown* and the *Prep & Landing* one too."

"*Frosty*. Oh, and *The Island of Misfit Toys. The Year Without a Santa Claus*." Kyle chewed bacon, grinning like a kid. "I guess I know what we're doing."

"You and me and Timmy, snacks and blankets and cartoons." He bounced on his toes, tickled as a pig in shit. "Hell yeah."

He pushed over, stealing him a hard kiss.

Kyle made a startled sound and grabbed on to him, but settled right down, letting him have it all. Mmm… salty and sweet and….

"Merry Christmas, cher."

"Merry Christmas, baby." Kyle's eyes flashed. "Presents?"

"I have one for you, yes. I brought it from home."

"Aw. Thank you." Kyle kissed his cheek and pushed him back lightly, trying to get up. "Yours are under the tree."

"Well, thank you. Come on. I'll help you get to the sofa."

"Walking boot," Kyle reminded him but took his arm anyway and smiled. "I'm not helpless, but the help still makes me feel special."

"I just hate knowing you're hurting." And he loved touching, loved having Kyle close. The last few weeks had been so soul sore.

"It's not that bad. Actually, in the boot it feels pretty good. I just overdid it at the show last night. I think I was pushing because I don't know when I'll dance again and…." Kyle sighed and coughed gently. "Hey, I forgot to bring my coffee, would you grab it for me?"

"I will, and you'll dance again soon. 'Til then, you'll choreograph. Hell, we'll go do things that ain't music or sex." He winked at Kyle, both of them cracking up.

When he got back, Kyle was on the couch with plenty of room beside him, the tree was all lit up, and Nat King Cole was on the stereo.

Merry Christmas to him. He grinned and went to snuggle, Kyle folding him right in. They sat there for a bit, just being close, Kyle all excited and smiling and telling him all about the people who had come to deliver the tree.

He opened a couple of large, brightly wrapped boxes that were under the tree for him, finding a warm coat, a hat, and a pair of thick-soled winter boots to keep his Cajun toes warm. Kyle really had been hoping he'd be back. Those were good city-walking boots.

"It gets so cold, cher?"

"Mm-hm. The wind is evil. Don't worry, I'll keep you warm." Kyle pointed. "That flat box is from Timmy. He was so cute when he gave me the box last night. He said you told him you needed what's in it."

"Must be gloves." He'd found Timmy a great glass pipe. It was a beauty. "My hands get freezy."

He handed Kyle the mask. "For you."

Kyle held it up and admired it, ran a finger over the little dancer with a smile. "This is so sweet. I love it. I'm going to put it in my studio. Is there a story? Did you get it somewhere amazing?"

"There's a shop in the Quarter. They sell all these masks, and I stopped in and this guy from Italy was there, painting them, just right there." He'd been missing Kyle like breathing, so he'd sat to watch, telling the guy all about his dancer, how fine he was. At the end, he had a mask. "He did this for you, because you're…." He didn't have words, so he shrugged, hands held open. "You're worth painting."

"Oh, Colt. That's so…. You're wonderful. This is so thoughtful, it will inspire me. Thank you." Kyle waved him back to the couch and pulled him down on it, dropping a kiss on his lips. "I love you."

"Good. Would be weird if you didn't." He petted Kyle's belly. "Loving you is a good thing, hmm?"

Kyle kissed him again. "Really good. Hey, speaking of love, I have one last little present for you." A wee box appeared, wrapped in sheet music, and Kyle had drawn little ballet feet and a guitar on it. "I hope you like it."

He opened the box, making sure to save the paper. He liked it; it could go in his wallet. There was a key in the box, a guitar pick on the keychain.

"I promise this isn't just so I don't have to get up and answer the door when you bring pizza home." Kyle looked at him, leaning in, one arm behind his back. "Home, you know? To our place."

"Yeah? Like… home." Colt's hands shook, because no one had ever offered him that, not in his memory. No one let him come home.

Kyle caught his shaking hands up and kissed his temple. "Home, Colt. I want this to be our home. I want you to stay. Will you?"

"Yessir." He could. He wrapped their fingers together, held on tight. "You make me want to play."

"You make me feel like dancing. The joy is going to blow the roof off this house."

"Well, you got a Cajun in it now. We do laissez le bon temps rouler, cher." Lord knew, he could do joy, especially where his dancer was concerned.

Kyle laughed and kissed him, eyes shining. "Bring it on."

"With all I am, swear to God. With every bit I got."

Chapter Twenty-Three

"Hey, Kyle." Timmy stood up and gave him a hug, then leaned over and touched a lever on the soundboard.

"Sorry, I'm interrupting."

"Nah, you're good. Just keep it low-key. They're finishing up. It's good to see you, dude. Colt didn't tell me you were stopping by."

"He doesn't know. I got done early. Thought I'd come pick him up. See if he wanted a date night. We haven't seen each other except, like, sleeping and coffee in days."

"He's totally working his ass off."

"I know. He's happy as hell about it too."

"I think he's at his best when he's living it, you know?"

"I know exactly." He'd been busy too. He was choreographing a new show that was opening in ten days. And after agonizing over it for a week, he finally did ask Colt about playing for his rescheduled exhibition.

"So how's the foot?"

He wiggled it for Timmy. "Perfect. I got sprung from rehab yesterday." He thought maybe Colt had been even more excited about that than he was. It was adorable.

"Right on. Oops. Hang on." Timmy tucked headphones on, and the booth got quiet.

Colt's face was a study in exhilaration, his lover lost in his work, in the passion of music. It was the hottest thing in Kyle's world.

He needed to do more of this. Stop by the studio, be supportive. Colt cleared the recording calendar for his opening weekend, and since his lover rarely performed live, this was the closest he could get.

Timmy nodded and stood up, held one hand up in the air, and after a few seconds made a fist. Kyle watched everyone in the room relax, grins and high fives all around. He hung back, just watching, taking in how at ease Colt was in that room.

Suddenly, Colt saw him, and a grin blossomed over his lover's face. "Cher!"

Oh. Oh, he'd walk through the snow a hundred times just to see that face. He smiled and waved back, knowing Colt couldn't hear him.

"Go on around, Kyle. I turned the recording lock off."

"Yeah?" He ran over and kissed Timmy on the cheek. "Thanks. Hey, Colt ordered a Looney Tunes DVD. Come watch it with us soon."

"Nothing I'd like better, dude."

Kyle ducked out of the booth and made his way around, carefully opening the door into the studio.

Colt was putting his six-string away, laughing at something this mandolin player the size of a mountain said.

"La! Cher! What a surprise." Colt came to him, offering him a deep, happy kiss.

Kyle accepted the kiss exactly as offered, pleased that Colt liked the surprise. "I got done early and walked over to see if you were anywhere close to finished. I thought we could go home together. It's snowing a little."

"Sounds perfect. Can we stop and eat? Timmy starves me!" Colt's laugh tickled his lips.

"Dude!" Timmy scooted around them into the room. "Did you just throw me under the bus, man? That Cajun lies!"

Kyle laughed along. "Mm. You gotta watch them, they're wily. And hungry all the time."

"True dat." Colt snuggled in close. "You gon' watch me, cher?"

"No, I'm going to listen." He tucked his arms around Colt. "You're going to watch me."

"Yo, get a room, Boudreaux!"

He looked over Colt's head at the smiling giant Colt had been laughing with a moment ago. "If you're offering, we'll take one at the Mandarin."

"Don't need a room. We got us a home." Colt took pride in their house, tiny little touches appearing everywhere.

Timmy laughed. "So there, Sam."

"Let's get you covered up and get out of here, hungry boy."

"Go ahead, Colt. We're wrapped here."

Kyle loved how Colt made a point of shaking hands, meeting eyes, exchanging smiles with each of the other band members, and he waited patiently for him to make the rounds. Then it was coat, boots, hat, toasty gloves, and out into the snow. It wasn't really sticking to anything, but it was pretty coming down.

"You have a good day, cher?" Colt wrapped one arm around his waist. "I was so glad to see you."

"I did. We ended early because we'd finished what I'd planned, and everyone was working so hard. This company is gelling really well. You're going to be impressed, I think. And I'm so glad I got here before you wrapped up! I loved just listening. Have you worked with them before?"

He led them around the corner and down the block. Planning on sushi unless Colt asked for something else along the way.

"I have. They like my sound. Asked me to go on the road with them, but that ain't my deal, you know?"

He had made his peace with Colt's inability to say no to people. In fact, he didn't see it so much that way anymore. It was more about the joy Colt took in being able to say yes. So, sure. Colt was tired some days, some days Colt took something to help him keep up, and Kyle didn't judge, didn't say a word because Colt always came home in one piece and slept in their bed and let Kyle take care of him.

He took Colt's hand in his as they walked. He knew Colt wasn't into the audience thing, but he wanted to be sure he wasn't the reason Colt was holding back. After all, there was no telling what could come along for him down the road. He'd toured before, he couldn't say he'd never do it again. "If you want to go, you should go."

"I spent a lot of life going. Right now, I'm happy." Colt grinned over at him. "You tired of me already?"

"Brat." He laughed. What a question. "Are you kidding? I'm very happy being served regular helpings of Cajun with a side of ballet."

"I am. I know. I am your magic man."

"You are." He didn't know what it was. Magic, fate, a higher power, plain old dumb luck. Somehow Colt had just fallen right the hell out of the sky and into his arms. There was no rational reason in the world that a sweet, gifted, beautiful, Cajun blues guitarist should cross his path. None. Zero. Magic was as good an explanation as any.

He stopped them, suddenly. They'd almost walked right by it. "Sushi."

Lord, Colt never would get used to how those guys could make bait and rice and seaweed taste so damn good.

Weird.

Fun, though, and he loved to share it with Kyle.

"Hey." Kyle walked past him, barefoot with a water bottle in one hand, and slapped him on the ass. "Come on. Bring your friend, there."

He shamelessly enjoyed the view as Kyle headed off toward the studio, then grabbed his guitar and followed.

"You looking fine, cher. I do love me some of that ass." He let himself follow like Kyle had a leash on him.

"Just some? I think you do a pretty good job loving all of it." Kyle laughed and dropped a sweatshirt on the chair by the door, long legs moving easily across the studio to stretch. Or flirt. It was sometimes hard to tell the difference. "I have been itching to move since the PT set me free yesterday. I was hoping you would play for me, music man. Start our rehearsals for the show. Pretty please?"

"It's my pleasure. You got a preference to type?" He settled on the sweet cushion that was his spot. The acoustics right here were cherry.

"Nope. You want to just see what happens? Improv awhile?"

"That is what I do, cher. Wind me up and let me go."

Kyle did a set of turns, three in a row and a couple of jumps that landed on one foot as if testing his feet out. "Feels good."

He didn't miss the pleased little smile on his lover's face.

Colt nodded, just about as tickled as Kyle was. His lover was born to move. He hummed softly as he let his guitar speak to him, rejoicing in Kyle's good health, in the snow, in the sushi and the laughter and the whole world, just now.

Kyle swayed to his music a little, marked out a set of steps and then tried them again. Then Kyle was off on a series of hops and spins, eventually moving right past him with a laugh.

He let his guitar answer Kyle's laughter, the joy bubbling through the strings.

It didn't take long for that give and take he remembered to come back. They stayed bright for a little while, and then Kyle stretched one leg long and high, suggesting another tempo, and he nodded as he caught on, moving into something smooth and jazzy.

    Kyle smiled at him, the look of approval suiting him to the ground. They got this.

    They'd lost it for a while, but truth had won out. They had won out. Colt wasn't surprised. Music was bigger than both of them.

    Thank God they'd had the good sense to figure that shit out.

JODI PAYNE spent too many years in New York and San Francisco stage-managing classical plays, edgy fringe work, and the occasional musical. She therefore is overdramatic, takes herself way too seriously, and has been known to randomly break out in song. Her men are imperfect but genuine, stubborn but likeable, often kinky, and frequently their own worst enemies. They are characters you can't help but fall in love with while they stumble along the path to their happily ever after.

For those looking to get on her good side, Jodi's addictions include nonfat lattes, Malbec, and tequila however you pour it. She's also obsessed with Shakespeare and Broadway musicals. She can be found wearing sock monkey gloves while typing when it's cold, and on the beach enjoying the sun and the ocean when it's hot. When she's not writing and/or vacuuming sand out of her laptop, Jodi mentors queer youth and will drop everything for live music. Jodi lives near New York City with her beautiful wife, and together they are mothers of dragons (cleverly disguised as children) and slaves to an enormous polydactyl cat.

Website: www.jodipayne.net
Facebook: www.facebook.com/payne.jodi
FB Author Group: www.facebook.com/groups/jodisgents
Twitter: @JodiPayne
Instagram: @jodipayne1800

BA TORTUGA, Texan to the bone and an unrepentant Daddy's Girl, spends her days with her basset hounds, getting tattooed, texting her sisters, and eating Mexican food. When she's not doing that, she's writing. She spends her days off watching rodeo, knitting, and surfing Pinterest in the name of research. BA's personal saviors include her wife, Julia Talbot, her best friend, Sean Michael, and coffee. Lots of coffee. Really good coffee.

Having written everything from fist-fighting rednecks to hard-core cowboys to werewolves, BA does her damnedest to tell the stories of her heart, which was raised in Northeast Texas, but has heard the call of the high desert and lives in the Sandias. With books ranging from hard-hitting GLBT romance, to fiery ménages, to the most traditional of love stories, BA refuses to be pigeonholed by anyone but the voices in her head.

Website: www.batortuga.com
Blog: batortuga.blogspot.com
Facebook: www.facebook.com/batortuga
Twitter: @batortuga

REFRACTION

JODI PAYNE AND BA TORTUGA

A COLLABORATIONS NOVEL

A Collaborations Novel

Texas artist Tucker Williams arrives in New York City for a gallery showing of his work and finds the city blanketed in snow. He meets free-spirited underwear model Calvin McIntire on the steps of the Midtown library and is captivated by a wild beauty that manages to compete with the demons that occupy his soul and fuel his work with their lust for blood and erotic imagery.

Unable to deny a new inspiration, Tucker sublets a studio and finds the city's energy almost as addictive as Calvin.

Tucker is obsessive, barely holding on to sanity as his art consumes him, and Calvin is dealing with demons of his own, trying desperately to protect his soul in a business where only his appearance has value. They each prove to be the perfect remedy for the other's personal brand of crazy until, in the midst of stress and exhaustion, they discover that a promise Calvin needs is the one thing Tucker can't give him, and their heaven turns to purgatory.

Can both men find a path toward wholeness in Tucker's beautiful but chaotic Texas home? In order for them—and their passionate relationship—to thrive, they'll need to adapt, share their psychoses, and find a true balance between New York City and rural Texas.

www.dreamspinnerpress.com

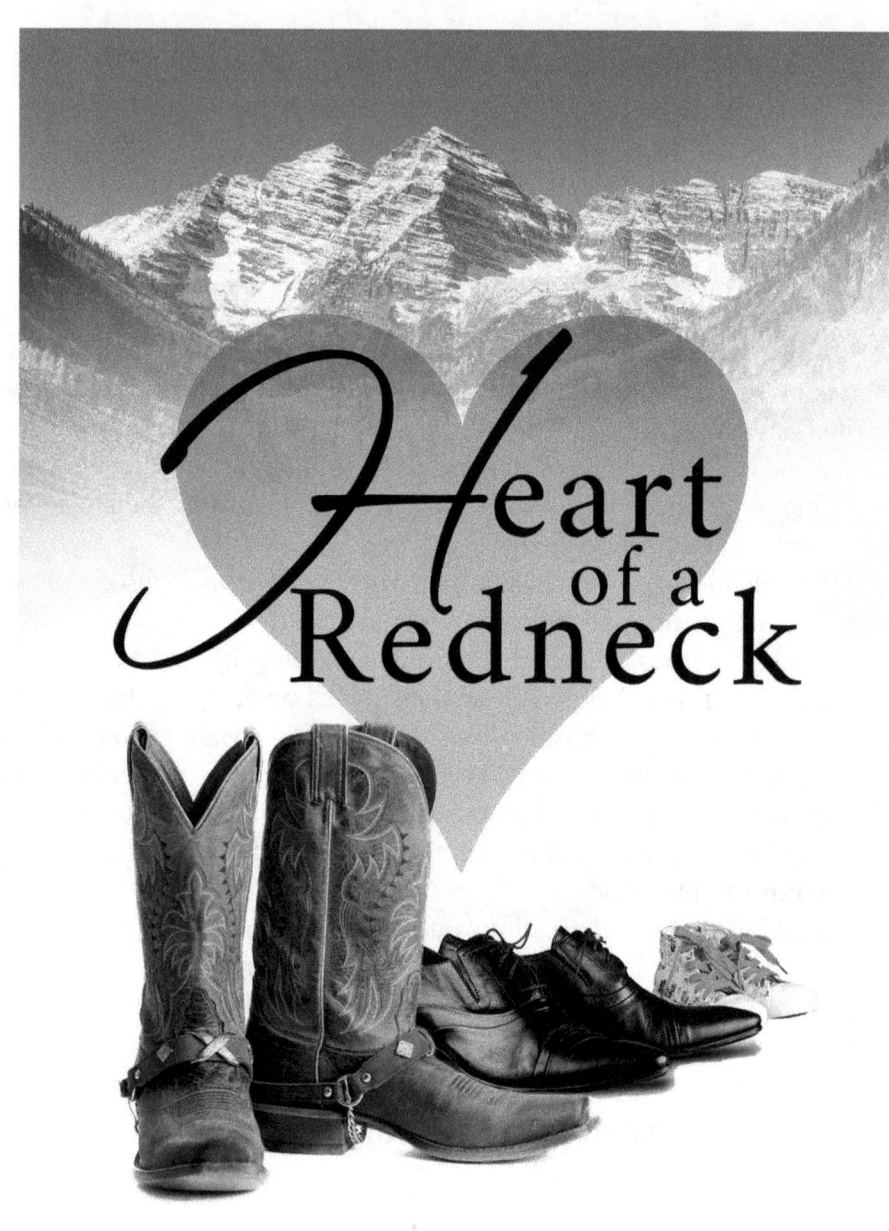

Heart of a Redneck

JODI PAYNE   BA TORTUGA

Colby McBride is a blue-collar cowboy trying to make ends meet laying tile in Colorado. A loner by choice, Colby works hard with his hands and finds his peace camping in the mountains outside Boulder. Gordon James is a white-collar restaurateur who owns not one, but two successful establishments in downtown Boulder. He's a sophisticated urbanite who is devoted to his work and is accustomed to getting what he wants.

The men are friends, but sparks fly when Colby falls in love and decides to show Gordon how much fun a good old boy can be. They're just beginning to explore their relationship when Gordon's sister's suicide leaves him with custody of his five-year-old niece.

Colby comes from a huge family and is eager to help with the girl and to prove his worth to Gordon. But neither of them is ready for the tremendous changes to their already busy lives, or for how this new relationship with Olivia challenges them, complicating the way they interact with each other.

They say opposites attract, but can these two very different men work together to join their disparate lives and form a strong, if highly unlikely, family?

www.dreamspinnerpress.com

Also from Dreamspinner Press

www.dreamspinnerpress.com

Also from Dreamspinner Press

www.dreamspinnerpress.com

CPSIA information can be obtained
at www.ICGtesting.com
Printed in the USA
FSHW010236030419
56900FS